It SOUNDS Like THIS

Also by Anna Meriano

This Is How We Fly

FOR YOUNGER READERS

Love Sugar Magic: A Dash of Trouble

Love Sugar Magic: A Sprinkle of Spirits

Love Sugar Magic: A Mixture of Mischief

It SOUNDS Like THIS

ANNA MERIANO

VIKING

VIKING

An imprint of Penguin Random House LLC, New York

First published in the United States of America by Viking, an imprint of Penguin Random House LLC, 2022

Copyright © 2022 by Anna Meriano

Hurricane image by archangel80889 from 123rf.com; *The Scream* image courtesy of Wikimedia Commons

Visit us online at penguinrandomhouse.com.

Library of Congress Cataloging-in-Publication Data is available.

Printed in Canada

ISBN 9780593116906

1 3 5 7 9 10 8 6 4 2

FRI

Edited by Kelsey Murphy
Design by Monique Sterling
Text set in Breughel Pro

This pandemic book is dedicated to the group chats that got me through.

It SOUNDS Like THIS

CHAPTER 1

"I'm not going to Homecoming, I'm playing at Homecoming," I explain to Mom, trying to coax the Kingwood High Marching Band Information and Parental Consent packet out of her hands so I can flip straight to the back page of signature blanks. I need her to sign before stumbling across any more actual information. "The football game, not the dance. And that's all months away, practically at the end of the season."

She waves her hand to dismiss my words before stubbornly flipping through the rest of the packet, laser eyes scanning as if the pages contain the secret to my successful high school career, or the hidden clause that will ruin it. I don't think she'll find anything objectionable, but sometimes she latches on to details—like the Homecoming dance—and turns them into another box for me to check off.

I'm not opposed to checking off boxes; I *love* checking off boxes. It's just that, going into sophomore year, my checklist is already full of an overwhelming number of super-important boxes that I want to check: get straight As, do well in my first AP class, prep for the PSAT, make friends with some teachers for future recommendation letters, keep up my extracurriculars (band), get leadership experience (first chair), and . . . How is Mom still reading the same page??

I thought that waiting until Sunday evening would make it easier to rush her through the packet, but I forgot that nobody but me cares about being late to church. Dad unhurriedly rinses dishes and loads them into the dishwasher, his button-down not yet buttoned over his T-shirt and his salt-and-ginger hair uncombed. Mom frowns at the dress code ("But they can't stop you from painting your nails, mija!"), dressed to reverently impress as always but showing no signs of getting ready to move. Even if we leave in the next minute and a half, we'll still be five minutes late to the latest possible mass. I take a breath and smile to keep my tone pleasant when I hint, "I'll be ready to leave as soon as this is signed."

Mom finally scribbles her signature on the last page and helps Dad finish the dishes while I tuck the forms into my brand-new folder and zip it safely into the polka-dotted backpack I picked out so carefully last summer.

It was supposed to give me good luck for my freshman year . . . so that didn't work out well at all. Maybe I should've asked for a new backpack this year.

I'm not, like, extremely superstitious, but then again, I am currently the driving force getting most of my family out the door to go to religious services because I want this year to go well. I technically have two more weeks of summer, but tomorrow morning is the first day of band camp, so basically the start of the year. And just to add to the pressure, it's actually my actual first day of band camp ever.

A week before camp was supposed to start last year, a tropical storm out in the Gulf agitated itself into a full-blown hurricane—Hurricane Humphrey—and aimed itself at Texas. The Sunday night when I should have been getting to bed early to make it to the marching field on time, I was instead clutching a flashlight, watching flood-water rush down our street and creep up our front lawn. We were lucky; the school was not. It took the whole semester to get things back in repair enough to have band, and by then the marching season was over. So, yeah, maybe I'm a little superstitious, and maybe I waited until the last possible minute to give Mom the forms to sign, and maybe I'm on my third Guadalupe candle burning itself out on my desk. But that's just because I need this year to go smoothly.

I do finally get Mom and Dad out the door and into the car. We're late, but not later than usual, so I count that as a win.

"What are you going to wear to Homecoming?" Mom asks while Dad maneuvers through the packed parking lot of St. Cecily's.

I hold back a sigh. "My uniform. I'm going to wear my band uniform. Because it's a band performance."

Mom tuts in disappointment and grumbles that I should be excited about the dance and the dress too, and I can feel her grumbling sliding inevitably toward complaining that I didn't do anything quinceañera-related last year, and then if I don't stop her, she'll be off on a pro-femininity rant. Her rants have less to do with me (I'm very pro-femininity, thank you! Not to lean too heavily on presentation stereotypes, but I'm literally wearing a pink skirt right now!) and more to do with Ellen, my sibling who doesn't do dances or dresses or femininity, and even though none of that is officially my problem, Mom has a way of unloading it all on me at least once a week. Also, since Humphrey tanked her small interior design business the same way it tanked Ellen's nonprofit job and my marching season, she's got a lot more time on her hands to pay attention to my business.

I'm actually lucky Ellen is at work today, or else there would have been a whole separate argument where Mom tried to convince her to come to church and she tried to come up with an excuse not to go to church and I would have ended up getting lectured about that too.

But the goal is to avoid all lectures on all subjects. Part of starting the year off right. "I guess I'll probably go to the dance after the Homecoming game," I concede. "But I need to ask Sofia about outfits." I'm not above invoking my best friend as a subtle reminder to Mom that I have good role models in my life.

"Oh, how is Sofia? I've barely seen her this summer—but you girls are always connected on your phones, right?"

"Right," I say, smiling past an unpleasant prick of emotion. Sofia hasn't come over much this summer. Maybe because she got an annoying boyfriend, or maybe because I was too loud about how annoying her boyfriend is. But we do talk on the phone, even if I'm bad at texting. And she's driving me to band tomorrow. Once the school year starts and we can't avoid each other, things will go back to normal.

Dad finally finds a parking spot, and we jump out of the car and speed-walk past the announcement board outside the chapel that reminds us to sign me up for Sunday school CCE classes (another box on my checklist, another piece in the puzzle of my schedule for the year). We make it into the pews just in time for the homily (church SparkNotes for latecomers), and then all I have to worry about is squeezing my eyes tight shut when the speaker calls for "all the intentions we hold in our hearts."

A *good year*, I intent as hard as I can. *Let us all have a good year.*

And specifically, let me get first chair, I have to add. I figure it doesn't hurt to ask.

CHAPTER 2

The band hall even *smells* like home. It smells like dried spit and perpetually dusty carpet and the layer of new paint from last year's post-flood renovations, peeking out past a whiff of old yellowed sheet music books and fresh-ink paper copies. One sniff and I'm catapulted back in time straight to last semester's concert season.

Except that it's August, not January, and that means we won't be spending all our time in this familiar room sitting in familiar concert curves.

This semester is marching band.

I pull the signed back page off my KHSMB info packet so I can add it to the pile on Ms. Schumacher's desk. There's a line of new forms to pick up: a welcome letter, a semester schedule, a sheet of contact info for all the teachers and student staff.

Sofia's hand smacks down on top of the pile of contact sheets before I can take one. "That's for section leaders only," she scolds. "And you promised you would stay outside until ten thirty."

"Aren't you excited?" I bounce on my toes, ignoring her cold glare. "I'm excited."

"You're a dork." Sofia sighs, but her eyes flick across the band hall and her mouth quirks into a smile. She can try to look cool with her high-waisted shorts and aviator sunglasses and new braces-less smile, but she's not fooling me.

She's also not cowing me. "Ms. Schumacher told me to come in." I gloat a little and watch Sofia's smile slip. "She liked my initiative."

Sofia drove me here, so of course she's annoyed that I'm getting credit for her arrival time. Rolling her eyes, she snaps, "You just had to get a head start on sucking up, didn't you?"

I laugh, not even ashamed that she's right. Nobody likes to talk about it, but getting on the band director's good side can definitely bump a person up a full chair position. And it's not like I haven't been very clear about my intentions. Ever since I was a fourth-grader starting music lessons in elementary school band and Sofia was my fifth-grade buddy assigned to help me learn the flute fingering chart, I've had one goal.

"This is the year I beat you," I tell her. "I can feel it."

Since that tiny elementary school band, I've always been second chair to Sofia. But at the end of last year I noticed that the gap was closing. The difference between our final sight-test scores was slight, and I actually creeped barely ahead on performance music. So I spent the summer beefing up my music theory and sight-reading. My family may have gotten sick of hearing me hack my way through unfamiliar études, but I'm going to get first chair this year, which means possible solos, a chance at convincing Ms. Schumacher to let me march with a piccolo (the dream), and, most importantly, a serious shot at being chosen for section leader next year. Sofia applied unopposed at the end of last year (the upperclassmen are all slackers), but when the process starts for next year's marching season, I plan to be a serious contender.

"Keep dreaming," Sofia scoffs. "Did you ever consider taking a path of less resistance? Osea, you can just switch to AP Music Theory if you want to pad your college apps so badly."

I open my mouth to protest that this is not all about my résumé, though it's also not *not* about that. I managed to scrape mostly A minuses as a freshman even with all the chaos, but I'm not naive enough to think that will impress the demanding forces of college admissions. I know the As and Bs and decent essays that were good enough to get my older sibling, Ellen, into the University of Texas won't fly for me in a couple years. I'll need *passion* and *leadership* and *commitment* and *point of view*, and all that for an above-average state school. I can't get back my first year of marching band, but surely if I passion committedly for these next three years, colleges can't fault me for that. That's why this year is Operation: Section Leader Material. Arriving early was the first step on a long journey to make Ms. Schumacher forget I'm an underclassman at a Hurricane Humphrey disadvantage and see me as the natural choice for next year's student staff. I'll pick up at least two years of leadership in an activity I'm devoted to, solidify my place in the band-kid social group, and maybe even experience some good anecdotes to build into a personal essay.

So yes, it is partly about college apps. But still, there are other reasons I want to beat Sofia. I love playing flute, and I'm good at it (and I love being good at it). I also love the whole idea of being section leader—setting practice times, organizing music, building section morale with bonding activities but still holding everyone accountable for learning their parts. I had a taste of what it meant to be first chair in eighth grade, after Sofia went to high school. Flutes are notoriously competitive, and it was a thrill to be at the top of the dainty dogpile. Being the de facto soloist, getting called on to demonstrate a particularly tricky piece of music, knowing my section mates were coming up fast behind me if I didn't keep improving . . . I loved it. I want it back, and I don't want to wait for Sofia to graduate again to get it.

I never get around to answering Sofia, because an authoritative voice asks, "Ms. Palacios, are you planning to join us?" Ms. Schumacher, a medium-old white woman who has traded her concert season button-downs and oxfords for a blue polo, baseball cap, and tennis shoes, raises one white-blond eyebrow at Sofia.

The other section leaders have gathered on the carpet around the band director's stool at the front of the band hall, and Sofia shoots me an exasperated glare like it's my fault that the disappointed-teacher tone is directed at her. It's not. With "Early is on time, and on time is late" being the rallying cry of band directors everywhere, Sofia should've known to be in position by 9:30 sharp. I keep my triumphant smile very small and slip innocently into the hallway outside the band hall while the pre-meeting kicks off.

I take a seat with my back against the Coke machine, arranging my flute case and backpack in front of me so there's no chance of forgetting them when I stand up. I also set a phone alarm for 10:20 so I don't lose track of time. I guess I could sit out in the parking lot by the wheelchair/pit-percussion-instrument ramp where most of the non-staff band members will gather before practice, but this hallway has two distinct advantages: air conditioning and silence. I close my eyes and send up a quick prayer of gratitude because it's a little bit unbelievable that I'm actually here, starting a normal year of high school.

I know that's a weird thing to think. I mean, nobody else seems to feel that way. I saw people on social media crossing their fingers (jokingly, I guess??) for another hurricane, like it was *such* a fun time when our whole suburb, along with most of Houston, was in shambles; when a third of our neighborhood was moving in with family or to cramped apartments, and another less lucky fraction was living out of hotels or shelters; when the school was so wrecked that it didn't even open until October, and even then it was all temporary classrooms and construction crews blocking off the hallways and teachers scrambling through a month's worth of material in a week's worth of class time; when the upperclassmen had to rotate through emergency off-site "internships" just so we could all fit on campus.

Even though my house stayed dry and my family stayed safe, last year was still a lot.

But it's okay. This year is going to be perfect. I smooth the semester schedule out on my lap and trail my finger down the list of dates. August is band camp and daily rehearsals, September starts the slew of football game weekends, October shows more games and extra rehearsal hours—and Homecoming, Mom will be happy to see—as we hit the final crunch before the UIL competition in November. Late November and early December have scattered optional commitments, but the season will be wrapping up by then. It will be an intense three months or so, but I can handle that.

Loud footsteps break my train of thought as somebody rushes in my direction. I tuck my legs a little more carefully under me as a figure jogs around the corner in basketball shorts and a sweaty tank top. I assume it's a jock coming into school for some cooler sport's practice until he slows and lifts his sunglasses and I recognize Neeraj, a South Asian junior low brass player who's just Like That—meathead jock personality with a band-nerd school schedule. He's in Sofia's grade and did band with us in middle school, so he's definitely a familiar face, and I can predict exactly what color Gatorade (blue) is going to drop from the vending machine after he nods breathlessly at me and slips in his dollar.

"What's up?" he asks after taking a long swig. "Uh . . . wait, sorry, I'm going to remember . . ."

"Yasmín."

"Yasmeeeeeeeen!" Neeraj nods and points at me while repeating my name in a drawn-out announcer voice for no discernable reason. Then he tilts his head thoughtfully. "You kind of look like a lost duckling without Sofia."

I consider being offended by that, but he doesn't say it rudely, and I can't exactly argue. Last year was a lot, and I didn't do a great job of, like, branching out and making a bunch of new friends. Or *any* new friends, except the rest of the flute section that I mostly just friend-inherited from Sofia.

I laugh along with Neeraj and decide to test out one of the first phases of Operation: Section Leader Material— putting it out into the universe. "Yeah, I have to get on band staff as soon as possible so I don't get left behind."

Neeraj isn't a section leader, but he's an upperclassman and a low-stakes way for me to practice being loud and proud about my intentions.

"Better you than me" is all he says, toasting me with his Gatorade. "I'm going to get a few more laps in; I'll see you in there." He jogs off, black hair and maroon string backpack flopping as he goes.

Seriously, who goes for a full run before morning marching practice?

I pop in my headphones and listen to Lizzo until my alarm goes off, then smooth out my skirt (and do a hair toss and check my nails) and walk confidently into the band hall, guessing (correctly) that the staff meeting would be broken up by now. I make sure Ms. Schumacher sees me again, early and eager to start, because I'm nothing if not goal-oriented.

The section leaders mill around the room, waiting for the rest of the band to show up. People catch up on summer gossip and make dramatic predictions about our chances at this year's state marching band contest, UIL. I drift over to stand with Sofia by the instrument cubbies, but she scowls and tuts at me. I wonder if she got called out in the meeting or if something's up with Andy, her low brass section leader boyfriend, who's on the other side of the instrument room, not paying her any attention.

Andy is the source of a lot of Sofia's recent bad moods. That's not a judgment, that's just an observation. She got sick of me observing it out loud over the summer, though, so now I keep my thoughts to myself.

The clock inches past 10:25. More and more people start crowding the cubbies, sliding black instrument cases into appropriately sized wooden shelves and then adding cleaning cloths and water bottles and lunch bags and sunscreen. We flutes have skinny cubbies, so we're all on top of each other like kids slipping shoes off for a trampoline park, but the low brass boys are causing chaos in their much larger corner, shoving each other as they see how many of them can crawl into one sousaphone-sized cubby. There's a muffled cry of distress from whichever poor kid got pushed in first. I shudder at the thought (claustrophobia), but I figure even the low brass players aren't trash enough to injure one of their members in the first hour of band camp.

Sofia steps back to chat with the seniors, Han and Katrina. Han is tall and Asian, wearing cutoff shorts that were definitely made from the ripped jeans she wore all of last year. Katrina is short and Latina (rounding out our Mexican flute squad) and wearing an extremely faded D.A.R.E. shirt that I'm fairly sure is supposed to be ironic. With the three of them in a huddle, there's just enough room to let in two Black girls, my sophomore buddies Mia and Laylah. We were triple stand partners last semester when the band hall was still half sheetrock and we kept "losing" our extremely limited music stands to those thieves in orchestra.

Laylah readjusts the green headband decorating the tight curls of her slicked-back bun and slips her flute, binder, and pencil bag into the cubby on my right, giving me a nod. I nod back and move to let Mia reach the cubby on my left on instinct. But Mia slots her thin body close against Laylah's thicker one, making a jumble of the neat space by stuffing in her flute case on top of Laylah's and adding a handful of crumpled but unopened breakfast bars and the tattered manila envelope we got all our music in last year. Instead of complaining, Laylah smiles and leans her head on Mia's shoulder, pressing a quick kiss to her cheek and whispering something. That's new!

"Hey, did y'all have a good summer?" I ask with a smile.

Mia winks at me while Laylah looks flustered. "Uh, yeah, it was fun. What about you?" In spite of her hesitant tone, Laylah twines her fingers tightly with Mia's, and the cuteness of it all basically melts my heart. I had certain suspicions that they were into each other, so I'm happy to be proven right.

"I had a good summer," I say, and then bite my lip. Should I feel bad that I didn't really talk to anyone in the past few months, didn't even know Laylah and Mia got together? "But it was also, uh, really boring. I just sat at home and practiced my flute a lot."

"Oh, I didn't touch mine," Mia admits, surprising exactly no one. She's a reluctant musician at best, fitting in with the general marching band nerd vibe (ripped jeans and anime T-shirts and big natural curls in pigtail puffs today) more than she actually enjoys the band part. Laylah nods along with her, though, which does surprise me. Laylah is usually super dedicated to everything, especially her flute. She wasn't in middle school with me, but she goes to my church, and we've done a few duets for Sunday school pageants and things like that. Besides Sofia, she's probably my main competition for first chair, especially since Yuki and Devin, Sofia's fellow juniors, are solidly middle-of-the-road, and our seniors didn't even put in enough effort to co–section lead with Sofia. But if Laylah spent her summer getting together with Mia instead of practicing, maybe she's lost her edge.

Maybe that's what helped me get the edge on Sofia too, since she started dating Andy at the end of last year. Maybe not dating anyone is my superpower. I'd be fine with that. Mia and Laylah's adorableness notwithstanding, high school romance seems to be mostly a scam designed to trick people into blowing their GPAs. I mean, I enjoy a good swoony rom-com or a secret crush or living vicariously through my friends' love lives, but real-life relationships . . . I'd rather have the extra practice time.

Of course, as soon as I think about secret crushes, Gilberto Reyes pops his extremely symmetrical face into the cubby room, calling a two-minute warning with the calm authority that makes him a perfect drum major.

My stomach flips gently at the voice (trace bilingual accent that feels like home) and the smile (warm and wide), but then I shake it off, refuse Mia's offer of cinnamon gum—even if we're not using instruments yet, I don't want Ms. Schumacher to think of me as a gum-chewer—and follow my secret-crush drum major into the main room for the official start of my first official marching band season.

This is going to be great.

Assuming no more hurricanes.

THE FIRST DAY IS SHORT AND (IF YOU ASK ME) A LITTLE anticlimactic, but Sofia says I'm going to wish for more indoor-only days once I experience a real marching practice (to which I reply that I'd sooner spend all day marching in the sun than participating in another awkward icebreaker or "learning" the B-flat concert scale and the school fight song, to which *she* responds that I don't know what I'm talking about).

I'm antsy after Sofia drops me off at home. Mom's in the middle of some drama with her sisters and is shouting into her phone, Dad's at work, and Ellen's out. I try to relax with Netflix, but pretty soon I'm pulling my flute case back into my lap and sliding the silver pieces together. I play last year's concert music because I haven't practiced it much since May, and my fingers move rustily through the once-familiar solo that Sofia performed onstage. My vibrato has improved a lot since then, even if my fingering isn't perfect. I wonder if I could beat her for a solo like this now.

Not that marching band would ever count on a lone flute to fill a football stadium with sound.

I play until the solo comes out smoothly, which is a little after Dad shouts his homecoming and Mom knocks to ask what I want for dinner. My flute is warm as I shake it out and wipe it down, my fingers stiff and the corners of my mouth and inside of my bottom lip sore. I snap my case shut with a satisfied sigh. This is what I wanted from today's practice. The pendulum melody swings between my ears, spilling out from my brain to my chest to my fingers to my feet. I steep in the music.

Dad's already at the table when I get down to the kitchen. Mom is pacing back and forth holding a bowl of kale salad, apparently still mad at her sisters. She's wearing yoga pants and an old flowery blouse, comfortable clothes for staying home and getting overly offended by family drama. Dad grabs me utensils while I set my plate down and Mom spoons out way too much salad, eyes narrowing as she sighs at me.

"You've been playing flute all afternoon, but have you even opened the PSAT book I got you?"

I freeze for a second, Mom's sharp tone scratching the record in my head. It's easy to get caught off guard when her anger switches targets. "I've opened it," I say, carefully leaving out the part where I haven't read it or worked any problems. Mom's clearly looking for an excuse to stay mad, so my job is to not give her one. I've always been good at Mom-calming, but my duties have gotten more important the longer she's spent waiting for clients to come back after the Humphrey slump. Without work, Mom tends to get way more into sister drama and Ellen drama and any drama she can stir up.

"That band director should know that you can't practice for hours and hours every day."

"I don't have homework yet," I remind her. "And Ms. Schumacher didn't really assign this. I just want to stay on top of my game. I'll do PSAT questions tonight." Mom tuts but gives a tight-lipped nod and turns her attention back to her own salad.

"How'd it go today?" Dad asks, helping me smooth over Mom's agitation with conversation. "Surely you can't be behind after all that . . . *beautiful practicing* you did over the summer?" He winks to take the sting out of his teasing.

"It was okay." I keep one eye on Mom while I weigh my words. "Actually we took it easy. We barely played, and we didn't march at all." Hopefully this shuts down the line of thought that band is too intense. But what if Mom starts to think it's a waste of time now? I amend: "But we did have a lot of things to get done! It was a lot of . . . administrative stuff." Is that what "administrative" means? Did I use it correctly? The more I think about it, the less it sounds like a real word, but Mom and Dad seem to accept it, and nobody looks mad, so that's good.

"Ooh, did you get the little hats with the big feathers?" Dad smiles wide. "Are you going to march in a parade?"

"No." I shake my head. "The new uniforms aren't in, and I'm pretty sure we don't have feathers." But not 100 percent sure, I realize. We're not really a football family, and Sofia expressly forbade me to come to any of her games. There's only one picture she deemed Instagram-worthy from her freshman marching season, but she's in the bleachers without her hat. I wonder if Ellen would know, or if being out of high school for five years has erased every last memory and replaced it with whatever you learn in college (plus whatever you learn from a year of underemployment). I don't know how I feel about feathers, but I guess I'll cross that bridge when I come to it. "We have one parade over Thanksgiving break, but that's well after UIL, when the season's almost over. We march at football games."

"UIL?" Dad asks. "Uncooked Iceberg Lettuce?" Mom and I groan as one.

"It's the state contest," I say. "They tell you how good you are compared to all the other bands. And then I think you can win prizes and move on to bigger contests, but our band usually doesn't. We're just shooting to earn a good score. It's, like, what we work for all season."

"I'm sure you'll be better than iceberg lettuce." Dad grins. "You'll be delicious, like this kale."

We finish our salad in time for Mom to fill our plates with chicken breast and brussels sprouts. She adds a slice of bread for me that Dad pretends to sneak a bite of just to make her laugh when she catches him breaking their low-carb pledge. With nowhere to direct itself, her anger starts to wisp away like the steam off the plates.

"Provecho," Dad says in his sincerely awful gringo accent. I love Dad a lot and respect the difficulty of learning a language as an adult, but when he speaks Spanish there's always a tiny part of me that's relieved that we aren't biologically related. I mean, my Spanish isn't *good* anymore, but I spoke it before I spoke English, so at least I can fool people with my pronunciation.

"I think you mean 'Get chewin'!'" I reply just as the back door opens and Ellen rushes into the kitchen, holding the long part of her undercut up in a topknot and looking frazzled.

"Please don't say that," she groans, crossing her free hand over her neon-green T-shirt with the GET CHEWIN'! slogan plastered across the front. "This is my home, my sanctuary, the one place where no one can force me to make or endure food-industry puns. Let me have this. Also lend me a hair tie?"

I giggle but hand over my elastic in apology, letting my sibling tie up her frizzy hair and loop a black apron over her grease-splattered black pants. Ellen has been working at Chewy's Cantina and Grub for about six months now, and she never gets less angry about it.

"What time are you off?" Mom asks, making a face (probably because of the smell of old fried food that means Ellen has reworn her shirt one too many times).

I freeze again and wish I could stop Ellen from sighing like it's a huge inconvenience to just answer "Eleven thirty." I've seen this fight play out enough times to recognize its beginning.

Before Mom can tut about it being "so late . . ." and Ellen can get grumpy about it being her responsibility to close at least once a week (and before Mom can imply that the rules should be bent for "people who are vulnerable," which will make Ellen mad because it's code for "girls"), I jump in.

"Oh, that reminds me. Nobody has to wake up early to drive me tomorrow, because Sofia said she has dibs on the car for the whole week." It's a calculated risk to bring this up now, but Ellen and Mom both seem grumpy enough to spell disaster if I don't interfere.

My Hail Mary works like a charm. Mom's anger and attention switch tracks immediately as she insists that today was a "special occasion" and that it's not safe to make a habit of riding with "a new driver." Sofia's been licensed for a year and a half, but I knew that Mom would still put up this fight, and I've been planning my argument for a couple weeks.

I start by reminding Mom how long Sofia's had her

license, then suggest that Sofia's mom wouldn't let her drive everywhere if it were dangerous. Mom and Sofia's mom are close, which is why we're so close, so that's a solid point in my favor. I have to spend a few minutes assuring Mom that we won't use any freeways on our (barely ten-minute) drive and that I'll text her as soon as I'm safely at the band hall (like I did this morning), but eventually she starts to nod along. And while I ease Mom down to a low level of disgruntled, Ellen snatches a granola bar and a handful of brussels sprouts and escapes to work. Her loud "See y'all!" as the door slams puts another slight frown on Mom's face, so I quickly compliment the chicken to get her happily explaining the seasoning.

See, this is why I know I have the skills to be a good section leader. Ellen moved back into the garage like a mini tornado amid the chaos of last year, and having her home again has been a true test of the conflict-resolution skills any good leader needs. Obviously Ellen isn't thrilled that her job hunt is going so poorly (worse now since all the nonprofits in the city that aren't hurricane-relief related froze hiring and budgets). Obviously Mom doesn't have an easy time navigating what it means to parent an adult stepkid (especially when she and Ellen clashed so much through Ellen's teen years). But as long as I can steer them away from dangerous topics—Ellen's nonbinary gender and veganism, Mom's centrist politics, the Catholic church doctrine, climate change, immigration policy, celebrity gossip, and that's just to name a *few*—we can all coexist in peace.

Everything is okay.

I'M THE ONLY ONE AWAKE WHEN ELLEN GETS HOME, restlessly revising my AP World History (WHAP) summer assignment. I'm mostly just resizing the boxes of the world religions table so that it's less obvious how relatively little I've written about Jainism. Our assignment sheet says to use the online textbook, but the textbook barely spent three sentences on some of the religions we're supposed to be writing about while dedicating whole chapters to others (zero guesses which), so I'm thinking I should pull in some outside sources. I also have a nagging Mom voice in the back of my head reminding me that I was supposed to work on PSAT questions, but I'm justifying myself by saying that I should finish all my real schoolwork first. I'll work on the PSAT questions soon; I know I need to.

Ellen pokes her head into my room after rummaging around the kitchen. There's something mysterious splattered across her face that I'm fairly sure isn't just her freckles. "Shouldn't you be asleep already?" she asks.

I shrug, rereading my sentence about the Ten Commandments—does it even make sense? Why do words jumble into nonsense every time I write them down? "I'm doing homework."

"There's no way you have homework from the first day of band camp," Ellen teases. "I know y'all are more intense than choir, but I refuse to believe it's that bad."

We do actually have a standing assignment to know a certain number of major scales by the end of the week (which might be a struggle for some of the freshmen if they didn't come from strong middle school band programs) and a "suggestion" to practice a certain amount every night. But I don't mention any of that because it barely counts as work and it's not what I'm doing right now anyway.

"It's world history for next week," I say. "I also still have to finish *Wuthering Heights*"—Ellen makes a gagging face—"and some packet about molecules."

"Sounds like a lot," Ellen says with a frown. "Make sure you get some rest, though." Ironic advice from someone who looks so thoroughly drained, reeking of oil and garlic. "It's just high school, you know?"

She leaves with a tap on the doorframe, and I scowl at my laptop before shutting it with an abnormally loud *click*. Ellen is my older sibling and I've always looked up to her, but the for-your-own-good lectures get old, especially when what worked for her doesn't make sense or apply to me.

It's just high school. Easy for Ellen to say. Her grades weren't amazing, but they were good, and they were mostly effortless. I'm not as smart as she is. My brain gets sick of reading or talking or thinking as much as she does. I don't remember trivia or collect news or ace standardized tests like her. But I can still beat her, or anyone, by doing the work.

That's how I'm going to get through my sophomore year. That's how I'm going to make first chair and section leader.

I reopen my laptop and add some Google research to my WHAP assignment for another half hour until I'm finally satisfied, then turn off the lights Ellen left on in the kitchen so I don't have to hear Mom's complaints about it in the morning, and then settle into bed. The dark silence feels too empty, so I twitch my fingers through the motions of my weakest scales for practice and then switch to the flute solo until the music fills my head and lulls me to sleep.

CHAPTER 3

After two long hours in the empty parking lot by the football field, my carefully chosen second-day-of-band-camp outfit is feeling distinctly less crisp and more damp. I went with a breathable athletic-wear blouse and a white tennis skirt, but I was not prepared for the particular hell of standing motionless in the late morning sun, slowly baking while Gilberto Reyes shouts at us.

He shouts rhythmic commands, loud and clear and worming their way into my brain until my breath hitches automatically in time to the call of "Band!"–(eighth rest)–"Atten-hut!"

The drum minor, Hannah Garcia, paces behind him with a hollow plastic block and a weathered drumstick, whacking a sharp metronome beat as we alternate moving our fists up to eye level and back down to our sides. I'm tempted to say something about loving Charles Wallace and myself, but instead I concentrate on making my motions *clean* and *explosive* like Ms. Schumacher keeps saying from the top of the oversized stepladder where she stands, looking at us from an approximate stadium view. If Hannah is our tempo, Ms. Schumacher's gaze is a looming articulation note: *staccato*.

Standing at attention, we hold ourselves still while Gilberto and Hannah patrol our lines, adjusting hand positions and foot angles and calling out trembling arms or roaming eyes. The problem is that we've been practicing this rigid position for over an hour, and the intensity is waning fast. Ms. Schumacher barks at a senior saxophone for scratching his neck but finally concedes a water break, which does more for morale than another round of making us chant the school motto or the call-and-response description of how standing at attention should look.

(I saw upperclassmen jokingly greet each other this way during concert band season last semester: "Feet?" *"Together!"* "Shoulders?" *"Back!"* "Chest?" *"Out!"* "Chin?" *"Up!"* "Eyes?" *"With pride!"* "Eyes?" *"With pride!"* "EYESSSS??" *"WITH PRIIIDE!!"*)

Sofia refused to teach me anything over the summer, but I figured it was just standing stiff and still with a super-serious expression like a bodyguard or those guys outside of Buckingham Palace. Actually, it turns out all the details matter, from the exact placement of your fists on your hips at parade rest to the way your fingers and thumbs overlap at attention. The two-handed fist I learned to make in volleyball, lining up my forearms to hit a pass, won't cut it, and neither will the loose right-under-left cup of getting communion at mass, ingrained like instinct from second-grade Sunday school. I practice the new way of folding my hands together while I sit on the curb with the rest of the flutes, trying to turn the crossed thumbs and straight wrists into another familiar pattern.

"You're a tryhard, you know that, right?" Sofia catches me practicing and rolls her eyes. She likes to act too cool for school, but I noticed that her name was never one of the ones shouted by a disappointed Ms. Schumacher, and that Gilberto never had to stop to correct the angles of her elbows. She might be in denial about her tryhard status, but I recognize and appreciate it. It's one of the reasons she's such a good band rival.

"I think you mean overachiever," I say.

"If you want to achieve carpal tunnel syndrome, adelante," Sofia grumbles. "Your hands are nowhere near as important as your feet, anyway."

"I've seen you dance." I raise a teasing eyebrow. "I'm confident I can outmarch your two left feet."

Next to me, Mia *oohs* while Laylah puts her hand over her mouth and Han snorts into her CamelBak. Their reactions surprise me, making my joke seem more mean-spirited than I meant it, and instead of retorting, Sofia tosses her hair and stalks toward the water fountain. I'm still sitting on the curb, but the whole exchange makes me feel off-balance, even more so when Han says, "You're probably right; Sofia's marching is weak."

I consider backpedaling, but I don't want to make this into an even bigger thing, so I try switching gears instead.

"Have you looked at the music for this year's show? Those runs in the third movement look tricky."

Han snorts again. "I can guarantee you I won't be playing those," she says. I guess my surprised face is easily read, because she continues, "Look, I know you're gunning for Sofia's chair, but some of us aren't ambitious like that. I play a flute hundreds of feet away from the audience. Nobody is going to miss my sound. As long as my horn angle is good, Ms. Schumacher can't even call me out."

It takes a conscious effort to keep my face neutral instead of scandalized. I knew Han wasn't one of the best players, but I didn't know that was a conscious choice. Like Mia and Laylah saying they didn't practice all summer, it just doesn't compute for me. What's the logic of giving up two weeks of your summer and countless afternoons and weekends for an activity you're going to half-ass?

I'm so busy grappling with this mystery that I wait

several seconds too long before saying, "I'm not *gunning* for Sofia."

Everyone kind of chuckles at that—even Katrina looks up from her phone to raise perfectly arched eyebrows at me. Wow, okay, I guess Operation: Section Leader Material is working a little too well. It's supposed to be a motivating rivalry, not a coup.

Laylah saves me (Why do I need saving? How did this conversation spin so far out of my control?) by saying, "Yasmín just has piccolo on her bucket list. She's trying to get those solos."

"God, there are people who want to play piccolo?" Mia asks. "Could not in a million years be me. I already need earplugs to play more than two lines above the staff."

I protest that the tiny piccolo is the cutest instrument and therefore the best, and Han rouses Katrina to tell a story about their freshman year and a horrifying sharp piccolo player who actually made Ms. Schumacher cry. Before long the staff is huddling, and then Gilberto Reyes gets on the megaphone and instructs juniors and seniors to move to the football field with him. Hannah Garcia waves for "freshmen" to stay with her on the asphalt.

"We're sophomores," someone reminds her, and she shrugs and corrects herself to "newbies," which honestly makes me feel worse. I grab a last mouthful of water (making a mental note to bring more bottles tomorrow since I'm almost out already) and return to the painted dot grid, ready to hold my fists in front of my head for another hour.

Eventually Hannah gives us a twenty-second water break and promises we can start marching when it's over. I glance wistfully at the football field, where the upperclassmen fly across the grass with wide synchronized steps, then switch to tiny steps without a hitch. I finish the last of my water and use my remaining ten seconds to whisper Sofia a speech-to-text message. She won't read it for a while, but it makes me feel better.

> Don't worry, if Hannah keeps teaching us in the slowest and most inefficient way possible, I'll never learn to march anyway.

MARCHING PRACTICE FILLS THE WHOLE MORNING WITH uncomfortable body positions, but at least the afternoon is music practice. My spine already knows how to stretch for a deeper breath, my fingers are familiar with propping up the weight of the flute body while still moving light across the keys, and my mouth tightens into a precise embouchure without complaint. We spend too long (in my opinion) on warm-ups, then we run through the entire packet of easy stand tunes (pitchy and rushed but recognizable, which I guess is all that matters when you're playing

"Gasolina" in the bleachers between plays of a football game), and then finally, when we have barely half an hour left of camp, Ms. Schumacher asks us to pull out our show music for halftime. I tap my foot impatiently while some of the freshmen panic that they didn't get their music in the mail and didn't know they needed to practice it, and try not to groan as the librarians scramble until everyone has the opening movement on the stand in front of them. Ms. Schumacher sits on her stool, nods around the room, and—starts *talking*.

She talks about the show as a whole, the feeling of resilience we're supposed to capture with our performance, how we're back after Humphrey better than ever, etc., etc., blah, blah, Houston Strong. The band hall AC, so appreciated after marching practice, feels like overkill now that we're sitting still. My fingers tap my flute keys, practicing the opening runs loud enough that Sofia glances my way and shakes her head. I huff and switch to twitching my fingers against the goose bumps on my knees instead. I want to play. I want to prove myself against these runs, this music. I want to calm the nagging worry that I didn't practice hard enough, that I'm unprepared and in for a rude awakening, that I'm not actually strong or resilient or good enough to make up for last year. I want to *play*.

But Ms. Schumacher just keeps explaining how she wants us to feel the music and the marching, and the clock ticks closer to 3:00, and when she starts laying out our weekly practice schedule for the semester, I know she's not going to let us touch the music today. Some clarinets and saxophones start sneakily removing reeds, and a telltale snap behind me means that either Han or Katrina is putting their flute all the way into its case. Ms. Schumacher doesn't even scold, just smiles and reminds us to practice the opener for tomorrow, and dismisses us fifteen minutes early!

I smooth disappointment off my face as I pack my flute away and drag my chair (and Han's) to the folded stack in the back corner of the room. The trumpets keep a few chairs out for sectionals—individual section practice time—and I feel a little jealous that flutes haven't planned any extra rehearsal time during this week. I can't even stay and work out my frustrated fingers in the practice room because Sofia's my ride and she's ready to go, waving me out of the cubby room instead of lingering with the groups making dinner plans or talking about a movie night for this weekend. I say goodbye to Mia and Laylah, dodge the freshman tuba who is inexplicably trying to carry five sousaphone cases stacked on top of each other, and follow Sofia to her sensitive—or, wait, her *sensible*—beige grandma car. Literally, the car belongs to her abuela, who moved in with Sofia's family after her condo got wrecked by Humphrey.

We don't say much as we crank the AC and pull out of the parking lot, and I'm not totally sure if it's just exhaustion from the day or something else. Sofia can't be that upset that I was impatient with Ms. Schumacher's talk, can she? Or is this about the "two left feet" comment? Uncertainty makes the quiet uncomfortable, and I snatch at a conversation topic.

"Can you believe we didn't touch the show music?"

"It's on purpose," Sofia says. "Ms. Schumacher wants this year to be, like, as unstressful as possible. We're supposed to be *easing* you newbies in."

I'm a little annoyed to be included as a newbie, even though it's true. "Are we going to schedule our first sectionals soon?"

Sofia sighs and turns up her nineties and aughts oldies radio (not a leftover from her abuela, who likes J Balvin and Bad Bunny, just Sofia's preferred aesthetic). "Not until school starts," she answers. Shortly.

"But shouldn't we get at least one in next week?" I argue. "We have some complicated parts to learn, and I know for a fact that like sixty percent of the section hasn't practiced, plus it'll help everyone get in the habit of meeting before school gets overwhelming."

"Ms. Schumacher already approved my schedule," Sofia snaps. "Take it up with her if you have a complaint, but I'm still the section leader."

Okay. Obviously my comments about one-upping her rubbed her the wrong way. At least now I know what Sofia's mad about, which means I can start to fix it.

"I do have a complaint," I say. "You run the section with an iron first. It's making it very hard for me to stage a successful coup."

Sofia shoots me a glare but snorts. "Why are you so obsessed with beating me? It's gone way past cute. There's such a thing as graceful defeat, you know."

Like opening the valve on Mom's Instant Pot, Sofia's teasing hisses with released tension. I take the opposite of offense to our anime-foils dynamic, the natural progression from our moms' game of comparing us to each other. Maybe we've gotten a little less careful and a little more aggressive about sniping at each other since middle school ended, but as far as I'm concerned, if Sofia's needling me then we're good.

"I'm not big on graceful defeat, but you're welcome to try it out," I say sweetly, and Sofia flips me off with a sharp smirk that doesn't totally hide her laughter. She's definitely the more likely of us to get her feelings hurt or hold a grudge, and not just against me. Mom sometimes says that she has a "strong personality," which I guess makes me the watered-down sweet tea to her espresso. I can handle whatever venom she spits and return fire while staying just inoffensive enough to get away with it.

It's a delicate balance, but I'm a pretty accomplished egg-shell walker.

My efforts are rewarded, because Sofia lets out a long sigh and then starts talking fast and animated. "So Han is a pain in the ass, and her marching seems to be getting worse every year. How do the freshmen look?"

I grin because gossip is our love language, second only to being rude to each other. "God, don't get me started," I say, even though the freshmen seem pretty nice. It's just relaxing to lightly trash-talk them in Sofia's car after a long day. The two new flutes are both tiny (as expected), one white boy and one South Asian girl. They both play into the exact flute stereotype by entering high school with a boyfriend they won't shut up about, and they both have long hair that flopped sweatily in their faces when we practiced pivot turning, and neither seems to have a good sense of rhythm. "At least the clarinets looked worse," I finish.

"They always do," Sofia snickers. "Reed-sucking weirdos." There's no real bite in her insult, but our clarinet section really doesn't do much to dispel the myth of being the nerdiest nerds of all the nerds.

"And there's one new saxophone who looks like he's going to cause drama," I add. Generally speaking, saxophones are either taller versions of the clarinet weirdos, or heartbreakers, or both.

"Why are marching band stereotypes so true?" Sofia sighs wistfully.

"Must be something they put in the cork grease." I laugh. "Or the . . . slide oil? Valve oil? What do they call it in your *boyfriend's* neck of the cubbies?"

"Lube," Sofia answers without missing a beat.

"Ewwwwww." This is what I get for trying to tease her. "Whyyy?"

"Grow up," Sofia calls over my whining. "Like you wouldn't willingly pour *slide oil* down Gilberto Reyes's naked chest if he ever gave you the time of day."

"Why are you like this?" I swear Andy's immature crudeness is rubbing off on Sofia, but I know better than to say it. I haven't changed my opinion that Andy is a genuinely obnoxious human, but after a few fights over the summer, I do try harder to keep that to myself.

"Why are *you* like this?" Sofia grumbles. "What do you and my mother have against the healthy expression of female sexuality?"

"I have a problem with you trying to healthily express *my* sexuality." Sofia's accusation does make me feel a little guilty, though. Ellen—whose voice is the one my conscience uses to lecture me about feminism—would not approve of making anyone feel bad for being horny on main. And I don't either! It just feels out of left field, like, what possessed you to bring naked Gilberto Reyes into the conversation? Where did that come from? Nobody wants that!

"Whatever. You seriously need to find someone to make out with this year, because I am not looking to baby-sit the forty-year-old virgencita forever."

I shrug. Makeouts are probably fine or whatever, but I'd rather impress Gilberto Reyes with my initiative and fingering.

. . . of my flute keys, I mean, ohmigah!

"Oh, let's talk about the flaquito low brass freshman." Sofia jumps to a new subject, which is a relief since I'm starting to feel totally squicked out. "He looks like a tuba will flatten him."

"True, but I saw him carrying a bunch of cases at once, so there's got to be some hidden muscle there," I protest. "He looks like one of Ellen's vegan friends, though. I always worry about their health . . ."

Sofia laughs as we pull up to my house, and I'm pleased that I can leave on a good note.

I unbuckle and hop into the driveway. "Tomorrow I'm going to kill the runs in the opener," I warn.

"You do that." Sofia shrugs. "Some of us have boy-friends to spend time with."

"And that's why this is the year I finally defeat you." I waggle my eyebrows before shutting the passenger door gently (because slamming is one of Sofia's many pet peeves). She can't fool me. Whether she admits to practicing or not, I know she's going to have those runs down cold tomorrow.

"Seriously." Sofia shakes her head, dropping the passenger window. "Is this some weird cry for help? Do I need to stage a tryhard intervention?"

I pause with my hand on the door, not sure what she means. "It's not a cry for help," I finally say. "I'm good."

"Sure." Sofia drags the word out skeptically.

"I'm perfect," I say more firmly. "This is going to be my year." I head up the walkway to my front door so that I don't have to meet Sofia's doubting eyes. "Hasta la vista!" I call over my shoulder in my worst Dad accent just to make her cringe.

Sofia tosses her hair and drops into her peak chilanga voice. "Ahí te ves, pendeja."

I wave back, utterly unbothered.

THERE'S A PLATE OF QUESADILLAS WAITING FOR ME WHEN I get home, and also an extremely suspicious email notification on my phone. I double-check with Mom to find out why the tortillas are orange (sweet potato) and whether the filling is real dairy or Ellen's tofu cheese (the former, thank goodness), and then I dig in while investigating the spam-looking message.

I would 100 percent delete and report this, except that the URL is just Instagram and . . . Kingwood High Marching Band related? I don't think professional scammers or even desperate social media clout marketers would go through the effort of finding out the name of my marching band, especially since I don't even have my own bank account or anything. So after tipping the end of my sweet potato quesadilla into my mouth, I wipe my fingers on my napkin and click the link.

Graphic design is clearly someone's passion, because the account my phone slowly loads is a perfect storm of bad Photoshop and fonts, clashing colors and outdated meme photos and general shitpost chaos aesthetics. Everything is vaguely marching band related, and one post names Ms. Schumacher directly. I tear my eyes away from the clash of colorful squares and force myself to actually read the description:

15
Posts

59
Followers

0
Following

KHMB Reflections
Public Service

We hold a mirror up to the petty realities of high school marching band. DM your spiciest band thoughts and we swear we'll keep them anonymous 😉. Will post ALL our DMs (just give us a minute, damn), but only the spiciest ones make it out of Stories.

| Follow | Message |

I raise my eyebrows. A gossip account? An anonymous gossip account?

I don't *hate* gossip. I come from a long line of chismosas and am a big believer in gossip-bonding. But gossip-bonding requires, you know, the kind of bond that forms when you lean in with a knowing smile, or the look of amusement on someone's face when you make the perfect snarky observation. A secret gossip website feels different.

Not that that's going to stop me from *looking*. I check out their Story highlights and see that the account is moving quickly for something that only went live today. There's already a highlight category for "KHMB Reflections info packet," one for "staffing decisions 👍 / 👎," one for "breakups and hookups," and—okay, wow. One for "hottest flutes."

Despite the temptation of that last one, I start by clicking the "info packet."

A series of colorful text walls flip past before I can read them. This is why I hate Insta Stories. I exit and start over, focusing my attention on the garish paragraphs before they disappear.

KHMB Secrets is the latest embodiment of a long-standing marching band tradition—anonymously shit-talking each other online.

The administration pulled down our corkboard in the ancient times, like the '80s or whatever, shut down our Facebook page in 2012, and reported our blog, but they can never crush the SPIRIT of marching band gossip.

That spirit lives on whenever a band couple falls apart thanks to a percussionist, whenever two woodwinds make out in the back of the band bus, or whenever a wildly unqualified section leader shows their incompetence.

Also, we don't take any responsibility for what y'all post here. If you don't like it, click away.

I mean, it kind of makes sense, I guess? I don't know about that last paragraph. Also, if this is such a tradition, why didn't we have it last year?

Well, we didn't have a marching season last year either. And it's not like Sofia would have willingly told me any high school band secrets from her freshman year.

I don't know if any of this is a good idea, but I do click "hottest flutes" because, come on, I have to see.

Hottest Flute final bracket: Sofia Palacios, the original flavor, the queen of the section, or Yasmín Treviño, the new and (not necessarily) improved. I've never seen two pretty best friends, so let's settle this once and for all, y'all!

Swipe through to see the matchups you missed!

Message at your own risk if you don't want your comments posted!!

This is so ridiculous. I can't believe anyone is participating in this. Surely no one is participating in this? My stomach holds itself at attention as I click Sofia's name. This is ridiculous, and I don't *care*.

I'm winning 63 percent to 37 percent. I slump a little bit in relief that immediately puddles into guilt. Okay, fine, I didn't want to be losing. But I didn't want Sofia to be losing either.

I swipe to see how the bracket progressed and start to get a better sense of how it happened. The account screenshots and posts all the messages people send while voting, and it's pretty clear that this isn't a purely aesthetic assessment. The comments are uncomfortably obsessed with boob size, for one, and I've got Sofia beat there. And there are also a lot of comments, especially in the Katrina vs. Han matchup, that got really specific into what it would be like to date them (I mean, I *think* they're talking about dating. If not, it's way, way, way more uncomfortable).

The account is posting comments with the usernames uncensored, like they warned, but most people are smart enough to send messages from burner accounts. The only person I see interacting with their real name is Andy—no surprise there. This whole poll is right up the toxic-masculinity alley.

I don't like this. Even the couple of nice posted compliments can't take the sting out of the whole sleazy contest. I want to do something, stop this somehow, erase the flashing emojis and numbers before anyone else can see them. I want to report the account for . . . I don't know, objectifying minors and also being rude and making people feel bad and weird.

But, I mean, obviously that's not new behavior on the internet. I'm probably overreacting. It's harmless fun, right? People just . . . like to talk about this kind of thing for some reason.

Am I a hypocrite for feeling like this is more dangerous than chisme?

I want to process my thoughts, so I try videochatting Sofia, but she rejects the call after only two rings.

Why do you refuse to text before calling? she texts. A second later she adds, You monster.

I stifle a sigh. I hate texting so much. People take forever to answer, and then I forget what I was planning to say, and then I can't hear their tone of voice, and my spelling sucks, which Sofia likes to point out. It's bad enough that I have to be in email and group-text hell for official things like school and clubs and group projects; I don't want to have to compose sentences every time I want to talk to my best friend. I can't even tell if she's seen the poll, and I definitely don't want to ask her about it if she hasn't. If I could hear her voice, I would know immediately. She'd give me that same tight congratulations she gave me when I got into the Duke Talent thing, and my mom was bragging so much that her mom started scolding Sofia for her performance a full year before. But staring at the word "monster" doesn't tell me whether it's monster (affectionate) or monster (derogatory).

When I don't answer after a while, Sofia texts, I'm hanging out with Andy. I'll call later if you're around.

I imagine that she's sighing a little, but that's the whole problem—I don't know for sure if she is. She could be laughing, or snapping her words because she's seriously sick of me, and how am I supposed to know how to respond when I don't know which it is?

I send a thumbs-up and several smileys, which feels reasonably safe for any occasion.

The problem now is that I still want to talk to someone. But there's no one else in band (or outside my family) that I'm really close enough to call out of the blue. I'm . . . comfortable with the flute section, Laylah especially, since we hang out at Sunday school, but I've had trouble cultivating our friendship beyond the times and places we're forced to be together. Maybe it's because I'm so bad at texting, and maybe it's because Laylah is a little shy, but either way it seems weird to reach out now. I have her number—I have the numbers of everyone in my section because Ms. Schumacher made us exchange—so I could just . . . send a text right now asking if she's seen the gossip account. But it feels stressful to put Laylah on the spot like that. Maybe she hasn't seen it and would be upset by the concept. What if she thinks I'm talking to her about it because I think she and Mia are gossip-worthy, and she gets offended? I spin my phone between my fingers, not sure what to do.

We had a flute group chat last year. That would be a perfect place to bring it up and just see what people are thinking, without forcing anyone specifically to engage.

We probably need to get a chat up and running for this year anyway. And I have all the numbers right here . . .

GROUPUS MESSAGE APP

Unnamed chat group: Yasmin T, Sofia P, Mia B, Laylah J, Han L, Katrina Q, 713-555-0123, 832-555-9876, Yuki H, Devin V

Yasmin T: Hi everyone! I wanted to start up a chat for us to chat and plan sectionals and other thigns. There is this new IG of marching band gossip also, so we can discuss our thoughs on that.

Yasmin T: 😜

Yasmin T: 🎺 🎼 ♻️

I put my phone down, letting out a breath and feeling the prickle of sweat between my shoulder blades. Textual communication technology should have quit while it was ahead with the telegram. Also, why do I already see typos in my messages?

Mom calls me to dinner, and I hurry into the kitchen because Ellen's off tonight and I'm afraid Mom might rope her into eating with us and then pick a fight, but luckily my sibling has plans with her nerdy friends and Dad is working late, so dinner is quiet and I can sneak glances at the group chat while Mom talks about rebuilding strategies for her business. Han and Katrina tease the freshmen and sophomores for being surprised by the Reflections account and inform us that getting anonymously roasted on a new social media platform every year is a rite of marching band passage. Mia has opinions on how online anonymity is going to embolden the shittiest kind of sexist/racist/ableist/queerphobic behavior: Look at how many posts are already mocking Hannah, never Gilberto, and how many comments there are just about the *existence* of a trans student. Her screenshots pretty much confirm what I was worrying about and match the Ellen voice in my head that's always pointing out systems of oppression. But overall people seem excited about the gossip, so I only react to Mia's message with a thumbs-up and don't say anything one way or another about my own misgivings.

I do end up winning the hottest flute bracket, and everyone teases me just as hard as they tease the boys for getting 0 percent votes in both of their first rounds. Nobody seems to take it super personally, so maybe I shouldn't either. Maybe Sofia won't.

After dinner, I encourage Mom to move the leftovers into Tupperware (instead of using plastic wrap like she usually wants to, which will annoy Ellen and make Dad choose between his environmentalist principles and his nonconfrontational/avoidant personality). I offer to do the dishes before Mom can get too worked up about the hassle, so by the time I'm done, it's really past time for me to shower, and I haven't even gotten to look over my music yet. Summer days always feel endless and empty; I forgot how quickly an afternoon and evening can pass when you spend the day at school.

Plus, I think all that standing at attention actually affected my muscles. My arms and shoulders feel a little slow when I work conditioner through my long curls, and my back protests when I bend to shave my legs. I finish as quickly as I can, rush applying moisturizer, and drape a towel over my shoulders so my hair doesn't drip through my pajamas. It's almost nine thirty, which leaves me only half an hour to practice before the house rules of Flute Curfew kick in. Better get cracking.

My mistake is grabbing my phone off the bathroom counter and checking it before I head for my music binder. I have missed calls from Sofia, three of them, and a series of texts that I can only see previews of. The one that catches my eye asks, Are you avoiding . . .

Oops. I guess I'm going to have to make an exception to Flute Curfew if I want to handle Sofia before I practice. Did she see the Reflections IG? Is she mad?

I call Sofia and then remember that she gets annoyed when I call without reading the texts she's already sent, so I put the ringing on speakerphone and try to skim the messages, but I can't decipher them fast enough, so I still end up on the completely wrong foot when Sofia answers and I ask, "Wait, what's going on?"

Sofia doesn't sigh or groan—a bad sign. "Hi, Yasmín," she says. "Do you by any chance remember the conversation we had less than eight hours ago?"

Uh . . . That's not what I was expecting her to say, so my brain takes a second to shift gears. I have a good memory for conversations (well, I have an okay memory for conversations; I have a near-perfect memory for conflict), and I assume she's not talking about the fun band gossip part of our car conversation. Which means she's talking about the other part, the "I'm still the section leader" part.

The part where she told me to stay out of running the flute section. A couple hours before I created a flute section group chat.

"Okay, wait, no. I wasn't trying to, like, schedule sectionals this week, though," I protest. "I was just thinking that we should have a chat for when we were ready to start scheduling! Plus I mostly wanted to talk about the gossip account—" I hesitate, remembering too late that Instagram might also be a sensitive topic. "Uh, that's what I was trying to call you about earlier. But you were busy with *Andrew*."

Sofia doesn't even tut when I drag out her boyfriend's full name.

"What's to talk about? Seems like you should be very proud of yourself." Her voice is tight.

"That's not . . . it wasn't even . . ." I can't think of a way to phrase it that won't make Sofia even more annoyed, that won't sound like I'm deprecating myself or fishing for compliments or adhering to Eurocentric, fatphobic beauty standards, but the vote clearly and objectively didn't tell the whole story. I know this because Sofia is clearly, objectively the prettiest person ever. She has amazing eyebrows and a natural fashion-model body type and never has to dig through her closet or the Marshalls sale section searching for something flattering because everything is designed to fit her. I can make my middle-of-the-bell-curve-y shape work, but only with a lot of time and Pinterest research. Through trial and error, I can definitely achieve cute and approachable and even hot. Sofia is, like, ethereal and arresting. So I want to tell her that she just lost the poll because immature high school boys found her too intimidating to date, but I don't actually think that will go over well, so I switch focus instead. "Whatever. They shouldn't have run such an objectifying poll. Do you think someone should do something about it?"

"About what?" Sofia asks.

"I don't know, about the account. Doesn't it all seem a little . . . you know. I mean, it's almost certainly against the honor code."

Yeah, we have our own honor code that's part of the (real) KHMB info packet. It covers time commitment, attendance at the games, uniform violations, zero-tolerance policies for drugs and alcohol, and the relevant section on hazing and harassment.

"God, you're a goody two-shoes," Sofia groans. "No, I don't think anyone should do anything about it. It's fun." Her voice is still a little too tight, but she pushes through. She might even sound convincing to someone who didn't know her as well as I do. "And by the way, this is not what we're talking about right now. You might be the *sexiest* flute"—she definitely used that particular word choice because she knows it makes me cringe—"but you are not in charge. I am."

Yeah. I know that. Obviously.

"Yeah, I know that, *obviously.*"

But I waited a beat too long to say it. Sofia's voice is icy cold when she says, "I'll see you tomorrow, Yasmín," and hangs up on me.

Which, okay, is not great. I have definitely dug myself into a giant hole of Sofia annoyance.

But it's going to be fine. Just like it was after the seventh-grade Duke Whatever Thing, just like it always is. I know how to handle Sofia.

I can fix it.

CHAPTER 4

Sofia thaws minutely the next morning when I greet her with a thermos of my mom's coffee. Kale-eating suburban mom plus Mexican equals total coffee snob; her brews are always organic and have a million special characteristics that I don't understand because it mostly tastes the same when you drink it with as much milk and sugar as I do. But Sofia appreciates all of Mom's dark or light roast, cold brew, whatever, whatever. She complains that I'm too perky and that it should be illegal to wear a skirt to marching band, but she takes the thermos eagerly.

Which just makes me smile because it's a step toward normal.

Morning marching practice is worse today since I'm starting out already sore and with a better understanding of how hot it's about to get. But it's also better because, after a half hour of warm-up and review, Hannah deems us freshmen and sophomores ready to start moving with the rest of the band.

We form a grid of bodies in the parking lot, each of us standing with our heels on one of the evenly spaced dots painted across the asphalt. We walk forward eight steps, the number meant to carry us perfectly to the set of dots five yards in front of us. Our first attempt is a disaster, the freshman flutes almost crashing as they both veer off course. I end up far ahead of my dot, while Mia, who should have been next to me, is almost three feet behind. Our chaotic lines break into equally chaotic chatter, and it's only when Gilberto turns on the megaphone siren that the arguing stops.

"Okayyy," he calls, stretching the word with a smile that makes up for the light sarcasm. "We'll try that again. Don't forget that you should be hitting a dot every two steps. Freshmen, we put seniors on the ends of every row on purpose—try to line up with them. Seniors, now isn't the time to adjust to your line, we need the little freshman fish to develop a sense of step size, so don't let them stop you from hitting *your* mark. Section leaders, step out and watch this time, please. What's our goal for today?"

"As one!" we all call dutifully. Hannah, Gilberto, and Ms. Schumacher have been making us repeat it (we step off *as one*, we move *as one*, that sort of thing). It's totally cursi (just like all the cheesy chants we've practiced), and Katrina and Han have been rolling their eyes every time we do it, but I don't hate it. *As one* is what I love about a full concert band. The feeling of melting into and strengthening the group with my work, my attention, my skills. It's where I want to get with marching, and I don't mind the reminder.

Plus it helps that Gilberto's voice is inherently charming—he could probably read Pinterest inspirational quotes and make them sound sincere. I would . . . *definitely* listen to that podcast, actually.

I miss the step-off because I'm distracted, and the clarinet freshman behind me gives a piercing scream when he almost crashes into me.

"Sorry," he whispers after we finish the even messier eight steps.

"No, don't be!" I respond, scrambling back to my dot that I overshot again. "I missed the step."

"And what the fuck was this knot of incompetence?" Andy, patrolling the borders of the block as the low brass section leader, sneers in our direction. I sigh, then feel bad for sighing, then feel annoyed for feeling bad. I don't have to pretend to like him just because he's Sofia's boyfriend.

"We just had a little traffic jam," the clarinet kid explains, which is either nice that he didn't throw me under the bus or clueless that he didn't recognize how completely my fault it was. And it's either brave or clueless to try to say anything to Andy, whose face looks like a smug cartoon villain. He's practically rubbing his hands together in glee as he prepares his response (which I suspect is not going to be encouraging or instructive).

"Look, bro, the next time you want to 'jam' with a flute in a tiny skirt, do it in the practice room like the rest of us."

Clarinet kid blinks and balks, round face turning red. My throat feels choked with something dark and burning even as I force myself to laugh and roll my eyes and turn back to the front of the marching block. I won't give Andy the satisfaction of acting upset. I definitely won't tell him how absolutely gross he's being, or how he doesn't deserve to have Sofia glance in his direction if he's going to use her to make "jokes" about his sex life. I take a breath. It's okay.

"Hey, Andy, help us out here?" a voice calls from one of the back rows. I glance behind me and see the skinny low brass freshman waving a hand. He also shoots me a weak smile, like maybe he did it on purpose to save me and the clarinet from having to march under Andy's mocking eye. Thanks, fish.

I step off correctly this time, landing just a few inches in front of my dot, and feel a pulse of pride when I look down. The block looks cleaner too. Improvement happens like this, each piece working a bit better than before and making the whole better, *as one*. Even including Andy. I guess.

By the end of marching practice, Ms. Schumacher looks downright pleased. She even lets us dig into the show music during indoor rehearsal.

As everyone packs up, Andy and his low brass goons run through the cubby closet shouting about a party they're hosting after the last day of band camp. But I'm not waiting for the chance to blow off steam a week and a half from now. I'm focused on the sign-up schedule for chair tests, which Ms. Schumacher just announced. The last day of camp is the day of the flute section tests.

Sofia has already signed up for the first time slot, which was easy since she literally hung up the sign-up sheet (well, the woodwind sheet. Percussion has been doing their own thing in the auditorium with Mr. Green all week and has their own testing schedule). I sign up for the second spot. I head home clutching my flute case like a hurricane approaching a city with poor drainage and aging infrastructure, ready to unleash a downpour of practice time until these runs are flooded under six feet of . . . spit? Okay, I might've lost track of the simile, but yeah. Sofia tries to ask me about the party on the way home, but I'm not letting her distract me. I have the rest of this week and next to get so good at marching and playing that Ms. Schumacher takes notice.

• • •

I'M SHAKING SPIT OUT OF MY FLUTE AND CRACKING MY
knuckles to get ready for one last run-through when Mom
comes into my room. The temperature of her entrance
doesn't escape me, the way she huffs and paces the room
before looking at me. My hand shoots out to tidy the papers on my desk before Mom opens her mouth and starts
her rant with "Your sibling . . ."

She only stumbles a bit over the beginning of the word.
She's mad, but not misgendering mad, so that's a small
victory. I let her rant about the latest argument—there's
always one starting between Ellen and Mom, usually because they just don't know how to listen to each other.

I listen to Mom, nodding and responding sympathetically while my eyes flick back to my stand and my fingers
ghost over the keys of my silent flute. My brain isn't
focused on the words Mom says but on the way her frustration boils itself off until she's standing still and quiet
on my teal carpet. The sooner she tires herself out, the
sooner I can get back to perfecting the tone of that one
high G.

"That reminds me," Mom says. "Ms. Palacios said she
can sponsor your confirmation. I think that'll be better
than any of your tías, right? She can be with you every
week."

My fingers freeze on the silver buttons. "Oh, really?"

I thought for sure I'd be choosing an aunt (or maybe a cousin) as my confirmation sponsor, probably whichever one most needed a US vacation and to hit up the Galleria in late March. I've already drafted most of an email to my CCE (Continuing Catholic Education, fancy acronym for Sunday school) teacher, Mr. Frederick, explaining that my sponsor lives out of the country and can't attend any of the lead-up events. I was not expecting Mom to have any problem with the plan, and I was definitely not expecting her to suggest Sofia's mom for the job. "I don't want to put her out."

Mom tuts. "Of course she doesn't mind. She's the one who suggested it."

I mean, it does kind of make sense. Ms. Palacios and Sofia are basically our local stand-ins for the family that's all in Monterrey. It's just that I was sort of counting on not having to talk much about religion with whoever my sponsor turned out to be.

I guess that's bad; it's basically the opposite of what confirmation is supposed to be: becoming a full adult member of the church, deciding for yourself to continue the path your parents set you on as a baby. It's not supposed to be just a box to check off between first communion and, I don't know, marriage/ordination/last rites. I should probably *want* to talk to my sponsor about what it means to be Catholic and how we should be living our faith, since the whole point of having a sponsor is to help you with that sort of thing.

But I just . . . don't? Whether it's one of my aunts or Sofia's mom, I don't really want to get into any of that. If I do, I'll have to confront their particular flavor of conservative Catholicism, the one that seems really focused on things like denying reproductive rights and feeling really strongly that the Catholic Church's outdated views on marriage should be legally enforced instead of reformed. I try not to be naive about the church—I know Papa Francisco didn't fix all the problems by asking people to spend more time standing up for economic justice and less time oppressing vulnerable members of society. But there must be Catholics out there somewhere whose values line up better with mine.

And I guess if I get a choice about it, I'd rather have someone like that sponsor me.

Mom is still looking at me expectantly, and "Your friend is too conservative" would definitely not go over well, so I grasp at the first out I can think of. "I thought I might go with someone younger . . ."

I'm mostly trying to pivot back to one of my primos in Monterrey—I don't know if any of them care about Catholicism at all, but I'm pretty sure they all got confirmed at some point or else I would have heard the tía grapevine complain about it. But Mom looks slightly horrified before I can even really finish my sentence.

"I don't think Ellen is really a good choice for this kind of thing," she says. "She barely even goes to church, and that's not really the example you want your sponsor to set, is it?"

Well, yeah, I didn't mean Ellen, who hasn't shown up for organized religion much since her own confirmation. But also, she volunteers multiple times a week at a Catholic nonprofit, and isn't that more Jesus-like than attending services? Even if Ellen's not a perfect sponsor choice, the way my mom panics at the very idea is Not Great™. It's always been her fear that I'll follow in Ellen's footsteps of being rebellious and sort of leftist and queer, which seems especially hypocritical considering Jesus's whole entire lifestyle! Mom tries to teach Catholicism as tradition and social status quo; Ms. Palacios is a perfect sponsor to continue the same line of thought. The more I think about it, the less I like it.

"I'll ask Sofia," I say instead. It's a good compromise. Sofia definitely falls under "role model" territory in Mom's book, but I know she's not on board with the church's rampant history of colonialism and abuse. Sofia isn't Ellen, trying to tear down and rebuild every system from scratch, but she's not the living embodiment of the system either. Mom shrugs, tapping her foot and huffing like she's trying to think of an objection. But eventually her nervous motion stills and she nods. "Well, that would be nice. You two are so close, and you're both good girls."

. . . Okay. Listen.

I have nothing against my "good girl" nature. I like being organized and goal-oriented and responsible. I like getting grown-ups to trust me. I like making peace and people-pleasing. But sometimes when Mom or Ms. Palacios or a teacher calls me that, uses that voice and that look to imply that I've won some sort of competition of worthiness against all the other girls in the world who are less straight-edge, less straight-A, less *straight* . . . Well, when that happens, sometimes I just want to go Princess Peach–style apeshit.

I mean, I don't, of course. I hold my smile in place until Mom leaves to answer a phone call from Tía Loli. Because I know that fighting with Mom would just make everything worse.

Besides, it's fine. I figured out a way to get what I want. That's how good girls do it.

I DIDN'T COUNT ON SOFIA SAYING NO.

It's Friday afternoon. The first week of band camp is over and done with, and I invited myself to Sofia's house because I haven't been in ages and I miss her mom's cooking (which rarely includes kale) and her giant white floof of a dog, Felpudo. Felpudo and I share an ancient cushioned rocking chair and give our best puppy dog eyes at Sofia when I introduce the topic of my confirmation sponsor.

"Ugh, I literally just finished my Sunday school purgatory last year. Why are you trying to drag me back in?" Sofia lies sideways across her bed with her head hanging off the edge, exactly where she collapsed ten minutes ago. She's grumpy because Andy blew off their weekend plans, which is another reason I invited myself over.

"Technically you didn't do a complete session last year," I remind her. "And Mr. Frederick said that it could be great to have a sponsor whose 'experience of the sacrament of confirmation is so close and vivid.'"

Sofia jolts upright, exciting Felpudo, who dives off the rocking chair and joins her on the bed. "Did you already tell Mr. Frederick I was doing it? Yasmín!"

I'm still trying to keep my chair from tipping over with the momentum of Felpudo's jump. "I didn't sign you up officially! I just mentioned it! And besides, our moms are both on board . . ." Okay, I'm realizing that maybe it wasn't super cool of me to tell Mr. Frederick and Mom *and* Ms. Palacios that Sofia would be my sponsor before I asked her. "Look, can I at least have you as my backup? I'll try to think of someone else that my mom will like, but can it be an option if I don't find anyone?"

Sofia groans and buries her head in Felpudo's glorious mane. "Whatever. Fine. I don't care."

I pat both of them sympathetically and then let Sofia switch the subject to the new TV series she's marathoning and the fandom drama she discovered on Instagram. Then we do a Felpudo photoshoot until her abuela knocks on the door to ask me if I'm staying for dinner and scold Sofia for letting the dog on her bed. I'm glad I came over. Things with Sofia feel more normal than they have all summer, and I have a tentative yes for sponsorship, at least. Now I just need to work on her enthusiasm.

THE SECOND WEEK OF BAND CAMP IS EQUAL PARTS AGONizingly endless monotony and instantly passing blur. I never quite find the time to learn the freshman flutes' names, but my feet learn to split five yards into eight equal steps so naturally that I can do it without looking down. My new drill-chart binder gets grass in the plastic pockets and dirt crusted on the corners as we work our way through the entire opener, forming lines and arcs and moving waves on the field. My spot is highlighted on every page, F6, and I study the charts at night and imagine stepping off from the twenty-yard line and weaving past the thirty, the forty. I picture stopping just left of midfield (or, well, right of midfield from my perspective, which always throws me off) for the first stop-and-play moment of the opener. I stand and mark time while I practice now, feet moving in place so my lungs can adjust to the extra effort and my body can practice compensating for the slight bounce of my flute against my lips. It's definitely not easy, and I can see the wide gap between where I am and where the juniors and seniors are. But by the end of the week, I'm starting to feel like I know what I need to do to close the gap.

I've also burned through several more velitas, just to keep up the good luck. And I know they're working, because the KHMB Reflections account deletes their hot flutes highlight and moves on to fanning the flames of a color guard/percussion love triangle drama.

Friday ends with a series of full run-throughs of the opener, one third of the show we'll be performing for the UIL competition at the end of the semester. Ms. Schumacher is going easy on us, not expecting us to have the full show rehearsable or even blocked by the end of band camp. Still, I'm gasping when we finally head inside, proud that I made it through all the drill, played decently, and didn't wreck any of our curves enough for the flute section to get singled out with notes. I'm also buzzing with nerves because the closer we get to the end of the day, the closer we get to our first chair test.

Ms. Schumacher calls us in for a pep talk about our "resilience." Last year I got sick of hearing that word, but now that we're finally more or less on the other side of the Humphrey carnage (knock on wood), it feels more real to say we're recovering so well, growing so much. Ms. Schumacher reminds us to keep our music and drill binders organized and to practice over the weekend. We'll start school year marching rehearsals with a bang, 7:00 a.m. every day. We're trying to take advantage of the cooler mornings and the lack of homework now, but then as the year goes on we'll transition to fewer morning and longer afternoon rehearsals. I'm not exactly excited about the early morning practices, but I am excited to show reliability and leadership skills by being on time to all of them.

"Flutes and clarinets, stick around," Ms. Schumacher reminds us casually, as if I'm not already perched on the edge of my folding chair, shoulders tense and fingers popping my flute keys in a low-decibel cacophony. "Saxes and trumpets can grab dinner or head home, but be on time for your evening tests. The rest of brass, I'll see you tomorrow."

I take a deep breath and roll my neck. Ms. Schumacher gathers papers off her stand and gives an encouraging nod before disappearing into her office. The chair test sign-up sheet is taped to her door, just below the blue-and-green KHMB-branded clock ticking ominously toward 3:15. While the general clamor of packing up instruments fades into the specific clamor of eighteen upper woodwinds re—warming up with a cascade of scales and last-minute practice, I keep an eye on Sofia. She waves at Andy while he tromps out of the band hall through the back door, and maybe I missed it, but I don't see him wave back.

"He's not staying to see how you do?" I ask, breaking my rule of not talking about Andy. That rule has worked to keep me on Sofia's good side, but oh well. I'm allowed to talk about him and ask simple questions about his behavior. I'm not *trying* to make him look bad, so it's not my fault if he does.

"Why would he?" Sofia snaps, sinking into a defensive hunch. "I'm confident I can beat everyone here. Besides, he has his party to host."

Which is another sore point; Sofia's annoyed I'm not coming to the party, even though neither of us is excited about it. She asked me to ditch family dinner to save her from the boredom.

"If he's not here for your chair test, then you don't have to be at his party. Problem solved."

She tosses her head and walks away, buried in her phone.

So I overcome my hatred of text to shoot her an emoji with its tongue sticking out, and then a message to get her mind off her annoying boyfriend and back where it belongs: You've gone soft taking your chair tests against slacker upperclassmen for two years. I'm here now, so you should be more nervous.

Sofia grimaces at her phone and then back over her shoulder at me, but then both our eyes flick to the clock. She holds her chin high as she adjusts course and walks into Ms. Schumacher's office.

"I'm glad this one doesn't affect our grade," Han whispers behind me. "The opener is so annoying. I'm never going to be able to play it anyway."

I turn to blink at her, and she blinks back at me before laughing and shrugging. "Okay, assistant to the section leader, chill out. I'm working on it."

I recognize (in theory) that she wasn't trying to give me a compliment, but my chest puffs up a little anyway, and my smile lasts until Sofia walks out of Ms. Schumacher's office looking primly pleased with herself. I gently clack all my flute keys, take a breath long enough to speed-think a full Padre Nuestro, and then walk across the nubby new carpet and into Ms. Schumacher's office.

Ms. Schumacher is calm and friendly, and I try to radiate calm, friendly vibes back at her as sweat starts to gather in the small of my back. She asks me to play a B-flat major scale, a C major scale, and a chromatic scale, and then asks if I'm comfortable with other major scales and hits me with A major when I say yes.

This is good. This is easy. I can do this. Hail Mary, full of grace . . .

"So let's hear your opener." Ms. Schumacher smiles absently. "Whenever you're ready."

The office is quiet—soundproof, I think, which is nice for this kind of thing—and cluttered with cardboard boxes of band-branded swag and drill charts and sheet music. Posters on the wall offer encouraging slogans and breathing tips. I breathe.

I play.

I didn't like music lessons when I first started on the piano—I hated to do anything I wasn't good at. I would get frustrated picking out boring and ugly songs on the keys, but then get overwhelmed by the slightly more advanced music I *wanted* to be able to play. My brain couldn't hold so many layers: each hand, each finger working separately, trying to read two or three or five different notes at once. Mom forced me to continue the lessons for two years, during which I felt like I wasn't learning anything but actually learned a ton of foundational stuff, so, fine, credit to Mom for that one.

Band was a horse from a different sack of flour (or whatever). I'm lucky we had it in my elementary school, so I was able to join right as I gave up on piano for good. My first impression was that band was so much *easier.* I didn't have to balance the entire Jenga tower of a song on my own; I could get a firm grasp on my single block and fit into the whole. I liked the way my flute depended on my breath—it felt like an extension of singing. My family has always loved singing, whether it was Ellen's musicals or Mom's Mecano and Maná. In band, I remembered that I liked music.

It's not easy now, of course. I used to be happy if I played the notes more or less in time. Now I want to master different types of vibrato and play not just with technical precision but with emotion and artistic expression. I love the challenge of being good at something but knowing I can get better.

Playing piano, I always felt the music was getting away, disappearing out from under me. Playing this piece, the runs I've turned to muscle memory, the long notes I fill with calculated warbling air, the precisely counted rest measures, I feel stable and safe and in control through the very last note.

"Thank you," Ms. Schumacher says when I finish. "Results will be posted on Monday. Good work, Yasmín."

She smiles bigger on the last sentence, like maybe it's not part of her scripted response. I leave the room, crossing myself by flicking the fingers of my right hand toward my forehead, chest, and each shoulder. Thank you. It went well, I think. I think I did good.

This year is going to be okay.

CHAPTER 5

Ellen brings me a slice of tres leches to celebrate the end of band camp and summer. She eats the vegan parts of dinner while complaining about the slow lunch shift. Then Mom starts in on her for complaining, and it takes me and Dad both soothing them to keep family dinner from exploding.

I feel bad for sometimes wishing Ellen hadn't moved back. It's not like she chose it; she used up her savings on months of job hunting and only found one barely paid internship. Everyone agreed it was best to take it, give up the apartment, and save while fleshing out her résumé. The idea was that either a full-time position would open up in her organization or she could find something else after six months of experience.

Then Humphrey hit and the nonprofit sector suffered

as everyone spent their disposable income rebuilding or donating to hurricane relief, and now Ellen's back to job hunting and waiting tables. While I do like having her around, there's definitely a level of chaos that follows whenever she emerges from her garage-apartment room. Plus, when she and Mom have a run-in, even if they avoid a real blow-up fight (which they are getting better at), it still ends up being me who has to listen to Mom process her bottled-up rants afterward.

I spend an hour after family dinner sitting on the side of Mom's bed, listening to her process. It's all *Ellen will never be gainfully employed if she has such a bad attitude*, never mind that the attitude isn't what made her old job lose funding. It's later than I expected when I head back to my room, so I decide to run through show music quickly. By the time I check my phone, there are twenty-some new messages from the flute chat. Sometimes the volume of texts really makes me regret starting this in the first place.

I skim through the messages, which mostly discuss Andy's end-of-camp party and not the chair tests, like I would have guessed. The early afternoon messages are a pretty even split between people who want to go to the party (Katrina, Laylah, and both of the freshmen, who are excited about their first high school party) and people who think it's going to be boring (Han, but Han thinks that about most things; Mia, but she'll go with Laylah anyway; Yuki and Devin, because going requires effort). Noticeably quiet in the debate is Sofia. I scroll further, not really reading until I finally reach the link Katrina sent just twenty minutes ago.

Y'all missed some drama, but don't worry, the Reflection gram's got you covered XD

KHMBReflections on Instagram: Shared from Andygreengrass . . .

The video autoplays on my screen, drawing my eye, so I click to hear and see better. The camera jostles through a party, with a bunch of familiar sweaty faces yelling over each other. Eventually the flashing colors resolve to show Andy, pressed against a closed white door, red SOLO cup clutched in his hand as he makes clicking noises and whines, "Here, fishy, fishy! Jonathan! JohnnyJohnnyJohnny! Jonathan Blooooooom!"

"Hey. Hey, guys. Guys!" The voice behind the camera hits the mic loud even though nobody on-screen pays attention. "What's going on here?" the voice asks, full reporter mode.

Andy doesn't react, but his low brass bud Trevor leans into the frame, holding a mostly empty beer bottle. "The freshman is hiding." His smirk holds steady as his head wobbles. "Like a little *wuss*," he shouts the last word loud enough that the audio garbles. "Because he's too afraid of getting a little seven-minutes-in-heaven action with a trumpet chick who's, like, at least a five or six!" Trevor kicks the door (jostling Andy, who yelps, "My beer!") and adds, "We're doing this for your own good, Johnny boy! You have to be a man to roll with us!"

I was grossed out from the beginning of the explanation, but that last part makes me full-body shudder. It's such a fucking nightmare sentiment on every level: toxic masculinity, objectifying women with numeric values, equating sexual experience with maturity—you're like seventeen years old, Trevor. Nothing you do or don't do in bed is changing the fact that you're an acne-riddled, fake-ID-wielding *child*.

The video is still playing, more low brass boys crowding the door and crowing at the freshman they have trapped inside, whistling, making kissing noises and moans, speculating about why he doesn't want to kiss the trumpet girl . . .

I click back to the flute chat. After the link, a couple of people sent laughing emojis. Han said, God, low brass boys will be obnoxious freaking boys with an eye-rolling GIF. And then a freshman asked about Monday's morning practice and the conversation moved on.

The thread is quiet now. Probably everyone went to

bed or is pretending they did to avoid answering texts. I call Sofia (she knows to keep her phone on "do not disturb" at night so I can't wake her), and when she answers I can tell she's still at the party.

"I'm mad at you," she answers. Which isn't an unheard-of way for her to pick up the phone, but there's something off about her tone. "You abandoned me to go to this party alone, and it's boring."

"I told you it would be boring," I say, pulling the phone a few inches off my ear to avoid the blare of music. I almost ask why Andy isn't entertaining her, but I have more important things to discuss than her boyfriend's subtle inadequacies. Like, for example, her boyfriend's glaring inadequacies.

"Everyone was talking about the thing with the low brass freshman," I say. "In the bathroom? It looked like kind of a mess."

Sofia tuts noncommittally. "Hannah came for like thirty seconds and then made a big deal about leaving when she found out there was alcohol. Being drum minor really makes her think she's too good for everyone."

"Oh, um, okay?" Not sure how that relates to my question, but . . .

"Yasmín, tengo sueñoooo."

Ah. That's the final clue I need to realize that Sofia's voice is Tipsy Sofia voice. Tipsy Sofia is a rare but memorable version that will complain about absolutely everything but has the attention span and attention-seeking tendencies of a toddler. Easy to redirect before she gets too set on being mad at any particular thing, but close to useless for information.

"Did the low brass kid leave?" I try again. "He's not still in the bathroom, is he?"

"Ugh, who cares?" Sofia grumbles. "He was being a party pooper. Pooper!" she yells loudly. "Why is it called a pooper and not a pee-er? Pee on the party, that's why he's an aguafiestas."

Because I suspect Sofia isn't listening anyway, I feel safe muttering, "It seems to me like el aguafiestas es tu boyfriend borracho, pero *okay*."

"Why are you mad at me?" Sofia whines. "¿Y con Andy? No me critiques como mi mamá."

"I'm just saying that your boyfriend was harassing his freshman, and that's kind of the opposite of what a section leader is supposed to do."

"Oh, because like you know exactly what a section leader is supposed to do?"

"The kid locked himself in a bathroom!"

"Whatever, Yasmín. ¿A ti qué te importa?"

"I don't care," I respond, but the words don't sound right. "I *do* care, because . . . because . . . Andy was being a jerk . . ."

"I only made everyone play Truth or Dare because I thought you would come," Sofia says. "Somebody was supposed to steal your prudish little heart so you'd stop hating on my boyfriend. But you never showed up."

"I told you I wasn't coming." I was very clear on that. What made her think I was going to change my mind? I mean, there was her seventh-grade birthday party when I made Mom reschedule a whole family gathering so I could surprise her at the ice rink. And last year she said she absolutely wouldn't participate in my *Pride and Prejudice* movie night because she hates period movies, but then when I chickened out of inviting anyone else, she ended up coming over and letting me put it on. So I guess I could imagine a world where I turned up at the party. But . . . I didn't realize it was that big of a deal. Sofia didn't beg me to come or anything.

I don't know; maybe I should have realized. We've been a little off this year.

"I don't want to talk anymore," Sofia says, and promptly hangs up.

Okay. That was pointless. Instead of feeling better about the uncomfortable video, I now feel worse. What if that freshman quits band because of those horrible boys? What if he feels totally traumatized? There's a whole section in the info packet about hazing, and isn't that what the low brass were doing? Or, like, worse than hazing, it was harassment, right? It definitely was, because if it had been me locking myself in the bathroom to get away from a pack of drunk guys screaming about my sexual preferences . . . And it doesn't matter the freshman's gender (which it's not like I even know for sure) because anyone could feel unsafe in that situation, and . . .

I do *so* know what a section leader is supposed to do. A section leader is supposed to make the band better. At the bare minimum, a section leader is supposed to *follow* the rules, like Hannah did. When the rules get broken, and people do things that will hurt the band members, hurt the band—a section leader is supposed to care. A section leader is supposed to do something about it.

And if I want Operation: Section Leader Material to work, I can't wait for Andy or Sofia to step up.

I creep through the kitchen and knock on the door to the garage apartment. Ellen's basically an expert on holding people accountable, and right now I want to borrow some of her conviction before the Mom in my head can convince me to keep my head down and focus on my PSAT prep, or before my nerves convince me to let this go so I don't make Sofia even more annoyed. I don't want to let it go.

Ellen gets on board immediately, always down for a good righteous cause. I guess there are some advantages to having her home.

"Are you thinking of fighting fire with fire? Make an anonymous account of your own and shame these dirtbags?" Ellen's eyes practically gleam as she proposes this extremely chaotic plan. Chaotic Good, maybe, but I'm just a more Lawful person myself.

"Uh . . . that seems roundabout. I think I'll handle this the traditional way."

Ellen's slightly skeptical—she likes to do things her way—but she helps me develop my plan. She also gives me a pep talk on Sunday night when I almost change my mind because tomorrow is the first day of school and do I really want to make a big dramatic fuss? And she drives me to school super early Monday morning so Mom or Sofia don't ask questions.

"You're doing the right thing," Ellen says, and it's comforting to know that, unlike me, she would never say that if she didn't believe it.

"Yasmín." Ms. Schumacher tucks a stack of papers under her arm and checks her watch when I knock and push open the band hall door. "I thought it would be Gilberto or Hannah, but maybe I should have known you'd be the first one here. Wanted to get in some practice time before the first day of classes?"

I shake my head, throat tight. "I came to see if I could talk to you about . . ."

Ms. Schumacher chuckles. "There's no talking about chair tests, I'm afraid. My decisions are final. See for yourself." She hands me a blue flyer, which I glance at but can't make any sense of while my heart pounds in my throat.

I take a breath long enough to pray to be brave like Ellen or Sofia. "I wanted to talk about . . . to report. I want to report something that happened."

The smile drops from Ms. Schumacher's face like a crisply cutoff note. "Report?"

I have it all straight in my head, how I'm going to tell Ms. Schumacher that there was a hazing incident at the party, how I have footage (screen-captured and cropped so the Reflections Instagram isn't named) that shows a freshman being harassed. I've planned for some skepticism, some pushback, maybe Ms. Schumacher saying that boys will be boys, but I know how I'm going to counter that. Ellen helped me find articles about the psychological and social effects of bullying and ostracization, so I have a lot of facts bouncing around in my head. The most important thing is that I'm going to argue for a specific action plan. I'm going to ask for all the section leaders to get extra training on the importance of building safe communities, and I'm going to ask for all the freshmen to have a meeting where they can express their concerns. It's a good course of action, I think. It will get things out in the open, not letting problems and resentment fester.

I hope it will give Andy a chance to realize what a jackass he was. And maybe it will also show Ms. Schumacher how I can be a leader.

That's not the point or anything, but it's not *not* part of the plan.

I have it all straight in my head, but from the moment I start talking, things don't go the way I expected. Ten minutes later—less, maybe—I'm in the main office with the principal, Mrs. Sanchez, and all three assistant principals, and they're talking over my head and passing my phone around, and nobody is talking about my action plan at all because there's something I didn't account for in all my mental preparation for this moment.

I forgot that the video shows underage drinking.

One of the APs, Mr. Dansey, whose ID badge includes the salsa dancer emojis after his name, promises me I can stay anonymous as Mrs. Sanchez dials parent phone numbers into her bulky desk phone. Ms. Schumacher holds a whispered phone conversation with Gilberto Reyes where she has to forbid him from running morning practice without her. After a lot of tense phone calls, the morning bell rings, and Mr. Dansey sends me to first period with another promise of anonymity. But as I'm leaving the office, I see an office runner leading the low brass freshman from the video in to see Mrs. Sanchez, and he sees me walking out. He looks confused, on edge, probably because he was summoned to the principal's office first thing on his first day of high school.

A wave of guilt makes me break eye contact. I think I just got a lot of people into serious trouble for this long-limbed white boy with a mess of ash-brown curls and a jumble of plastic and string bracelets climbing one wrist. I didn't ask him how he felt about the party or the video. I don't know if he wanted to be dragged into any of this.

I duck my head and scramble to class, feeling small and sweaty. I thought I was doing something right, something that would make me Section Leader Material, something I could write about in my college essays. Now I'm afraid I just did something I'm going to regret.

MARCHING BAND IS LAST PERIOD FOR WOODWINDS AND brass, which is great for bleeding straight into afternoon practice (and evening practice later in the season). But today it means that by the time I walk into the band hall, everyone already knows that our entire low brass section is fucked. Minus the freshman and Neeraj, who skipped the party, they're all suspended from school for two weeks and suspended from marching band for the entire season. Everyone knows that Andy's mom, who is (predictably) kind of a Karen, is probably the only reason they aren't all expelled.

Everyone also knows exactly who turned them in.

Laylah looks like she's considering what to say to me while I slide my stuff into the cubby with my head down. Mia doesn't consider, just fake-coughs the word "snitch" at me before flouncing away.

"I didn't think . . ." I say softly to her back.

Laylah grimaces. "Yeah . . . sorry, but maybe you should have *thought*, you know? We don't like those guys either, but . . ." She sighs, waves her hands at the whole band hall, the whole band. It's marching season. You need brass for a marching band. The sousaphone was quite literally invented for this. I've never seen a band score well at UIL with less than four tubas. There's no replacement for that sound. Without Andy, without that whole crew . . . we're dead. I killed our chances.

"It's not that I don't like them!" I try to explain. Ruefully, I remember Mr. Dansey's promise that I could remain anonymous. "The freshman . . . I just wanted them to apologize for that. I forgot about the alcohol policy."

Laylah gets the look on her face that I recognize from whenever our Sunday school teachers say something about the sanctity of life or family values. The "I want to believe you mean well, but it's straining my suspension of disbelief" look. I don't think explaining is helping my case. It doesn't matter what I thought I was doing; it matters what I did.

Outside of the cubby closet, nobody's moving chairs

into concert arcs. Instead, everyone's gathered in huddled clumps whose whispers turn to shushing as soon as I get close. Ms. Schumacher is nowhere to be found. A couple percussion kids from last period are spreading info instead of going to their next class. I hear at least one voice speculate whether we'll even go to UIL this year. Whether we'll cancel the season.

I pull out my phone to look less like I'm trying to eavesdrop. The flute chat is dead silent—which makes no sense, actually. There must be a new thread that doesn't include me. I swallow hard.

The Reflections Instagram has taken down the video, nearly all of its posts and highlights, anything that might get flagged by school administration. There's just one story left.

KHMB STATUS:
season threatened by
Hurricane Yasmín

The late bell rings, changing exactly nothing around me. I'm about to retreat to a practice room when Sofia enters the band hall, the heat of her glare making my throat go dry. I tried to call her at lunch. I even texted. I wandered the halls looking for her when I didn't find her in the band hall—even checked the cafeteria in case she was hiding in there. But now that she's walking toward me, I kind of want to turn the other way and run like the coward I am.

"Well?" she says, staring me down in the middle of the hundred or so pairs of eyes all pretending not to watch us.

I take a breath. Maybe I can still, I don't know, do some damage control. If I talk to Sofia now, if everyone sees her listening, maybe they'll understand what I meant. Maybe Sofia can grant me absolution in the eyes of the rest of the band. I mean, she has every reason to be extremely pissed on behalf of her boyfriend, but . . . she's still my best friend.

"I'm so sorry," I say. "I only wanted to talk about hazing. I would take it back if I could. I'd do anything to make this right."

Sofia stands still, eyes sharp and laced with bitter poison. Nothing about that look says "understandable mistake" or "all is forgiven" or even "give me time and we'll get through this." The look says "revenge is a dish best served right the fuck now." I brace myself for the takedown.

But then Sofia says, "Okay."

"Okay?"

She raises her hands like I've defeated her, but I get a sense it's the other way around. "Okay."

"I'm sorry," I say again. Sofia just nods.

If all was really forgiven, she would be fondly calling me ten kinds of asshole. If she was working through her normal anger, she would be ripping me a new one. I have no idea what to do with this calm. I have no idea what it means.

Ms. Schumacher's office door opens. She looks haunted, but asks us to sit on the carpet while she pulls her normal stool to her normal spot. She explains everything the rumor mill has already processed about the low brass section. She says she's disappointed, but for all the wrong things. For partying, for breaking the law, for posting evidence online. Doesn't she care about the rest of it?

"You should all know better," she says, but I'm the one people look at. Then she says, "I know we're all wondering where we go from here."

My breath catches. They're not really going to cancel the season, are they? But even if they don't, are we going to be able to show our faces at UIL? Will we be one of those bands that cobbles together a halftime show for the benefit of the football parents and never competes on our own? Or maybe that sad scenario is still out of reach for us. Even our show tunes will suffer without low brass.

"I've talked to student staff about our options," Ms. Schumacher says. "And we all want to hold ourselves to a high standard. We want to go to UIL"—there's a half-hearted cheer and some scattered claps, but most people still look worried and confused—"and that means we're going to have to be flexible." Ms. Schumacher takes a long beat, looks around the room. "So. I'm asking for volunteers to switch instruments to fill out the ranks. It won't be easy, but none of us signed up for easy, right?" She half laughs, and I think maybe she's trying to sound inspiring, but it comes across more as pleading. "That's all I've got for today, folks. Talk with your sections and let me know who will be joining low brass. The rest of the period can be study hall." She heaves a huge sigh and slides off the stool, heading back to her office and leaving the door just open enough that she's technically supervising.

What. The. Hecking heck?

Switch instruments? Fill out the ranks? How is that even going to work? It's not *totally unheard-of* for a wood-wind to pick up a brass secondary instrument to be more useful during marching season, but that's when they have an experienced section around them. A whole low brass section made up of people who've never touched the in-strument before this season? Will that be any better than no low brass at all? Tubas are loud. There's no hiding in the music; every messy cutoff or blurted note will be on display. And Ms. Schumacher is just expecting people to jump into playing one, or the equally loud euphonium, for three-ish months and then march at UIL. That's impossible. That's a nightmare. That's . . .

Every single flute is looking at me.

"Well?" Sofia asks for the second time today. Her look is still a challenge, but now I'm clued in to its meaning.

I did say I'd do anything to make this right.

I almost drown crossing the sea of gossiping band kids to get to Ms. Schumacher's office. She looks as excited to have me as I am to volunteer. "Yasmín, if your section is trying to force you—"

"No," I cut her off. "They're not. I want to do it. I . . ." I can't say I need to do this, because that will sound like peer pressure. "It will be a . . . cool challenge."

Ms. Schumacher grimaces at me. "Okay. You can go to the instrument closet. Gilberto is signing out the horns. I'm guessing you'll be learning euphonium?"

I shrug. The low brass section includes the full-body-wrapping sousaphones (which we sometimes call tubas because they're just the marching version of the same instrument) and also the smaller but still gigantic euphoniums (sometimes called baritones because . . . I don't even know why—low brass is just a confusing mess). Why am I joining this section I literally don't know the first thing about? I try to keep my smile steady.

"Okay." Ms. Schumacher nods. "Have . . . fun." She looks down at the binder in front of her, frowns, and crosses something out with a thick black Sharpie.

Maybe my name. Maybe my chances to ever lead the flutes.

I slink to the cubby room.

Gilberto Reyes's eyebrows spike when he sees me, but he quickly smooths them out with a smile. "Hey . . ." he says in that slow, temperature-taking way. "How are you holding up?"

His kindness is like a spotlight, and I'm about to puke from stage fright. I open my mouth and say nothing, and then I shrug and say nothing, and then I laugh awkwardly and still say *nothing*. I have had dreams about marrying Gilberto Reyes, and I absolutely do not want to talk to him about this.

"Keep your head up," he says. "Hannah's been warning Andy . . . I should have done more to keep him in line. Putting a freshman in the middle of that shit, that was bad."

Of course Gilberto Reyes gets it. I pick my debilitating crushes very well, thank you. I'm so relieved I forget to be tongue-tied. "That's all I wanted to say! But it became this whole . . . zero tolerance isn't even a good system . . . and now I play euphonium, I guess." Brilliant and charming, I am not.

Gilberto winces. "Actually . . ." He looks at his clipboard, at the mountain of instrument cases behind him, back at me. "So we've been due to buy new baritones for a while, and obviously that got sidelined last year, so we started with a shortage already, and Jonathan and Neeraj have theirs, and then Elias checked one out during lunch—I had sort of talked to the trumpets already, which wasn't super cool of me, I guess . . ." I definitely don't follow, until Gilberto runs a hand through his (glossy, perfect) hair and explains, "We don't actually have any euphoniums left. Just tubas. But maybe Elias will switch, if you're worried about carrying it. I can go ask him if you want."

I laugh. There doesn't seem to be anything else to do. "No, that's okay. Just . . . what do you have?" How much can a marching tuba—a sousaphone—really weigh? A lot more than a flute, probably! I think of how my arms ached after holding my horn up last week. "I'm going to die either way, aren't I?"

Gilberto whistles a long descending glissando. "Uh . . . yeah, it's pretty bad all around. I mean, the bright side is that you're not, you know . . . the tiniest flute we have?" Gilberto bites his lip like maybe he should have shielded me from the objective fact that I'm not as skinny as Sofia, which is more annoying than pointing it out in the first place. He rushes quickly forward, "Anyway, with baritones, the weight is so far forward and all on your arms, so a sousaphone might be better in the long run. It'll be more like . . . a crossbody bag that weighs between twenty and thirty pounds!" He lets out an unconvincing laugh as he uses his foot to scoot a case toward me. "This is, well, the Dragon. Tuba D, but I think they had to give it a nickname to avoid it getting a worse *D*-themed nickname." His smile quirks up at the corner, and my head (probably) explodes because Gilberto Reyes obliquely mentioned dicks in my presence and everything is awful and my skin is on fire. "So you can just sign here . . ." Gilberto holds out his clipboard. I sign a blank line, then only think to read after he's pulling it away, and all I get is "Instrument something Rental something Agitation."

Or, wait, that's probably "Agreement." The agitation is in me because Gilberto Reyes touched my hand when he took back the clipboard.

"And then you can add your name . . ." He passes me a silver Sharpie and shows me a long list of crossed-out names down the side of the case. Most recently, Trevor Jones, Andy's awful bestie. I cringe as I write my name as small as possible under it. Yasmín Treviño. Tuba D.

Gilberto snaps a photo of my signed agreement and then gives it back to me to get the parent/guardian signature by tomorrow. He explains that I can take the Dragon home now, if I want, or I can leave it at school and work in the practice rooms.

"Thanks. I . . . uh, I guess I'll . . ." I stare at the case. What if I can't move it? "I'll just leave it for now."

Gilberto nods. "We'll get your new section together soon. Tomorrow, probably. We get that this is a lot." We both laugh again, as if that helps. My marching season is slipping away for the second time, and I can't cry in front of the drum major I want to impress. Ha ha.

"If you want a suggestion?" Gilberto waits for me to nod before he continues, which is another excellent quality. "Take the mouthpiece home tonight. Since you're a woodwind and all, the embouchure is different. I imagine you'll feel a lot better if you can make a sound tomorrow."

My stomach is flopping like a magikarp now, both because this is officially the most attention Gilberto Reyes has ever paid me and because I don't want to learn a new embouchure. I don't want to start over being the clueless kid who can't play anything but a screech. I don't want any of this.

But I also can't change it now. And Gilberto Reyes, in his infinite and crush-worthy kindness, is giving me good advice for how to start making myself less clueless. "Thanks." I reach for the silver clasps that keep the case closed, unlatch them with a surprisingly loud CLUNK, and pull up the top half of the case, hoping nothing crashes.

The Dragon is huge and silver, and its wide dented maw roars at me from its soft black felt nest. I leave that and the curving middle segment alone, reaching in to snatch the tiny mouthpiece like I'm afraid the new horn will snap at me. Gilberto nods encouragingly when I hold it up, like maybe he's impressed I could pick it out of a lineup.

The mouthpiece is *relatively* tiny. It's still three times as wide as my flute, and I'm officially baffled as to how I'm supposed to put my mouth around it. It's kind of shaped like a DivaCup (thanks, brain, for that mental image), and I feel like I should remember how brass players use these things, but all I can recall is that the word "buzz" is somehow involved.

"You can let me know if you need any help," Gilberto says. I stop examining the mouthpiece and shove it into my pocket, shaking my head because I do not need Gilberto Reyes staring at my mouth or making me look at his mouth. I just want to leave so I can be awkward and clueless where no one can see me. "Okay," he says. "Ms. Schumacher will probably email tonight about the plan. After-school practice isn't happening today, but we'll get everything rearranged and the charts adjusted by tomorrow, so we'll be able to jump back in . . . Well, she probably already told you. Good luck."

I nod and scurry out of the cubby closet, the mouth-piece that barely fits in my pocket digging into my hip. I made an impression on Gilberto Reyes; he knows who I am and even offered support. It's a tiny raft in a flood of disappointment, and the irony of the whole situation threatens to capsize it, but I try to hang on anyway.

Everyone in the band hall is staring pointedly away from me. It looks almost like an average lunchtime, with everyone clumped in groups on the floor with the occasional folding chair dragged into the circle, backpacks open and phones out and snacks trading hands. But the laughter is missing, and I don't know what to do because I can't just go sit with the flutes like everything is normal. The wrongness of the whole day freezes my feet to the ground. This isn't lunchtime or a fun free hour off work. This is about as much of a "vacation" as the weeks post-Humphrey, and I can't be the only one wondering how we recover from this.

I mean, obviously I'm not the only one. That's why no-body will so much as glance my way except . . .

On the other side of the band hall, surrounded by nearly as much empty space and as many turned-away heads as I am, one pair of eyes meets mine. The low brass freshman (Jonathan? I've heard his name a couple of times now, but I'm only 90 percent sure) gives me something that might be a nod, and that tiny approval unfreezes me enough to go back to my spot next to Laylah. At least one person doesn't hate me for what I did. Two, counting Gilberto. I busy myself with my algebra book. Laylah gives me a wry smile and a piece of extra lead when my mechanical pencil runs out. Three people who don't hate me. I keep trying to make eye contact with Sofia, hoping to get the count up to four.

It's a long, tense hour before the bell rings. Mom insisted on picking me up today, so I don't have to follow Sofia out to the parking lot, but I do it anyway out of habit. She stays calm and cold, only looking at me when I'm standing next to her open driver's-side door and impossible to ignore anymore.

"What? I thought you didn't need a ride."

I'm not sure what I'm supposed to say. I'm not sure how to ask if she's too mad to ever drive me again. "Uh, Ellen offered to drive me tomorrow," I lie. "If it's easier for you?" I try to watch her face, but she's flipped her sunglasses on, and I have no idea what I might be missing.

"Okay," she says. "Flutes have morning sectionals anyway."

Her dismissal slams shut like her car door in my face. I'm not a flute anymore. I step back as she reverses out of her spot and drives away.

I twirl the mouthpiece in my pocket, the one I don't know how to use, that belongs to a beast of a tuba as unfamiliar as a real dragon. Then I head to the corner where Mom's probably stuck in a line of traffic.

I'm low brass now. And as much as it hurts, I have no one to blame but myself.

CHAPTER 6

I am *planning* to tell my family what happened. I honestly mean to do it in the car, but Mom has a million first-day-of-school questions, and once we're home she wants me to walk her through the school website and how to access my online grade portal, and then she wants to go over all my handouts and syllabuses (syllabi?) and make notes in her planner—and make sure *I'm* making notes in *my* planner—and then Dad comes home and wants the first-day scoop, so I have to start from the beginning again. It's nice to eat dinner and just focus on the normal parts of the day until they seem realer than the lumpy mouthpiece haunting my pocket with its silent reminder that, even if I don't let a single lie out of my mouth, nothing I'm saying about my day is anywhere near truthful.

I retreat to my room as soon as dinner ends. It's my

first moment alone since I knocked on Ms. Schumacher's door. My first second to breathe without holding myself together for someone else's observation. I can feel the tight knot in my chest begging to be released.

But I need to get to work.

I start with Google because I need a plan. YouTube videos make the most sense to me, so I watch three-fourths of two beginner brass videos before I get the courage to hold the mouthpiece against my lips and blow.

It does not make the sound from the videos. It doesn't really make a sound at all.

I find an even more basic video and watch the whole thing this time. I drop the mouthpiece into my lap to work on my messy raspberry-blowing, "free buzzing" my air until it comes out in a steady (but not smooth) stream. My lips hate everything about this almost immediately. They tingle and itch with the unfamiliar vibration, like when Sofia and I borrow her mom's massage footrest and turn it up to the highest setting until it feels like ants are eating our feet. I rub my face until it stops feeling like ants are eating my lips. Maybe it's better with the mouthpiece?

It's worse. How does anyone manage to play these things for more than ten minutes at a time? I thought I knew pain from two years of mashing my lower lip against a flat metal plate while wearing braces, but this mouthpiece feels like it swallows half my face and bites down.

I resist the urge to fling it across the room. I'm not frustrated. Okay, I'm frustrated, but it's normal. Music is frustrating sometimes.

I drain my water bottle, which is an instant relief. Maybe I'm allowed a snack break. I'll try again in an hour or so.

I move to the kitchen and graze on bagged popcorn (the snack everyone in the house can agree on). After about thirty seconds my brain starts itching for something productive to do, so I inch toward the side table where my backpack lives. I don't really have homework yet, but I have a reading packet for WHAP that I can start on early, and math pages due next week. If nothing else, I can check the school district calendar and add all the vacation dates into my planner, ideally while listening to music so techno that it's never been touched by a real woodwind or brass instrument.

I take my backpack and a last handful of popcorn to the kitchen table. The mess I find when I unzip the biggest pocket looks like it belongs to someone else, someone who leaves their binders crammed out of order and with their spines facing the wrong way, edges overgrown with the weeds of stray worksheet corners. How out of it was I today? I brush salt off my hands and start pulling the binders and papers out, setting everything back in order. For a second, things seem manageable.

Then I pull out a crumpled blue flyer, loose at the very back of the pack. I have a vague memory of zipping it in while I rushed out of the band hall this morning. Ms. Schumacher didn't mention it again. I didn't look at it.

I look at it now.

Chair Test Results — Flutes
1. Yasmín Treviño
2. Sofia Palacios
3. Laylah Bowin
4. Devin Chu
5. Saanvi Yerramsetti
6. Mia Palmer
7. Katrina Villas
8. Gregory Avioli
9. Han Yi
*Chair challenges may be issued starting on September 3rd. Full section chair retests will be October 15th.

I check three times to be sure. Holy shit. I did it. *I did it.*

I . . . almost did it. I could have done it. I had done it, and if I had just *kept my big mouth shut and minded my own business*, it would be done. This would be my life. Not making fart noises with an instrument I probably can't lift in a section that's doomed to failure and a band that hates me for dooming us all to failure! I could—easily— have just *not done anything* and I would be perfectly on track.

FUCK!

I'm glad the front door opens when it does, because three seconds later I would have been ugly-crying. I chew my lip and stare at the ceiling and blink my way back to a mostly probably normal facial expression, and then Ellen walks into the kitchen smelling like salsa and grease. Smiling, she says, "Hey, I've been texting you all day. How did it go? Are you going to lead some community-building activities?"

And, well, so much for holding it together.

Ellen makes tea. "Is there maybe a silver lining here?" she asks. "Like, in sports, playing a different position can make you better at your main position, because you know what the other players on the field . . . are . . . thinking . . . Yeah, this doesn't make sense as I'm saying it. Ignore me. Sorry."

I hiccup into my manzanilla. I hadn't even thought about my flute skills, which will absolutely take a dive if I spend the semester practicing tuba instead. By the time I get back to my section, I'll be edgeless. "This can't be happening."

Crying to Ellen—often over tea—is a tradition, at least. But it's not the same as when I would cry as a kid and Ellen would capture the bug or sound out the frustrating word or color with me to distract me from whatever fit I was having. It's been years since she's had the answers for my tears.

Ellen scrapes something brown and crusted off her Dickies. "I'm sorry, kiddo." She sighs, sounding like Dad. "None of this— I'm sure it feels, uh, crappy. Like, wow, okay, suddenly your life got totally derailed because of something you couldn't control, and now the next step is just daunting and . . ." She coughs. "But, you know, you just have to, um, be gentle with yourself, right? Take care, and don't worry, and I'm sure it will work itself out . . . somehow."

"Yeah. I guess. Thanks."

Ellen snorts, but I'm lacking the energy to try to sound more sincere. Because of the blatant projecting, Ellen missed one major difference between her situation and mine. I had control over my disaster. I brought it down on my own tattletale head. Which means I don't have time for self-pity. I made this mess, and I'm the one who has to fix it.

I finish my tea in one gulp. I have a lot of raspberries to blow.

CHAPTER 7

I stop by the band hall on Tuesday morning. I can't help myself. I linger by the vending machines for a few deep breaths, but soon the draw of the muffled music and chatter overcomes my nerves and I pull the door open purposefully.

Morning rehearsal was canceled, but it looks like almost the entire band showed up anyway. Percussion and color guard members (who usually use the gym or auditorium for their rehearsals) overfill the space, luckily keeping their twirling and tapping sticks to themselves. The practice rooms down the back hallway are all full, and the flutes and the French horns seem to be trying to hold sectionals at the same time, Sofia practically shouting to be heard.

My chest aches a little at the sound of the tricky flute

part of the opener, and my lips ache as I watch the French horn players buzz into mouthpieces much smaller than the Dragon's. Is there a French horn joining my new section? Will they have an easier time learning to play another brass instrument? Am I going to be hopelessly behind, even compared to the other beginners?

Sofia huffs loudly, and my eyes snap to her on instinct. It's not exactly new, this undercurrent of warm jealousy as I watch her wield her power. But it's usually more tinged with admiration, and excitement to work my way up and meet her at the top. I don't like the bitter edge of my feelings today.

I start to notice people noticing me. I suddenly don't want Sofia to catch me here, watching her run sectionals with badly concealed envy. So instead, I navigate through the crowd to hide in the cubby closet.

I turn the wrong way immediately, veering toward the left wall of flutes instead of the larger cubbies on the right. Catching myself, I groan and spin on my heel, only to realize I'm not alone. The low brass freshman is here, watching me be bad at walking. He stands by the cluster of massive cubbies I'm supposed to consider mine now.

"Hi." I smile to cover my surprise. This is my section mate now, so I should definitely act happy to see him. "We never actually met. I'm Yasmín."

The kid nods and pulls his phone out of his pocket,

hiding his face behind it and his slightly overgrown curls. "Saw," he mutters, and it might be part of a longer sentence, but it's impossible to tell at that low volume.

"Sorry?"

"I saw on the . . ." He waves the hand holding the phone very slightly toward the door, then tucks his chin back down and keeps scrolling the tiny screen.

Okay . . . Is he mad at me? I thought he wasn't, because I thought he nodded at me yesterday, but I guess I could've read it wrong. He's allowed to be mad at me. Everyone's allowed, but him more than anyone. I just hoped . . .

"Eight," the kid mumbles, and I can't tell if he's talking to me until he waves his phone toward the door again. "We only got eight, and it seems like you're the only . . . so it was easy to figure."

I take a few steps toward the door, following his gesture, and now that I'm looking, I notice a bunch of new blue flyers taped up on the inside. Chair results for each section. My chest aches again, and I distract it by forcing myself to read each sheet. The flute flyer shows Sofia on top, undisputed queen as always. I spend an extra second reading the names of the flute freshmen, trying to commit them to memory before I remember that it doesn't matter anymore. My eyes slip back up the page. Sofia Palacios. First chair.

Why am I doing this to myself? Is this what the

freshman wanted when he pointed me this way?

Um, obviously not, my more rational brain steps in to remind me. My eyes skim the tops of the other blue flyers until I find the one labeled LOW BRASS. There's my name, at the very bottom (I'm assuming that it's just alphabetical, but it still stings). I force my eyes to move slowly up the list.

Section—Low Brass
1. Caleb Bowman
2. Elias Ayala
3. Jonathan Bloom (SECTION LEADER: phone number 713-555-4272)
4. Jonathan Gottlieb
5. Lee Parker
6. Milo Xia
7. Neeraj Shankar
8. Yasmín Treviño
*Chair test scheduling TBA

I read the whole list. Carefully. Twice. The mumbling freshman was right—there are eight of us. More than half of them don't even ring a bell, and the ones that do— Lee, who is trans and plays the French horn, and Milo, who I'm fairly sure is the Asian clarinet player I crashed into that one time—are freshmen. Except Neeraj, the lone upperclassman who's somehow still not the section leader, every other name here is either definitely or probably a freshman. And not only that. I check the list a third time. I get why the boy behind me was mumbling about knowing which name was mine.

"Am I the only girl?"

The mumbling freshman makes a mumbled noise that might be confirmation or a laugh or nothing. I fight the urge to growl. I mean, I knew low brass was traditionally full of people with, in the best-case scenario, big himbo energy, and that low brass girls were in the minority. But I didn't factor that in when I was standing in Ms. Schumacher's office, stubbornly declaring that this would be a fun challenge.

Not to totally deny my new section any benefit of the doubt, but I wasn't imagining the "fun challenge" of being the odd one out, being talked over and ignored and weirdly coddled and mascotized. I've been to summer math camp; I know how important it is to find at least one other girl to sit by so you don't drown in obnoxious behavior. I mean, Milo seems nice, and Neeraj is less obnoxious than the rest of his former section, and maybe Lee has as much reason to hate toxic masculinity as anyone else. Maybe it's possible that these boys will be more mature than the ones I remember from middle school . . . but it seems risky to count on it.

What am I getting myself into?

I must sigh too loudly, because the skinny mumbler mumbles, "O . . . kay," and even drops his phone hand. "If you need anything . . . number's on the . . ." I lean closer because he's impossible to follow. ". . . whenever . . . Bloom."

The morning bell rings, and the band hall erupts into chaos, and the mumbler disappears with his head in his phone screen and his backpack hanging from one shoulder while flutes and French horns and people from the practice rooms rush to cubby their instruments.

Which means I don't get a chance to confirm.

But I'm 80 percent sure the mumbling freshman just told me he's my new section leader.

I wonder if it's too late to switch to AP Music Theory.

I HIDE IN THE LIBRARY FOR LUNCH. NOT SUPER MATURE, but it's been a long week and it's only Tuesday.

I tell myself I'm not being a coward. I'm being tactical. Taking lunch to collect myself means I can start afternoon rehearsal strong, greeting my new section with a big friend-making smile firmly in place. It'll be good. It has to.

When I return to the band hall for sixth period, the whiteboard says: OUTDOOR MUSIC PRACTICE: FULL BAND (INDOOR SECTIONALS: LOW BRASS)

I'm almost late, slipping in just as the tardy bell chimes because my English teacher went on a "the bell doesn't dismiss you; I do" power trip. The band hall is already emptying out, and my new section leader, Jonathan Bloom, sits on a lone folding chair in the center of the room, chin on his fist like a phone-scrolling statue in the middle of all the swirling bodies. Just one chair? Ms. Schumacher has thoughtfully provided us space to get our act together without the rest of the band looking on and judging, so I assume we'll be sitting here.

I'm sure Sofia sets out chairs for flute sectionals.

Jonathan Bloom doesn't look up as I approach, his head buried in his phone and his shoulders slumped under his faded blue T-shirt. I get solidly into his personal space, but still no reaction. My big friend-making smile probably falters.

"Uhm." My half cough, half sigh garners no response. "Hi," I try again. "Jonathan?"

He startles, shifting so I can read his shirt, which says GO AWAY in tiny white letters. He mutters something under his breath, forcing me to ignore his shirt's instruction and lean closer.

"Sorry, can you speak up?" Has no one told this kid that section leaders have to give instructions? At audible volumes?

"I lost the thumb war," he repeats, which honestly

doesn't make things any clearer, but at least he's louder. "Because the other Jonathan cheats. So I'm Bloom. It was that or they were going to make me be J2-D2, and Star Wars is overrated. You probably need your horn or whatever."

The whole speech is delivered in that monotone that's usually used on parents or teachers or other people you don't want to be talking to (ouch), but it is a speech and I do hear it, so I guess that's a start.

"Okay, Bloom it is." I smile. "I've only seen like half of one of the Star Wars-es with the girl main character. I mean, I know the general idea and the memes and stuff, but . . . My family is all Trekkies."

Bloom nods and fiddles with the string bracelets on his wrist. I guess sci-fi franchises are the wrong angle to crack him. Or maybe he really just doesn't like me at all.

"So, music practice today?" I ask. "Do you want help setting chairs out?"

A frown flicks across his face as he glances at the corner where the folding chairs live until they're needed. "Oh. Um. You can . . . or you can just get your horn."

Neeraj exits the cubby closet with his euphonium assembled and then heads to grab his own chair, so I follow him and take a chair under each arm, dragging them to form the beginnings of a circle before I go to the closet.

Because it should have been set up before now. Because this sectionals is going to be chaos enough already.

Because my section leader didn't exactly tell me not to. Not because I'm avoiding the Dragon.

The Dragon lies in wait for me anyway, already out of its cubby and on the ground near a handful of other tuba and euphonium cases with a group of freshmen buzzing around them, looking as wary as I feel. Some of the cases are open, but none of the instruments are assembled yet.

"Hey." I wave as I approach, taking a breath to refresh my flagging smile. Five pairs of eyes blink wide at me. "Yasmín. Former flute. New tuba. What's up?"

A wave of dismissal passes over the faces in front of me. I hate that I recognize it.

"It's fine," one of the freshmen, a white blondish/ brownish-haired kid in a polo shirt, taps his chin while he considers the open case in front of him. "I basically have it." Everyone goes back to crowding around him and ignoring me.

Except one person does step toward me: the clarinet— former clarinet—Milo, with the chubby face and the Gudetama lazy-egg shirt.

"Yeah, we upper woodwinds are out of our league here." He laughs nervously and nibbles a thumbnail. "Uh, oh, I'm Milo."

"Yeah, of course." I'm relieved that at least one person is being normal and friendly, and also that he's including himself in my ostracization instead of inching away. "I'm glad, or, well, I'm sorry that you ended up here, but I'm glad to be playing with you."

Milo snorts and switches to biting the nails of his other hand. "No, it's totally fine." He lowers his voice conspiratorially, "I just think it's cool that you actually got rid of Andy." His eyes hold a glow of vindication that surprises me coming from his otherwise smiley, nervous face.

"I wasn't *trying* to . . ."

Milo shrugs innocently. "I'm just saying, the kid is a jackass. He got what he deserved."

Okay. Maybe Milo can be my section friend.

There's a clang, and a short Latino kid with bushy eyebrows stares in comic shock at the sousaphone bell he just dropped on the floor. The sort-of-blond guy in the polo shirt is now holding a tuba mouthpiece and a skinny L-shaped pipe in each hand, a baffled expression on his face. A freckled Black kid in skinny jeans with schmancy headphones hanging around his neck has propped up the curled body of the sousaphone and mutters to himself while spinning the screws that surround the top opening. And the last freshman boy, bulky and pale and dressed in an oversized plaid button-down, leans against the wall in the shadowiest corner of the closet with only his white-blond buzz cut visible over his defeated facepalm.

"Maybe Andy deserved it," I whisper to Milo. "But does the band deserve this?"

Milo grimaces. The plaid-clad boy hiding in the corner looks up long enough to warn the hipster headphones kid to watch out for the spit valve, and the hipster drops his part of the tuba in disgust. The kid in the polo shirt has connected his two pieces but now seems content to stop there, resting on his laurels. I can't watch this obra de desastre any longer. I march to the doorway.

"Hey! Section leader!" I call. "Your section needs some leading in here."

Bloom looks up from his phone sheepishly, and Neeraj sets down his euphonium and jumps out of his chair with a confused, "What's up?"

"None of us know how to assemble the horn," I say as they walk toward us.

"Hey," polo-shirt kid complains, "I basically had it."

"We have no clue," the short Latino kid with the eyebrows admits, cheerfully dumping the bell into Bloom's arms. "Did I break that?"

Our first lesson lasts about fifteen minutes, and it covers basic horn storage and setup, plus a quick and dirty rundown about advanced care and transportation. Bloom's instructions are sometimes drowned out by Neeraj's affirmative refrain of "no doubt, no doubt," but by four p.m., we all have our horns out of our cases and the pieces put together, ready to play.

Theoretically, at least.

Slipping the Dragon over my shoulders for the first time feels a bit like being swallowed whole. This thing is *big*. It's heavy across my chest and back, more boa constrictor than dragon, and even though I just tightened the screws holding the tire-sized bell in place, I'm terrified that they're going to come loose and give me a concussion any second.

And this is just sitting in a chair with it. How am I going to take you onto the marching field, Dragon?

Once we're all seated in a circle with our instruments, Bloom lets out a sigh that might be relief or disappointment or gathering his courage, and then he starts reading off his phone, the words pouring out both allegro-fast and legato-slurred.

"Hi welcome everyone we're going to start by buzzing into our mouthpieces that's how you make a sound with a brass instrument if you already know how you can do that now and if you don't you can just try."

There's a long silence. Neeraj helpfully plays a rumbling note on his euphonium, which encourages the kid in the polo shirt to do something similar but a little deeper and more wavering on his tuba, and the kid in plaid (who is no longer in the corner but who has still scooted his chair a little bit away from the circle) blatts out a cracked note. Milo, sitting next to me, lets out a laugh that seems more awkward nerves than insulting, but the kid who cracked turns red and frowns. There's another silence, more uncomfortable this time, and then a distinct two-note slur that sounds exactly like a disappointed horn is saying "womp-womp."

The kid with bushy eyebrows waggles them playfully as he sets down his euphonium. Everyone chuckles a little, and even the plaid-shirted guy looks a little less embarrassed.

"That's good," Bloom nods at Eyebrows.

"Yeah, I practiced with the mouthpiece last night, and I'm a trumpet, so . . ." Eyebrows gives a cocky head toss.

Elias, right? I think Gilberto said the trumpet player who switched was named Elias. Thanks, crush anxiety, for fixing that in my memory. Gilberto probably gave Elias the same advice he gave me, only it seems to have worked better for the trumpet.

Now I've got four of the seven boys named (Milo, Neeraj, Bloom, Elias), which means I should be able to process-of-elimination the other three . . .

Wait a second. I should not have to super-sleuth my way to knowing my section members' names!

"Any brass player can do lip slurs," Polo Shirt is saying, and he does a not-great "womp-womp" of his own, with an ugly blatt in the middle.

"Can we maybe back up for the woodwinds?" Milo asks.

Bloom clears his throat and scrolls on his phone again, reading aloud, "Brass instruments use the vibration of the lips to produce sound so we can practice buzzing into our mouthpieces to—"

"Can we . . . ?" I interrupt. People turn. Am I imagining a couple of eyes that look like they're in danger of rolling? This is the thing Sofia was so mad about, my second-guessing her leadership, thinking I knew better than she did how to run everything. If I had been less annoying, would she have made more of an effort (any effort) to keep me around? Am I going to end up making all the new low brass hate me just as much as the old low brass must?

I hesitate, and Neeraj jumps into the empty space of my indecision. "Yeah, I think the flute is going to need a little more help, bro." He nudges Bloom. "Do you have, like, a lesson for beginners?"

"Do you?" Bloom whispers back.

"Nah, man, you know I barely know how to play this thing." Neeraj slaps his euphonium with one hand and catches it from toppling off his lap with the other. "That's why you're the thing."

"I have a . . . this." Bloom gestures at his phone. "I'm getting . . ."

"I was actually going to say," I interrupt their quiet bickering, "that we should . . . Wouldn't it be a good idea to introduce ourselves?" I switch my statement to a question and smile as sweetly as possible. *Please don't hate me.*

"Oh shit, introductions. You gotta start with introductions, bro." Neeraj elbows Bloom harder this time.

Bloom sighs. "You want to start?" he asks Neeraj, who immediately touches his finger to the tip of his nose.

"Nah, that's a lot of responsibility," he says. "Sounds like the section leader's jam."

"I'm Bloom," Bloom says, his voice still monotone but also dripping with resignation. "I'm the section leader because I'm the closest to knowing what I'm doing, but the bar is low. I don't know. Will you go next?"

He's looking at me, eyes somewhere between hopeless and hopeful. I get a nice spike of adrenaline as I breathe and mentally rifle through a list of possible icebreakers.

"Yeah, hi, I'm Yasmín. I used to play flute. I'm a sophomore, and . . ." I need some fun facts, ASAP! "Should we do favorite colors? Truths and a lie? Uh, there's a story behind how I got my name . . . ?"

"Favorite color," someone says, at the same time Milo says, "I want to hear a name story," and at least one other person groans.

I hold my chin up and keep smiling because the whole point of icebreakers is that they're a little awkward. "Right, so, when I was born, my mom looked at me and I guess she thought I looked super white and blue-eyed, so she named me after the white flowers." I glance down at my definitely not lily- or jasmine-white hands. "Obviously that didn't stick, but the name did."

"I named my little sister Rosy because she was so red when she was born," Polo Shirt says, a surprisingly un-pompous smile on his face. "My parents should not have let a four-year-old pick. Oh, I'm Jonathan." He waves around the circle, looking like he'd love to walk around and shake each of our hands. "I won the thumb war to keep my name because I don't lose. I played trombone before, so this isn't such a big change for me. Happy to be here."

"Cool." Bloom nods first at (the other) Jonathan and then at me. "Uh, I guess we're not going in order, then, so . . . ?"

"Yeah, I'll go!" the trumpet with bushy eyebrows volunteers happily (of course he does). "I'm Elias Ayala. My name is a tongue twister! I'm a freshman too—we're practically all freshmen, right? Or fresh-women? Fresh-people? Fresh-students?" Elias shrugs, knees bouncing. "And I think Yasmín wanted to do icebreak-ers because she doesn't know us, because she's not a freshman—fresh-woman—so we should probably tell her that most of us are in at least some classes together. So we're all ice-broken. And housebroken, I hope. But never heartbroken!" He winks at no one in particular. "Also my favorite color is the best color: gold."

"Gold isn't really a color," Jonathan says, his pomp-ousness back in full force. "*Golden* is the color . . ."

Elias looks very offended, and Bloom elbows Neeraj to intervene.

"Yo, I'm Neeraj. Slack-off senior except I'm a year early, so I'm the just-chill junior. My favorite colors are Rockets red and white!" He tugs his basketball-branded T-shirt as he shouts that last part. Then he points across the circle at Milo. "Take it away, bro."

Milo fidgets. "Uh, sure, I guess. I'm Milo, I don't know how my parents picked it, but I like it because it's the character from *Phantom Tollbooth*." He shrugs at me and bites a fingernail. "I like red because money and luck and everything."

There's a long silence, and Bloom swings his head around the circle to stop at the two guys on my right. "Caleb? Lee? Can one of you . . . ?"

Almost a direction. Maybe he can learn to be a section leader after all.

"Caleb," says the freckled Black hipster. "Saxophone until recently. My name is just from the Bible or some-thing. I like black. And pink. And Blackpink." He makes the little K-pop finger heart, and Milo squeaks excitedly next to me.

"I'm Lee," says the boy in plaid. "Lee Parker. Uh, we haven't been doing pronouns but we should, and mine are he and him. French horn. And one fun fact about my name is that when I was picking it, I was *this close* to choosing Peter."

Oh, rats. Ellen has definitely talked to me about normalizing asking pronouns so that it's not always trans people who have to bring it up. I make a mental note to carve it deeply into my list of icebreakers.

"All right, all right." Neeraj nods approvingly. "So we've got Spider-Man here"—he points at Lee and then moves down the circle—"then Caleb K-pop." He emphasizes the "kay" repetition before continuing down the line by pointing to me. "Brown white girl; Milo-Danny Phantom; this-kid-talks-too-much"—Elias squeaks in indignation—"then plays-to-win Jonathan; and then our fearless leader, Bloom, who we aren't calling Jonathan anymore. And me!"

"Okay," Bloom says. "Uh, thanks, everyone. Hi." He glances down at his phone, back around the circle. "So, like I was saying, if you already know how to make sound, that's great. But if you can't, don't worry. We can definitely go over more basics, starting with posture, positioning, and then move on to buzzing and embouchure . . ."

He doesn't transform into a vibrant extrovert or anything, but he does speak a little more clearly and look a little more relaxed as he walks us through the basics of our instruments. The power of icebreakers.

Posture is what I expect—straight and tall. We detach our mouthpieces to practice, and I'm really glad I worked on this exact skill last night. I'm still bad at it, but I accidentally sat between the saxophone and the clarinet, so at least I don't feel as alone with my embouchure struggles. Bloom looks a little pained by us, but eventually he has us put our horns back together so we can play a real note.

"Just keep buzzing," Bloom says when we're all set up on the edge of our seats. "Like we did. Everyone, right now, as much as you want. Just . . ." He lifts his euphonium, which looks more like a giant trumpet and doesn't wrap around like our tubas—I mean sousaphones. Is it okay that I use "tuba" and "sousaphone" interchangeably now that I'm actually playing one? Because I definitely do.

Bloom starts playing one long repeated note. Neeraj joins in on a different pitch, quickly followed by Elias and Jonathan.

Okay, credit where credit is due. Bloom planned this moment well. The noise of the section takes off some of the pressure as I breathe and set my lips to play my first note on the Dragon.

I buzz into the mouthpiece like we practiced, but instead of a manageable whine a few inches from my mouth, noise rumbles around the Dragon's long tubes and comes out in a low roar above my head. An unsteady roar, broken and hesitant. A pubescent dragon.

I try again, putting a little more air behind my buzz. The Dragon blurts a smug chuckle at my efforts. I roll my lips together and straighten my spine before angling back into the mouthpiece. Funky lip vibrations aside, the Dragon is still a wind instrument, and I know how to use my wind.

My next note starts messy and stutters in the middle, but there's a moment, maybe two, when the Dragon sings.

I hold that sound in my heart and try to make it happen again.

Bloom sets down his horn and shuffles around the circle, offering suggestions as he goes. I hear him tell Milo to unclench his jaw and then repeat the same advice to Caleb on my other side. I guess I'm lucky not to be unlearning years of reed embouchure. Bloom tells me to keep working on holding a steady tone, which feels obvious, but I continue failing at it. He gives Elias the trumpet and Jonathan the trombone a fingering chart so they can start playing notes on purpose (but considering there are only three keys—valves?—I have a lot of questions about how that's going to work).

"The rest of you should just keep working on tone for today," Bloom says, holding up his hand to stop our random attempts at notes. "And please get as much practice as you can. Ms. Schumacher has a list of resources for private lessons, or you can ask me for help or use the practice rooms or whatever. Oh, and we're going to take rehearsal time for our own practice for a little bit, but we also need to pick a time for extra sectionals at least once a week. So, uh, I'll email out a poll or something at some point for that."

"Some point?" The words leave my mouth before I can consider whether I should stop them. I get another round of eyes on me. "I mean, I can make a list right now. We just need day and time preferences, right?" I reach for my backpack under my chair. I'm still not trying to overstep, but I don't think I'm wrong to interpret Bloom's "at some point" to mean "I've forgotten to do this once, and I probably will again." I know some people hate this kind of organizational stuff, but it's honestly relaxing for me, so I don't mind doing it as long as Bloom isn't going to mind me taking over.

Bloom blinks at me, but he doesn't seem to mind. "Uh, okay. Knock yourself out. I have to get the new drill charts passed out, so . . ."

I set up a quick form to pass around. Elias and Jonathan fight to be the first to fill it out, which could be a good sign (our top newbies are forming a rivalry that might push them to be better) or could be a bad sign (our top newbies are forming a rivalry that might cause tension in the group). Bloom gets us brand-new drill charts and then music, which looks . . . shockingly slow and simple.

I guess I didn't expect flutelike flurries of notes, but still. Ms. Schumacher worked hard to simplify the marching for us too, I realize as I check out the drill charts. I try not to feel offended. The season is going to be hard enough as it is.

After we organize our new papers, Bloom has us practice a concert B-flat (not the scale, just the note), and I fight to wrangle the pitch out of the Dragon.

"Relax your fingers," Bloom suggests, as if I'm not hanging on for dear life.

An hour passes quick, and even with frequent breaks, my lips are noticeably swollen when Bloom finally tells us to pack up. We still have to go outside and start relearning drill with the rest of the band.

"This was a good start," Bloom tells us before we head outside. "I think it's gonna be . . . You know, we'll survive this."

Neeraj whoops and Elias grins, and the general murmuring and laughter around the circle seem positive. I give a quiet "ha" a second late; I don't want to be the only person who finds Bloom's speech underwhelming.

But I was hoping to do more than survive this year.

Not much chance of that now. It's clear that music is going to be rough—I don't see how I can possibly catch up with Elias and Jonathan, much less Bloom and Neeraj. There is no path to first chair for the foreseeable future.

And if I can't even work toward being the best, what am I doing here?

My fingers twitch in answer, the trickiest run of the opener on flute. The part I aced in my chair test.

I'll get back there. This is a temporary penance, so I have to survive and prove I'm a team player, and soon enough the semester will end and I'll be back where I belong. Maybe my glorious return will be as epic as this semester's victory would have been.

Marching goes about as well as can be expected: not great. I maybe took for granted how helpful it was to march between Sofia and Devin, who generally knew what they were doing. It becomes harder to fit yourself into a curve when your entire section line is a wobbly off-beat mess of stumbling steps. Jonathan gets extremely red-faced when it becomes clear that he's not the best at stepping on beat, and Milo shrinks every time we get called out for terrible form, apologizing more and more profusely as the rehearsal goes on. Even Neeraj looks embarrassed at our performance.

The KHMB Reflections Stories don't hold back. We even have our own highlight now—Low Brass Laments:

> Really? None of y'all seniors could've stepped up to give us a real tuba section?

> **New low for low brass, amiright?**

We're supposed to believe this is the sober version of the section??

Hurricane Yasmín is now its own highlight as well, and the posts are brutal. If I thought switching sections would earn me automatic sympathy and goodwill, I miscalculated.

We'll have to earn goodwill by not being garbage, I guess.

I'm not used to losing this much time to social media. Usually Sofia's the one who keeps me updated on the lives of our elementary school friends, all the drama from the grade above me, and any big news moments. I'll occasionally scroll for dog photos or cottagecore aesthetics, but mostly I'm on Instagram to like Sofia's photos and not much else. Now I suddenly get how addicting it can be to scroll.

Homework is a soothing escape. I hole up in the peace of my room with my headphones playing cheesy ranchero tunes, and every item ticked off in my planner is concrete evidence that I'm managing. My Spanish paragraph comes out a little short and my WHAP reading gets a little skimmed, but my list shrinks and shrinks until it's down to one item, the one I wrote at the bottom of every day in my planner before school even started.

Practice flute.

I stare at the unchecked box for a long time, and then I close my planner and call Sofia.

"Hotline for marching disasters, what is your emergency?"

I snort with relief. She answered. She answered and she made fun of me. I swallow a dramatic lump in my throat and reply with snark of my own. "Yeah, I'm calling to report a flute section that couldn't adjust an arc to cover *one* missing person despite having several experienced upperclassmen and a whole new drill chart."

Marching practice wasn't great for the infant low brass section, but at least we weren't the only ones struggling.

"You've got some log in your eye there," Sofia snips.

"Look, I don't blame you. I guess I'm just impossible to replace."

Sofia sighs. "Did you call for a reason?"

I think I mostly called for this. To hear Sofia's voice, to tease and be teased. To know that even if all isn't forgiven yet, I'm on the right path to get there.

"Yeah, can I get a ride tomorrow? My mom's on a lecture streak, and Ellen's working."

Sofia sighs loudly. "Bring coffee."

I grin at my seafoam accent wall (Mom was testing paint samples a couple years ago). We're going to be okay. "Bring your A game to the field tomorrow."

"You really are an unshamable force of nature." Sofia tuts. "Hurricane Yasmín."

The nickname sinks my rising mood faster than

Humphrey sank downtown. Sofia says it so easily, like it just rolled off her tongue, like it belonged there.

I force a laugh. There's a measure of uneasy rest. Sofia's always been good at social media.

"Are you, uh, the mastermind behind that?" I ask, failing to make my voice sound light or jokey. "All the posts and everything?"

"Seriously?" Sofia asks. "There have been like eighty submissions about it—I promise I have better things to do with my life."

"Yeah, no, I wasn't saying you did all of them, I just . . ."

"You just thought it was somehow my fault your colossal screwup ended up part of the band-meme zeitgeist? Unfortunately I think you did that one to yourself."

I'm a little lost and a lot embarrassed, and I need to find my way back to the path of forgiveness that I've stumbled off of (and down a cliff and into a piranha-infested river).

"Sorry," I say. "I'm just . . . sorry. These new boys are getting on my nerves. I miss the flutes." It's the conversational equivalent of rolling over to expose my belly, and I think it will work.

Sofia *hmms* like maybe she's considering asking me to elaborate or maybe she's thinking, *Whose fault is that?* but then she just says, "Oh, Abuela needs me downstairs. Gotta go. But . . . you should text me about it."

I hate texting, but after Sofia hangs up, I start typing a message.

First off, my new section leader is antisocial and awkward . . .

Sofia answers with laugh reacts and skull emojis. I'm definitely playing up my frustration for the petty comedy, but if that's what it takes to get back on Sofia's good side, I don't care.

I squeeze in twenty minutes of flute practice before bedtime. My shoulders and fingers feel light as I play, and all the Reflections posts and the frustration and the confusion start to fade away.

I'll get back soon. I'll put things back the way they should be.

CHAPTER 8

Sofia picks me up with Andy in the passenger seat.

I do understand why she might think it's poetic justice to surprise me with this, but she doesn't have to look quite so smug when I almost drop her requested coffee thermos.

I only have a few seconds—the time it takes to recover the coffee and open the back seat door—to decide how I'm going to play this. I figure Sofia wouldn't have bothered with the dramatic reveal if she wanted us all to pretend like nothing happened. So either Andy is pissed off and looking to be mad about it or—harder to picture but still possible—he could be feeling genuine remorse for his part in the disaster.

Even on the extreme outside chance that he is here

to apologize, being rude or blaming him will only make matters worse. So by the time the door's open, I've picked my path.

"Ohmigod, Andy. I'm so glad to see you. I am so, so sorry about everything!"

Sofia tuts, and Andy looks taken aback. The enthusiasm feels a little phony in my mouth, so I try to remind myself that I mostly do feel sorry about getting him kicked out, while I slide into the back seat and slip Sofia's coffee into her cupholder.

"I had no idea Ms. Schumacher would bring in the APs—I can't believe how out of hand it got, but I definitely should have known better. I'll do anything to make it right."

"Anything?" Andy asks, eyebrows hopping up his forehead suggestively in the rearview mirror. Sofia reaches across the gearshift to push his face toward the passenger window.

Ugh. For a second I hear Milo's faux-innocent voice saying, "That kid is a jackass," and I almost grimace before I catch myself.

"Uh, yeah, sorry." I end my performance there, afraid of laying it on too thick or failing to sell my sympathy now that my heart's not in it. Why is Sofia dating this jackass anyway?

Andy shrugs, stealing a (long) sip of the coffee I

brought for Sofia and smacking his lips. "Whatever. Ms. Schumacher is a bitch anyway. My mom got me into AP Music Theory, so that's an easy 5.0 added to my GPA. And, like, society has evolved beyond the need for marching band. Bunch of weird, incestuous nerds."

There's an undercurrent of hurt in his bravado, but I still turn to the window to roll my eyes in secret, struggling to find sympathy.

"You'll be back for concert season, though," Sofia says, with maybe a hint of a question mark in the darting movement of her eyes off the road to read his face.

"Who knows?" Andy shrugs again. "There's not much I care about in concert band except the spring trip to Schlitterbahn."

"And *me*," Sofia shoots back. Andy grunts over another gulp of her coffee.

I hate him. I know I'm not supposed to hate people because it leads to the dark side and is not WJWD and whatever, but I hate this jackass with my whole entire heart.

I mean, it's *fine*. I already ruined his life. He's not worth my hatred. Really.

"How are sectionals going?" I ask Sofia pointedly, hoping to twist the knife a bit in Andy's missing-marching-band wound. "Are Han and Katrina pissed about learning new drill? Are the freshmen keeping up?"

Sofia brings the car to a carefully measured stop at

the intersection before tossing a venomous glare over her shoulder. "Worry about your own freshmen, Yasmín."

Andy snickers and finishes the coffee, and I spend the rest of the ride working my way back from hating his guts to just not liking them.

Because hate leads to that Star Wars meme, and because of my own peace of mind, and WWJD and whatever. Not because he doesn't deserve it.

THERE'S PLENTY TO WORRY ABOUT WITH MY FRESHMEN. Bloom spends half of our morning sectionals (which have replaced our morning marching practice) waiting for people to show up, and he doesn't even say anything when we do get settled twelve minutes after we should have. Neeraj and Elias, the late(est)comers, both make half-assed excuses, but Neeraj is sweaty from his run and Elias has Starbucks.

We break up into "people who need to learn the music" and "people who still need to learn what valve oil is." Bloom gives us a rambling lecture on instrument hygiene that would've been more effective as an email with a YouTube link, then sets us on B-flat to practice rhythmic tonguing and tone and not making our horns sound like dying livestock. It's encouraging that I'm more middle-of-the-pack than bottom-of-the-barrel, but it's not enough to dissipate my annoyance.

Milo is the bottom of the barrel. I'm actually worried that he'll quit—if he can't make noise on the horn, Ms. Schumacher won't force him to stay, right?

"Do you want to practice together at lunch?" I ask as we pack up ahead of the morning bell. I'm hoping for extra bonding time plus a chance to get Milo's skills up.

"I would really prefer to forget the sousaphone exists for as long as possible." Milo shrugs and grimaces. "Maybe next time." He stomps away with his book bag sliding off his shoulder.

"Yeah, I'm kind of with him." Caleb gives an indifferent shrug before he follows Milo out of the band hall.

Indifferent is all I've been getting from most of the boys. It's pretty much consistent with the way they dismissed me as "the flute" on the first day, but that doesn't mean I'm going to accept it. This semester is going to be long if I don't have at least a couple of friendly stand partners. If Milo really does quit . . .

I catch Lee as he's leaving and match his step into the hallway. "I like your shoelaces," I say to get his attention. They're flat with rainbow stripes, tied in that cool way to make a pattern.

Lee looks up and tilts his head at me. "Are you . . . thanks? I, uh, stole them from the president?"

"Huh?"

"Huh?" Lee's whole face starts to turn red. "Nothing.

Never mind . Ignore me." He spins and starts to walk away.

"Wait," I say, not sure what I said wrong. Maybe the problem is less that the boys are indifferent and more that I have no idea how to connect with people.

Lee stops and glances back at me, looking confused and still red. Maybe I need to be up-front about my intentions?

"Sorry, I just feel like I haven't really gotten to know people in the section yet."

"What do you want to know?" Lee asks, chin rising like he's responding to a challenge I've issued.

"No, nothing specific." I raise my hands, not sure how I've missed my intended tonal mark so badly. "I just . . . wanted to be friends?"

Lee furrows his brow. Then he shakes his head. "Sorry, I'm not really the group-hugs-and-slumber-parties extrovert type. And you have your flute friends already, right? Just let sleeping loners, uh, be alone." He pulls away with quick steps down the hall.

Ugh. Okay, so I came on overly friendly and scared him off. Part of me definitely itches to run after him and try to keep explaining myself, but that would probably be the opposite of effective, and also the opposite of boundaries. I'll just . . . try to be more chill next time. I'll just get him to like me slowly. I can win over an introvert. Probably. Hopefully.

Or maybe it's not too late for me to talk to Ms.

Schumacher. To tell her this was all a big mistake, that I can't be a tuba, that I give up. Maybe the rest of the section will vouch that I'm just not low brass material, too bright and shrill to be anything other than a flute.

Problem is, the flutes don't want me either.

I go through the day with this gloom cloud over my head, totally forgetting to take notes for pre-calc and zoning out during the WHAP video (not the "WAP" video, tragically). When lunch rolls around, I don't feel like socializing. So I get to the band hall as quickly as I can and drag the Dragon into a practice room.

I'm not in here to cry. I'm in here to practice, because none of this is worth it if we don't end up with a semifunctional low brass section for UIL. I fumble less with the assembly this time, but in the tiny broom-cupboard space, the Dragon feels drowningly large and sounds furious about being caged.

I warm up with a few notes that go from sounding terrible to sounding still pretty bad. So what? I might not be able to handle any of my human section mates, but I am not about to lose to a hunk of metal. I'm going to play a B-flat scale, and it's going to be recognizable.

The Dragon snorts an incredulous honk of a laugh at this goal, but I adjust my mouthpiece and try again.

B-flat. The Dragon prefers to be sharp.

B-flat. It tries being inaudible.

B-flat.

B-flat.

C.

D.

I have to stop there and look up the fingering for E-flat because I get so excited that my notes sound like notes. My mouth is tingling, and I hitch my shoulder where the Dragon rests.

B-flat. Sort of.

C. Definitely.

D.

E-flat.

F. Not really, but I'm counting it.

G.

A. For "awful," apparently, but I'm not stopping now.

B-flat!

I'm a little out of breath and my mouth is dying, but that was basically almost a recognizable scale! Ha ha!

I attempt the scale four more times and get one and a half decent runs. Then, just to get fancy, I try some arpeggios. The Dragon lumbers up and down the steps where my flute was featherlight, and my lips don't have a sense yet of where they should be for each note, and even though there are only three(ish) buttons for my fingers to mess with, I still find it tricky to switch between them.

But the progress is there. I'm at least successfully mounting the Dragon to ride.

I stop with ten minutes left of lunch, just enough time to snack on the carrots Mom packed me and the Hot Cheetos I bought from the vending machine. I'm rolling the corralled Dragon back to the cubby closet when Gilberto Reyes comes out of Ms. Schumacher's office.

"Was that you in the practice room?" he asks, eyebrows raised. "I thought it was the French horn. You're taking to brass nicely, aren't you?"

I flush. I forgot the soundproof practice rooms are better at blocking the whisper of a flute than the shout of low brass.

"Oh, thanks, I feel like I'm struggling . . ."

"Gilberto!" Hannah passes with an armful of papers, snapping a finger as she goes. "Stop flirting and hurry up!"

Gilberto pulls a goofy face at me before shrugging and trailing after Hannah. "I'm coming," he singsongs sweetly.

My face is on fire. I feel like I might barf. Playing (or failing to play) the Dragon is suddenly the least of my worries.

I don't know what's worse: that Hannah thought Gilberto was flirting with me or that he didn't deny it.

. . .

I don't think I've ever Thanked God It's Friday as hard as I did this week, but before I know it, Mom's waking me up for Sunday school and I realize that my weekend is on its last legs.

I actually like going to Sunday school. My sleep schedule is so shifted from marching band practice that 8:30 feels like sleeping in, and then I get an hour of class and an hour of mass and we're home ready for lunch by 11:30 (right about when Ellen wakes up).

Mom drops me off outside the tiny elementary school attached to our parish, St. Cecily's, and I walk down the quiet hall with my footsteps echoing on the shiny floors. My teacher, Mr. Frederick, never makes us start on time, so the twelve or fifteen students of our confirmation preparation class lean against baby-sized desks and flirt or tease each other with a backdrop of phonics posters and early chapter books.

Laylah's in her usual seat at the front of the class, and I take my usual seat next to her. She smiles and waves like usual, but there's an unusual hesitance in her eyes and an unusual awkwardness in our normally companionable quiet.

"So weird that I've barely seen you all week," I say, hoping to plow through the weirdness head-on. "The only thing I know about the section anymore is how many times Ms. Schumacher calls your lines out in rehearsal."

Laylah laughs, ponytailed curls bouncing. "Yeah, no, we've been good. I mean, Sofia might actually decapitate Han if she keeps leaving a gap for you in all our formations, but . . ."

I smile, imagining Sofia getting more and more frustrated as Han highlights my absence. "Oh, Han." I sigh. "Échale ganitas, the barest minimum of effort, please."

Laylah rolls her eyes but smiles, the tension lifting along with the corners of her mouth. When Mr. Frederick finally calls for everyone to sit down, Laylah's telling me about Mia's family's new house, built almost six feet higher on the lot that got submerged by Humphrey last year.

"So I've got a complete set of forms from about half of you," Mr. Frederick announces. "And if you're not sure what I'm talking about, please assume that you owe me something. That's enrollment, retreat permission, AND sponsor commitment forms. Three forms. Count 'em with me, please; the list is on the board if you weren't listening: one, two, three."

Oh crap. My sponsor form. I definitely did not get Sofia to sign it this week. I am zero percent sure she'll agree to sign at all now. I'm never late turning in forms!

If Sofia refuses, what's my backup plan? Her mom? That would be one heck of a can of awkward worms.

Should I try to come up with a more convincing argument for why Mom should let one of my tías do it? I don't see that working unless I explain why I don't want Sofia's family to be involved, and I don't feel like dealing with her opinion on . . . everything that's going on.

Mr. Frederick assigns us a page in our workbooks, a discussion question about how we see the Holy Spirit at work in the world. He lets us work in groups, so I lean over the desk and brainstorm with Laylah, deciding that the Holy Spirit is working through Beyoncé, Lizzo, and Megan Thee Stallion, AOC, community organizers, and both of our grandmothers.

"I see the Holy Spirit at work when people forgive their peers for horrible season-tanking mistakes," I joke, and to my relief, Laylah laughs.

"I see the Holy Spirit at work when my mom asks about my *girlfriend*." Laylah shimmies a tiny happy dance. She points to the page of "symbols of God's work." "See? The rainbow is right there."

"I see the Holy Spirit at work when Sofia makes fun of me."

Laylah frowns. "I'm struggling to see that one, honestly."

"No, really," I say, "that's how she shows affection."

"I guess?" Laylah shrugs, suddenly very interested in writing in her workbook.

"What?" I ask. Laylah doesn't meet my eyes, which makes me suspect that Sofia has been making fun of me behind my back, which is definitely not Holy Spirit–inspired. But it can't be that bad, right? "I know she's mad at me right now. I mean, you wouldn't have been as cool with everything if it was Mia I got kicked out, right?"

Laylah grunts, but she looks up after another pause. "Anyway, you have your whole new section now! Do you see the Holy Spirit at work in any of them?"

"Uh, sure." It's my turn to shrug. Between Lee telling me I have the flutes and Laylah telling me I have the low brass, I'm starting to feel like an unwanted hot potato. "I see the Holy Spirit at work when any of us hits the right note."

Laylah laughs, and our brainstorming gets less focused on the Holy Spirit and more on marching band jokes, and pretty soon Mr. Frederick is dismissing us with another reminder about sponsor forms. My mind wanders during mass, turning over Laylah's obvious discomfort when Sofia came up. Are things that bad? Is Sofia so mad that she trash-talks me to the rest of the section all the time?

Oh well. It's okay even if she does. I'm on the path to atonement, but that doesn't mean I get results as soon as I take the first step. That's why it's a path. I'll get there.

Mom finds Sofia and her mom outside the church, in front of the eucharistic minister sign-up table and free coffee and doughnuts. Mom and Ms. Palacios start trading family chisme (no, Ellen's job hunt hasn't turned up any opportunities; yes, Sofia's abuela is still considering whether to rebuild or sell the lot). Sofia hangs back, tapping on her phone and giving me a quick nod as if she's just casually living her life when clearly she's ignoring me.

I retaliate by typing out a text to interrupt her scrolling: How do you like sleeping instead of joining us in CCE?

Sofia rolls her eyes when her phone buzzes, but she types back, It's delicious. Was Mr. Frederick scintillating as usual?

Laylah and I talked about why the Holy Spirit hasn't improved my tuba playing.

Sofia laughs at that, covering her mouth but hiding nothing. "Or your flute," she says out loud, before turning determinedly back to her phone.

Mom and Ms. Palacios continue chatting as the crowd thins out. Dad hangs by the car but looks happy to watch the clouds drift across the sky.

I'm not ready for the conversation to be over, but Sofia refuses to look up from her phone and *talk* to me.

It's hard to believe in an omniscient, omnipotent, and benevolent God when you hear our former clarinet play, I text, and watch Sofia's eyebrows arch and the corner of her lip twitch when she reads it. Then I earn a full-on chuckle when I add, Or our section leader speak.

Ms. Palacios starts to wrap things up. Mom puts an arm on my elbow to make me put my phone down to say a proper goodbye.

"See you." Sofia waves with a slight eye roll. "You can *text* if you need a ride."

Slight emphasis because she knows I would rather call, but I still grin. Whatever Laylah thinks, I see the Holy Spirit working to get Sofia to forgive me.

MONDAY CRUSHES MY OPTIMISM FAST. WE HAVE A SUB IN pre-calc, so everyone just chats or plays on their phones, but since I don't really have friends in class it feels like a waste, and I'd rather be doing worksheets. WHAP is another solid chunk of boredom as we sit through a PowerPoint. I'm having trouble keeping my eyes open by the time lunch rolls around, and I consider sneaking to the back of the library for a nap. But, no, I need to be in the band hall. Between hiding in the library and using the practice rooms and the occasional club meeting or tutorial, I didn't sit with the flutes at all last week. It's time to stop hiding. Also, if I go to the band hall, I can keep fighting the #HurricaneYasmín stigma (down to a handful of highlight posts this week, and only a couple handfuls roasting the new low brass).

But then Sra. Mendez wants me to stay behind to talk

about my compositions, which are bad, and apparently she doesn't care that my English compositions are equally bad because this is an "upper-level Spanish literature course" and "No es suficiente hablar; escribir también es importante, mamas."

I nod as much as I can and promise to try harder and not just rely on my speaking to get through the class. But also, it doesn't hurt to tell Sra. Mendez (in Spanish) what a great teacher she is. Eventually she lets me go with an assignment to rewrite my last essay. Which, fine, I guess.

The band hall, while obviously a safer space for nerds than the cafeteria, is not free from the obstacle course of social pressure that exists whenever teenagers get to choose who to sit with. Showing up late puts me at a disadvantage because everyone's already found floor space and spread out their lunches and last-minute homework. I step lightly to avoid a cluster of clarinets in the doorway and approach the flute corner.

Sofia sits closest, with her back to me, lecturing a freshman next to her about something that happened in sectionals. Laylah is on the opposite side of the group, snuggled with Mia where the walls meet. She gives me a little wave that Mia copies, but neither of them has space to make room for me.

Sofia glances over her shoulder. She doesn't stop talking, though, and she doesn't turn.

Fine. I expected to be nobodied to some degree. "Hey," I say as brightly as I can, taking an extra step so I'm hovering a little too close over the freshman's personal space. "How are things in the treble clef?"

Sofia looks up. The freshman, and Yuki and Devin and even Han, look intently at the floor or their suddenly open textbooks or their Lunchables stacks. Not a good sign at all, and my instincts start screaming to abort, retreat—but come on. This is still my section, even if I have to push through some awkwardness.

"It's going fine," Sofia says, voice calm and polite. "That reminds me, we should really discuss when we're having those extra sectionals to learn stand tunes. Ms. Schumacher obviously has bigger concerns, but . . ." She turns away, the freshmen frantically flip open their planners, and I stand where I am for about three seconds longer than it takes to realize what's happening.

Nobody makes room for me. Nobody changes conversational tracks to include me. I have no choice but to take a step back and turn away.

The weirdest part is how innocent it is. Sofia isn't saying anything to provoke me, isn't shooting daggers with her eyes or telling me to get lost. I would know how to deal with any of that behavior. She's just handling section plans. It's a perfectly reasonable thing to be doing right now, and it just happens not to be any of my business.

I scan the band hall, face hot. Am I supposed to sit by myself? Will somebody snap a picture for Instagram? Will everyone say it's exactly what I deserve?

No. If I can't sit with the flutes, I have another option, right? Isn't that supposed to be the bright side of my situation? I scan the room, heart dropping when I catch sight of Milo sitting with the other clarinets. But there. Behind the open door leading to the practice room hallway, I see half of an arm adorned with string and plastic bracelets. I head toward it and find Bloom sitting with Caleb, the hipster saxophone. I hang in the doorway, half smiling, fully wanting to puke. "Uh . . . hey?"

The air is thick as I imagine that I'm about to repeat my humiliation. Nobody wants Hurricane Yasmín wrecking their lunch break. But then Bloom looks up and immediately pulls his knees to his chest, nodding at the empty space left behind. It's a lifeline, and he doesn't even seem to realize that he's offering it. Like the space already belonged to me.

Caleb shifts back too. I sink into the small linoleum spot, trying to look casual instead of desperately grateful and eager for acceptance.

Nobody says anything as I unpack my whole wheat and turkey breast sandwich. Were the boys talking before I got here? Should I say something now?

I take a bite of sandwich. Bloom scrolls his phone

while Caleb nods slightly along with whatever's coming out of his over-the-ear headphones. It's actually relaxing not to have to keep up with conversation, I guess. And besides, they made room for me.

After a few minutes, Bloom dumps the crumbs of a Doritos bag into his mouth in one quick motion and then starts stuffing trash into it, slinging his backpack over one shoulder and standing up with a tiny wave before disappearing out the back door.

He's weird and quiet, but I don't worry that he's secretly mad even with that abrupt departure. I can't imagine him talking badly behind my back.

Caleb and I keep eating in mostly comfortable silence. Weird that I feel more welcome here, across from a freshman I've barely talked to, than in a group of all my closest flute friends. Pure power of suggestion, maybe, making me think I fit in with my "section." Or maybe Caleb is just chill.

"So," I say, because I guess Lee was right about me being an extrovert. "Do you miss the saxophones?"

"Sorry?" Caleb shifts his headphones and puts down his limp toaster strudel. "Did you say something?"

I don't get to repeat myself, because Elias crashes into the hallway with all the subtlety of a blaring trumpet, juggling a hot lunch Styrofoam tray and a phone and one of those giant zip-up binders that already has way too many papers straining its seams. The binder slams to the floor in what might generously be called a semi-controlled drop, and Elias gives a wordless yelp as his body follows it down to land next to (and semi–on top of) Caleb.

"Whoa, man." Caleb steadies Elias's arm to avoid getting splashed with any of the colorful puddles on the tray of mystery nutrition. "What's up?"

"Not much." Elias's downward momentum spreads seamlessly outward as he kicks out his long legs, slides his tray to one side, and leans toward me with his phone hand outstretched.

"Hey, Yasmín, want to be in my video?" His eyebrows arch into enthusiastic spikes that match the swoop of his gelled-up bangs, and he gives puppy dog eyes to top it off. "I'm showing my cousins about band. You could just say hi and your instrument and whatever. What do you say? You know Spanish, right?"

"Uh, yeah." I shrug. "I guess I can?"

"Wow, so you're going to go all mosh pit on me and not even ask if I want to be in your viral TikTok?" Caleb asks, lips pressed together and eyes wide in joking-but-not-really disapproval.

"Shut up, it's just for my little cousins," Elias says. "I don't even have content like that yet." He reaches for one of my avocado oil kettle chips, which surprises me so much that I'm too slow to stop him. "These don't have meat, right? I'm vegetarian," he says, and then snaps the chip up when I shake my head in bewilderment.

Caleb shoots me a look like, "What is happening?" and I shoot him one back like, "I don't know, but make it stop." He snickers into his fist while I miss my chance to stop Elias stealing a second chip.

"So why can't I be in your video?" Caleb presses. "Your cousins are racist, or . . . ?"

"No, man, my cousins are in Mexico." Elias tuts like we should have known this, even though it definitely doesn't answer the question. "The video has to be all in Spanish."

"Great," Caleb says, raising his chin. "I speak Spanish."

"Oh. Wait, you do?" Caleb nods. Elias tilts his head. "But, like, for real?"

"Yes, for real! Man, whatever." Caleb covers the indignant squeak in his voice by regaining his thousand-yard hipster stare and sighing loudly.

"Wait, wait, sorry," Elias says. He claps his free hand on Caleb's shoulder. "I'm just a dumbass sometimes. Are you Dominican or something?"

"Mexican and Panamanian, both from my mom," Caleb says, relaxing a little into the magic of the shoulder clap. "Y mi abuela vive en mi casa y no acepta el espanglish, so no me pongas a prueba, cabrón."

"No mames." Elias beams. "My dad's hondureño, so I get my Mexican from my mom too." They both turn to me expectantly.

"Oh, uh, I don't know." I'm still trying to catch up with the train wreck Elias brought to Caleb's and my peaceful lunch corner. But I guess the same magic that let me sit here also means I'm in the conversation now. "I'm just Mexican. Family in Monterrey. Failing Spanish, actually." I flip my binder open so my most recent essay is visible.

"Wait, so you don't even speak Spanish?" Elias laughs. "You definitely lose Mexican points for that."

"I speak Spanish!" Maybe my voice jumps a little, the way Caleb's just did. "I just can't do the writing. Anyway, we don't have to do the 'who's more Mexican' thing just because we have three diaspora people in a room together, do we?" Sofia and I have seen this play out often enough that we've dubbed it the Rule of Three, but that doesn't mean it's not annoying to go through all the time. The way Caleb laughs and rolls his eyes makes me think he feels the same.

"I'm just saying, though, I think I would win," Elias insists. "I visit my cousins all the time. I've got the culture."

"Dude." Caleb shakes his head. "You just told us you were *vegetarian*."

I snicker over Elias's protests. I like Caleb.

"Man, shut up, have you seen those videos about the baby chickens with their little bloody beaks and shit?"

"Oh, I've seen them." I sigh. With Ellen being vegan, I've seen everything.

"But have you tasted my abuela's caldo de pollo?" Caleb teases. "Or, like, any legit Texas barbecue?"

Elias shakes his head. "And their sad little peeps and everything. I'm straight, but that broke my heart." My soul cringes at that, because why do some boys have such fragile visions of their masculinity that they think feeling emotion puts them in danger of losing it?

Caleb doesn't miss a beat, but puffs out his chest a little as he replies, "Well, I'm gay, and my cold gay heart feels nothing but the pleasure of consuming flesh."

I snort around a mouthful of chips. For a second, I'm afraid that the easy conversation will die a toxic death and I'll have to talk to Bloom about calling out homophobia in the section, but then Elias repeats his shoulder-clap thing and Caleb tilts his head and nods, his posture relaxing, and both boys smile and continue bickering. Are shoulder touches some secret shortcut to forgiveness that I've never learned? Is this a special talent Elias has been granted to make up for sticking his foot in his mouth so often? Can I use this to relate to the rest of the low brass, or does it only work between boys?

"So record your video already, dude," Caleb says,

reaching for a carrot off Elias's tray and donating a handful of his Hot Cheetos. Is this how my new section bonds? Why don't they eat their own lunches??

"Yeah, okay." Elias raises his phone. "You still want to say hi too, Yasmín? Sorry." He shrugs at Caleb. "It's just that my cousins will be happy to see a girl."

"There are plenty of girls in band." I roll my eyes.

"But does it really shock you that none of them will talk to him?" Caleb asks.

"That's not it!" Elias says. "I mean, well, yeah, that's pretty much it. But that's because I don't know anyone yet. I'm laying the groundwork. So, uh, Yasmín, if you want to help out by introducing me to your girl Sofia . . ." The puppy dog eyes make a second appearance.

I roll my eyes hard enough to get the point across, and Elias sighs and finally hits the record button on his phone.

When Sofia leaves out the back door for fifth period, I'm *almost* too busy giggling at Caleb's on-camera reaction to the cafeteria meatless-loaf to notice her cold stare.

I FEEL WEIRD ABOUT TRYING TO GET A RIDE HOME WITH Sofia after the lunchtime rejection, so I text Ellen before marching practice ends and confirm that she's not closing and can pick me up when she gets off work. That gives me about an hour and a half to spend in the practice rooms, which I pretty desperately need anyway. As a section, I'd say we've gotten past the point where we can't play and have landed smack in the middle of the part where we play like crap.

Setting up the Dragon is pretty routine by now. Marching with it still isn't, which is why I needled Bloom into requiring push-ups at the beginning of every sectionals. He and Neeraj might be used to carrying twenty-five pounds of horn upright, but some of us aren't.

Thinking about push-ups means I should probably do push-ups. Since there's just barely enough room to lie on the floor of the practice room, I justify doing forty half push-ups on my knees instead of twenty full ones. Then I hoist the Dragon onto my sore shoulders, set my tired lips against the mouthpiece, and try to play a B-flat scale on the first try.

An hour passes quickly, and I decide to pack the Dragon up and attempt my Spanish essay revisions until Ellen shows up. But then, when I'm in the cubby closet, Ellen texts to say she's going to be later than she thought. I *could* work on Spanish homework for that long or get a head start on history reading, but the band hall has cleared out now and it's such a perfect opportunity . . . and my flute case is tucked into the back of my cubby, where I hide it every morning just because I haven't had the heart to stop bringing it and because Mom would definitely ask questions if I did.

I leave the Dragon in its lair and bring my flute back to the practice room I was using. Why is it so satisfying to close that thin-windowed door and shut the world out again? The room feels emptier without the Dragon, more peaceful. It's been a minute since I've practiced my flute. I feel weird about that.

I shiver at the bite of cold metal on the back of my knees when I settle into the too-wobbly-for-concert-arcs folding chair and wince at the unharmonic creak of the music stand when I adjust it. I slot the head and foot joins into the body of my flute, testing the angles and rolling the mouthpiece forward. I play.

Something like fear dissipates when I hear the clean piercing note, leaving behind an irrational relief that grows as I slide effortlessly through a couple of major scales and a chromatic. It would have been silly to think I would lose years of muscle memory in a little over a week, but I still feel a thousand times better knowing that my embouchure will form and my fingers will remember their steps in the complicated dance of sharps and flats. I do have a fleeting thought: Do we really need so many buttons? But I forget it pretty quickly.

After some warm-up and a little bit of goofing around with Lizzo songs, I turn to the show music. Not because I think I'm going to perform it, just because it's difficult and pretty and often stuck in my head, and I have it in my binder. It's a hill to climb, and I need the exercise.

The show music trills out of my flute, and a tiny bit of calm clicks into my mind and body. At the end of CCE last year we had an all-day retreat with a bunch of nuns-in-training to "get us excited" for confirmation prep this year. The nuns-in-training talked about vocation, the little voice that calls you to the thing you're supposed to do in the world, the thing you were made for. They were all called to serve the poor, teach classes, spend their days in prayer, and other holy stuff like that. Their little voice told them to do those things, and they felt peace when they did. I always feel guilty, because if I really listened to my little voice, I think I would just listen to music and play my flute all the time and become a hermit. Not a musician, not a performer. Just music and peace.

The nuns-to-be also taught us a meditation, one where Jesus was calling your name. They talked a lot about Jesus calling. I always got tripped up imagining that—what language is he speaking? With what accent? Anyway, he called and you had to tear down a brick wall to reach him or something. I didn't totally get the metaphor, but I remember the brick wall when I'm in the practice room, where it isn't much of a stretch to picture my fingers ("slow, lazy fingers," my very Russian piano teacher used to say) digging out bricks chunk by chunk, turning red and raw from scraping the mortar, catching glimpses of the other side, where everything is beautiful, and getting closer to it with every new effort.

I don't notice the face in the window until someone knocks on the glass.

"You're really good," Gilberto Reyes says after I jump up and open the door. My brain is in overdrive coming up with reasons for him to be here listening to me play, and belatedly I remember that there's an official time that's the latest we're allowed to stay in the band hall at night, and it's entirely possible that I blew straight past it.

"I'm sorry," I say, checking my watch. 8:37. Which means I'm probably supposed to be gone by 8:30 and Gilberto was trying to be polite. "I haven't gotten to practice much since . . ."

Gilberto flashes a crooked grin, and my eyes latch on to the mole under his left eye. Why is it so important that I memorize the placement of the mole under his left eye? Can he tell I'm staring at the mole under his left eye?

"And," I add to stop my brain from running wild, "I'll practice my actual instrument a lot more, I promise. I just wanted to . . ."

"No worries, you're welcome to practice." Gilberto holds up his hands. "I'm always here late, so you're not keeping me. I'm not rushing home to anything." His grin falters for just a second while I try to figure out exactly what he's saying, but almost immediately his smile reappears. "It's nice here."

"Yeah." I watch his eyes travel along the walls of the practice room. He loves it as much as I do, doesn't he? "It's really nice."

My phone buzzes, loud against the music stand. I answer Ellen's call and quickly pack my flute in its case. Gilberto Reyes waves silently while I run to gather my backpack and then rush out to the parking lot. As we pull onto the street and Ellen apologizes for picking up a twelve-top right as her shift should have been ending ("But the tips were so good; they were very drunk and very sweet"), I notice that the lights in the band hall are still on and the door is still propped open, not locked up. I guess Gilberto Reyes really isn't rushing home.

I mean, I do need to practice, and he did say I was welcome. Maybe I can make a habit of this. As long as Ellen can keep picking me up.

CHAPTER 9

Mom pops her head into my room on Friday morning, asking why she's barely seen me in the two weeks since school started, and if I want to go to Costco on Saturday.

So now I finally have to admit to myself that I've been avoiding her.

The longer I wait to tell her about the section switch, the more awkward it'll be when she finds out. I know this. But I just haven't been able to bring it up. I wanted to tell her when I knew I could explain without breaking down. I have to approach this carefully so Mom will get it. The last thing I need is to try to tell her when I haven't made up my mind how I feel about it yet, when I'm still likely to cry. If I don't present this with a wall of perfectly chipper logic, then I'll have no defense against Mom's snap judgments and frantic opinions and endless questions, and then it will turn into a storm of emotion as bad as any Ellen provokes. Mom will be on my side, of course, whatever that means to her. She always is. She's just so forceful that sometimes even her support feels like it will blow me away.

I agree to the Costco trip, though, obviously. I'm not trying to get on the wrong side of Mom's intensity.

I turn in my revised Spanish essay and crush a math quiz and generally wrap up the week feeling good about myself. We still have sectionals scheduled for the first hour of marching practices, because while we're starting to get the hang of our new drill charts, our show music is still about 45 percent random sound burps and 20 percent unintentional silence. I pull my chair up between Milo and Caleb and wave Elias's phone away when he tries to film me assembling the Dragon. Jonathan proudly jumps in to give a thorough (if pompous) walk-through of the process, only to get disappointed when Elias explains about the language barrier and then perk up when Neeraj suggests translation or captions. Bloom is quietly waiting for everyone to settle down when Ms. Schumacher enters the band hall, pulls a chair up to our rowdy circle, and takes a seat.

The vibe immediately shifts. Bloom stiffens and starts mumbling orders, and we start our first run-through of the show music in record time. Neeraj actually plays instead of inventing excuses to ignore his sheet music.

Jonathan and Elias stop fighting to see who can drown the other out and start matching pitch, and even Loner Lee makes an effort to sit up straight and look less disaffected. As a result, almost 70 percent of the show comes out in unison, and I notice multiple moments when we sound like we're all playing the same note.

"This is great, really great," Ms. Schumacher tells us when we finish the closer. We all sit on the edge of our seats, and nobody even snickers when Ms. Schumacher praises our progress and tells us how much she believes in our work ethic. "I thought I could just run you through it a few more times, with your permission, Mr. Bloom?"

My jaw aches by the end of the hour. I'm not playing as well as I did on our first run-through, and it frustrates me that with all Ms. Schumacher's personalized advice, I seem to be moving—no, I'm being dragged helplessly by the Dragon—in the wrong direction. I trip over every accidental in the opener, and nothing I do succeeds in making my notes staccato in the closer ("Less water balloon, more ax," Ms. Schumacher coaches us fruitlessly).

"Well . . ." she says, when even Bloom's notes start cracking. "This has been great, but we'd better get out to the field. Instruments can stay inside. Keep up the great work, all of you. Great job."

We nod, and I wonder if anyone else's confidence plummets with each "great."

"Mr. Bloom," Ms. Schumacher says when we start to put up our chairs and horns. "Make sure you have extra time blocked off for sectionals next week. From now on, I want you all to be with the full band during rehearsal hours."

The searchlight of her upbeat smile dims when she turns and head for the fields.

"Ha. Nailed it." Neeraj spreads his arms wide to clap Bloom and Jonathan on the back. "We're off the bench."

Lee tugs the straps of his thick leather bracelet, and next to me, Milo flicks the red phone charm hanging out of his pocket. I'm probably not the only one panicking at the thought of being held to a normal band standard, both musical and physical. We've been having light marching days without instruments, and my muscles are not prepared for three hours with the Dragon on. I could be doing better—I should be doing better.

Across the circle, Bloom meets my gaze and shakes his head slightly. When I tilt my head, he gives a wide-eyed shrug. I can't tell exactly what he's trying to say, but I think he's shaking his head at my doubts, so I keep them to myself and give a little clap instead. I try to mirror Neeraj's easy confidence, letting it hang in the air like a veil hiding the daunting task ahead of us. To my surprise, Milo and Caleb actually join in. Bloom nods once before hauling his horn to the cubby closet. As he passes me, he whispers, "Thanks."

Which is funny, because why does my reaction matter?

The sun hangs low, softening the day's heat as we fill in the ten-yard gap between the trombones and the percussion line for the first set of the opener. We're capable of full marching run-throughs of all three show movements, but unless we can get our music up to snuff, Ms. Schumacher has hinted that we might perform only the opener at our first football game. I know that's a thing some bands do, but I also know (from upperclassmen and from chatter on KHMB Reflections) that it's not a thing high-level competitive bands do, and it's never been a thing we do. In two weeks, we'll have an absolute concrete metric for how far "Hurricane Yasmín" set the band back.

I try to make each one of my steps explode with energy, but I'm still restless as our line struggles to cross smoothly through a line of trumpets. I weirdly wish I had the Dragon heavy on my shoulders; at least its echoing roar would make me feel like I was making a difference.

Bloom passes around bug spray at the next water break. The darkening sky shrouds the faces of Ms. Schumacher and the DMs on their tower, the flutes huddled together at the opposite end of the sidelines, and my section mates next to me. I pass the spray back in Bloom's general direction and sip my water, listening to the boys' chatter. Milo, silhouetted against one of the field's floodlights, is trying to join the clarinet huddle, but Caleb holds his arm and whines that he's betraying us, making poor Milo stammer flustered protests and promises to return. Neeraj has coaxed Lee into a heated debate (well, Neeraj is heated, at least) about which Overwatch heroes are OP. Sadly, I now have at least a passing knowledge of what that means. Elias is teasing Jonathan, who is quick to rise in sputtering outrage to the slightest provocation. Grass tickles my palms as I lean back, and for a second it's like the whole field is a giant loud practice room.

"Gather around," Ms. Schumacher calls through her megaphone, climbing down from the tower to wrap up practice. The air fills with more happy chatter as we all realize she's calling it a bit early. I drift to the huddle, ending up on the outer edge of the clump with Bloom on one side and Milo on the other, even though we aren't trying to make concert arcs. "I used to be a front-row person." Milo sighs wistfully. "Low brass is transforming me into a back-row person. I even catch myself trying to sit farther back in class—except then I can't read the board." I snort and nod. Weird how taking up position in the back of the group (instead of the front, where the upper woodwinds always stand) is starting to feel natural.

Ms. Schumacher reminds us (unnecessarily) that the first football game is fast approaching. This is met mostly by cheers and only a few nervous screeches. She tells us that we'll have a day of uniform fittings sometime next week and that she'll be weighing how much of the show we should perform at our first halftime. "This will be a big milestone, but don't forget that it's just the kickoff of the season," Ms. Schumacher says. Once the season picks up, we'll have games nearly every week for most of September and October, maybe longer if our football team actually does well. She talks about how far we still have to go to be ready for the rush of fall. She urges us to practice.

"Since it's Friday," she says, nodding at Hannah and Gilberto, "your DMs and I have selected a section of the week." The trombones, who won the meaningless but still semi-coveted honor last week, whoop and call for a repeat. "This section has shown great improvement in marching fundamentals even though they have an experience disadvantage, but their hard work at learning brand-new music is the reason we feel they've gone above and beyond. They really embody the spirit of resilience we're embracing this season. Congratulations, low brass!"

It's hard to tell in the harsh fluorescent shadows, but I feel like every head turns back as Neeraj whoops and Elias gives a series of fake-tearful acceptance-speech thank-yous. I catch Sofia, half her scowl illuminated and the other half vanishing in darkness, rolling her eyes and leaning to whisper something to a snickering Yuki. Milo shakes my shoulder excitedly, and I give a half-hearted smile back.

This is bullshit.

The week the trombones won, they were the only section that didn't need a single arc adjustment for two full practices. Our big "improvement" was that we only got lectured for being out of step every *other* run-through today and only brought the entire band to a screeching halt three times.

It's a pity win. Just like Ms. Schumacher telling us how great we're doing. We're not doing great. We're doing so bad, the leadership feels sorry for us.

There's a soft tug on my elbow. Bloom's whole head is backlit, so I can't see his expression at all, but I guess he can see mine.

"It's fine," he mumbles, low enough that I doubt anyone else hears him. "It makes people happy. We'll win it for real next time."

It's comforting that he knows too and that he does in fact hold us to a higher standard. Sometimes it's hard to tell, as soft-spoken as he is. But there was an intensity in the way he squeezed my elbow and said "next time." He's not happy with a pity win either.

Good.

. . .

"Shouldn't we all exchange numbers?" I ask when the section stands together in the cubby closet after practice.

"Why?" Lee asks, frowning.

"I've got everyone." Bloom shrugs. "From the staff list, you know."

Caleb pulls his headphones off one ear. "Wait, I missed it, what's happening?"

"Yasmín's trying to get some digits," Elias editorializes.

I roll my eyes. "I'm just saying. We're a section. We should be in contact. Maybe set up a group chat. We have to schedule more sectionals now."

"To be perfectly honest, I don't know if y'all could handle me in a group chat," Elias admits.

"To be perfectly honest, I agree," Jonathan snarks back.

"Well, it sounds good to me," Caleb says, whipping his phone out of his pocket and handing it straight to Milo, who nearly drops it (along with his jaw) as he squeaks in surprise.

"Uh, yeah, we have a clarinet group chat, and it's cool." Milo recovers, typing his contact into Caleb's phone. "It can't be just a woodwind thing, right?"

"No, trumpets have one too, but they kicked me out the second I switched over." Elias trades phones with Milo next, and they both start typing. Bloom, Jonathan,

Neeraj, and I add our phones to the round-robin.

I remember the flute chat going silent the day I reported Andy and his crew, but the sting of that rejection isn't as sharp as I expect it to be. I give Elias a smile in solidarity.

The circle gets kind of quiet, and I realize we're all looking at Lee, who still hasn't produced his phone. His right hand wraps tightly around the bracelet on his left wrist.

"I don't . . . I never really give my number to people," he says, shoulders hunching defensively and eyes on the ground. It reminds me of the way he acted when I said I wanted to be friends. "I had to change it once in middle school because people were spamming . . ."

Okay, so maybe I didn't need to take it so personally when Lee wanted to be a loner.

"That's okay," Milo says softly, words tripping over Caleb's "No pressure" and Bloom's "If something urgent comes up, I can always . . . you know." Elias, not the subtlest, asks, "What, like telemarketers?" and Jonathan gives an equally confused shrug. But it's Neeraj who puts his hand on Lee's shoulder (that shoulder clap again!) and leaves it there until Lee's grip on his wrist relaxes.

"You don't give your number to people," he says. "But we're not *people*. We're your section."

Lee tilts his head, a shaky smile flashing on his face.

"You're a Bastion-loving weirdo," he snorts softly. "Fine, whatever. It's 832 . . ."

We all rush to type the number into whichever phone we're holding, and pretty soon the group chat is up and running and full of psychedelic GIFs courtesy of Elias. "I'm going to name it Low Brassholes," he warns. "I've been waiting for a chance to make that a thing."

"It's definitely not a thing," I tell him, but the chat name appears on my phone screen, undercutting my point. "I refuse to let that be a thing."

It takes a lot more chatter before everyone clears out and I can take the Dragon to a practice room in peace. But the Low Brassholes—I mean the *group chat*—continues buzzing periodically for another couple hours.

"So," Mom says, "¿cómo estás, mija linda? You've been busy all week."

I scan the busy Costco parking lot for spaces. I'm not avoiding Mom's question, I'm just . . . watching intently to make sure these other suburban power-shoppers don't try to sneak in somewhere that's rightfully ours.

"Yasmín?" Mom asks.

"Yeah, I'm busy with band. Remember, they warned us it would be a big commitment."

Mom *hmms* absentmindedly and honks her way into a parking spot only one row from the door. The Karen in a minivan who lost out gives us serious stink eye, but Mom gives an ice-cold smile back. We're halfway to the entrance when she continues her line of questioning. "Your packet said that after-school rehearsals wouldn't go on after dark this month. You've been coming home much later." Her side-eye as she passes up a cart with wonky wheels gives me a warning vibe.

"Yeah, I told you I was staying to use the practice rooms."

"You can't practice your flute at home anymore?" And there it is. Now that she's asked that question, I officially have to choose between telling her about my exile or lying.

So, as we walk in past the back-to-school clearance and the first hint of Halloween decorations, I take a deep breath and tell the truth.

Mostly.

"Yeah, well, I've actually been practicing something new . . . I got this really cool opportunity, actually. Ms. Schumacher thought I could help the band out a lot by playing a different instrument."

"You practiced just fine at home all summer."

"No, Mom, that's—I'm not playing flute anymore." Honestly, she has the info packet memorized after a quick scan but she can't hear when I'm trying to ease her into some shocking news?

"What?" Mom looks at me like I'm a mislabeled

party-pack of Cheez-Its in the middle of the produce aisle. "Of course you are. Why—"

"I had to switch! To tuba!"

The declaration gets me some weird looks, and I shrink back against the apple crates. Mom tilts her head and purses her lips at me.

"I don't understand. You *had* to?"

"I mean, I had the opportunity to. I did. Whatever, Mom, the point is, I can't bring a sousaphone home to practice."

"Why on earth would they make you play a . . . I thought you said tuba?"

"Nobody made me, I . . . Ms. Schumacher asked . . . I volunteered . . ."

"And your college applications?" Mom asks, voice rising. "How will this look? Why would you volunteer for something so silly, Yasmín? And without discussing it with me first!"

Now we're both getting looks.

"Mom, porfa, it wasn't anything to discuss." I feel cornered, which is how I would have felt no matter when and where this conversation took place, but it feels extra unfair in the massive grocery aisle. "I didn't have a choice. I mean, no, I did have a choice—I had an opportunity and I took it because . . . because . . . it's my fault all the tubas got expelled, so—"

"*Expelled?*"

"From band! Not from school!"

Mom abandons her cart and paces the aisles, muttering to María, José, y Jesucristo, which she usually saves for the comfort of her (or my) bedroom. I trot behind, doing my best to explain the situation, how it's all going to work out for the best, how Ms. Schumacher is sure to reward my hard work with a leadership position next year plus a glowing recommendation letter. How great it looks that I took responsibility, alerting her to the problem. How Ellen and I made sure I was looking out for the safety of the new students . . .

"So this is how Ellen gives you advice?" Mom asks, and I mentally kick myself for dragging her into this. Mom paces straight out of the store and back through the crowded parking lot, and I keep explaining how this might become a college essay, an interview anecdote, a really, really good thing.

". . . and we even won section of the week. Ms. Schumacher is happy with us. Okay?" I ask. We've been sitting in the car for a few minutes, Mom tapping her fingers against the gear shift but not moving us out of park. "It's fine, Mom. I'm learning a lot. You know, lots of music majors and professional musicians play multiple instruments—*NOT that I'm planning to go into professional music!*" Mom's look of horror softens somewhat, but her lips still press tightly together.

"Well." She inhales softly. "I'm glad you're making the best of it, mija. I just don't understand why you wouldn't want to stay on your flute."

"I do want— I would like to— It's fine. I'm good." That's what I need to tell her. That's what I need her to understand. If I stay on-message, if *I* believe it, then Mom will believe it.

"Mhmm." Mom raises her eyebrows. "Well, do you want to just go home?"

"Absolutely not. I came for new camisoles and a giant bucket of chocolate-covered almonds, and I'm not going home without them." I smile, and it feels real, and Mom smiles back and turns the car off. I hop out again, a little more exhausted but a little lighter.

"And Sofia?" Mom asks suddenly. "She couldn't help keep you where you belong?"

I drop my eyes to the asphalt. I can't find enough belief yet to explain *all of that* positively. "It wasn't her decision."

Mom stays pensive through the walk back into Costco and then loosens up as we find my camisole pack. By the time we reach the chocolate aisle, she's pestering me about signing up for a Saturday PSAT prep session: "You only have until October, right around the corner! I don't want you to go in with no real-life practice."

"It's over two months away, and I'm practicing with

the book." The PSAT can't be around the corner. The test is practically at the end of marching season—only a couple of weeks before UIL in November. Maybe my reading-passage scores aren't perfect yet, but they're a lot better than my tuba playing. I have to believe I have plenty of time to improve both.

But I let Mom talk me into signing up for a Saturday session, on a weekend in September that doesn't conflict with a football game. I dutifully add it to my planner when we get home, flipping through the last days of August, our first football game coming up in two weeks, the ramp-up of games and rehearsals and unit exams through the end of September and beginning of October, then Homecoming, the PSAT, UIL . . .

It all looks mostly manageable in my planner. There's no box to plan the days when KHMB Reflections posts will take up more space in my brain than they should, or the days when Sofia's cold shoulder will keep me up late inventing plans to earn forgiveness. I know exactly what I need to do to get through this semester, every step written clearly in ink. But I don't know if I can follow the plan. I don't know if I'm good enough to make this all be good.

So I just have to keep working. If I do, I can't help but get better.

I add an extra hour of PSAT prep to my schedule for tomorrow. I haven't been practicing much. I can do better.

New Monday, old problems. My Spanish essay comes back again, with another note to stay after class. Sra. Mendez asks me if I made my best effort, which is frustrating since I did, twice! If she would just give me an F on the assignment, I could focus on acing tests and quizzes for the rest of the quarter, or figure out some over-the-top final project for extra credit. Baking pan dulce for the whole class? Dressing up as Frida Kahlo and doing an oral presentation? So many options, all less painful than an essay! But no, I got the teacher who believes in the *writing process*, so I'm supposed to keep working on this pinche essay until I graduate. Sra. Mendez gives me until the end of the week to finish a new draft. "Make me see it," she says.

Oh, and I got a B on my WHAP quiz. Not good enough.

I eat lunch with the low brass again, not brave enough to attempt to sit with the flutes. But I catch Sofia watching me as I pass. Maybe she regrets her behavior. Maybe she's starting to forgive me. Or maybe her eyes just track motion, like a predator.

Sixth-period music rehearsal is disjointed because the DMs and most of the section leaders are busy getting the uniform closet up and running. Ms. Schumacher makes us play our duet with the French horns over and over until it sounds less like garbage. Bloom was not volun-told to do uniform inventory, which is good because I think he's the only one of us playing every note. When we're finally meeting Ms. Schumacher's standards, she switches to grill the saxophones on their tricky bit, but that becomes a low brass issue too when she notices that we're not keeping a consistent tempo for the saxes to fit into. By the way she claps the beat at us, brow furrowed in frustration, I'm guessing we're not about to win section of the week again, even out of pity.

Gilberto Reyes interrupts our humiliation by calling for the first group of woodwinds to come check sizes for their uniforms. I still find it weird to switch from the section that's always first, the alpha in the alphabet-like order of instruments, to the section that's always called last. While the uniform closet works its way through outfitting the flutes and clarinets, saxophones, trumpets, and French horns, Milo and I share longing glances over our shoulders before shaking out our buzzing lips and trying to play the full second movement *again*.

Finally it's our turn. Elias and Jonathan shove each other to be first, then complain when they find out they have to take off their shoes. I stand at the back of the line by my favorite practice room, far from dirty-sock stench and bickering. Lee hangs back with me, fidgeting with his leather bracelet and tapping his phone.

"You're a sophomore," he says, surprising me a little since I assumed he was in his own world.

"Yeah." I wait, but Lee doesn't continue. "Why?"

"I don't know, what do we have to do? Is it just shoes?"

I don't actually know how the fittings work because of Hurricane Humphrey, but it's easy enough to take a few steps forward and see Elias and Jonathan trying stiff blue jackets with green trim on over their Fortnite T-shirt and salmon polo (respectively).

"Yeah, it's chill," I report to Lee. "I think shoes just come off to try the pants. I mean bibs."

"Cool," Lee says, shoving his phone in his pocket. "I'm excited for the bibs, actually. Or is it just bib? Bibber? Whatever. Big overalls fan."

"Ha, I can see it," I say, upping my actual enthusiasm because I don't want to pass up a bonding opportunity. "I'm excited for the weird hats. My dad wants them to have feathers, but I hope they're just really shiny. Either way, should be a fun adventure!"

"I thought tubas don't wear hats?" Lee asks.

Oh. Damn. I think that's right. I guess my disappointment must show on my face, because Lee hesitantly pats my shoulder. "Maybe they'll give us berets?"

The shoulder not-quite-clap cheers me up considerably.

The line moves fast, and soon I'm in the closet, cold linoleum sucking warmth from my toes as I try on bibs for the first time. They're a strange item of clothing that look like tuxedo pants had a secret affair and subsequent love child with overalls (no, I don't watch too many daytime dramas and novelas when I'm home sick, why do you ask?)

After the saxophone section leader has me sign a sheet saying I've been assigned a size medium bib (pair of bibs?), I move down the line to the jacket station. Milo, who went in front of me, jokes around with the clarinet section leader who wrote down his size, and when Sofia steps out from between the rows of jackets ready to help the next in line, he says, "Oh my gosh, it's like fate! Once a woodwind, always a woodwind!"

I smile hopefully at Sofia, waiting to see if she agrees. She technically smiles back, but it's a dead smile, polite as the polar ice caps. "T-shirt size?"

Her professionalism makes me want to needle her. "I don't know, Milo," I say, "the woodwinds aren't the ones winning section of the week. Maybe we made a good call joining the better half of the band." The fact that Milo is laughing at something his former section leader said and not listening to me at all is a slight setback, but the jab wasn't for his benefit anyway.

Sofia rolls her eyes and flounces to pull a jacket off the rack. "Try this," she instructs. "*Quietly*, if possible."

I'm not sorry I got under her skin. I'm glad. Once in elementary school, when Mom and Ellen were always at each other's throats and Mom and Dad fought their quiet war of wills, Mom explained that sometimes people fight because they love each other. She told me that the opposite of love isn't hate, it's indifference. It's not super mature, but I have to check to make sure Sofia's not indifferent.

I try on the jacket. It's tight around my shoulders and doesn't want to zip over my chest. "I always forget you're not my size," Sofia purrs. She stalks back to the jacket rack, stopping to take a jacket with a broken zipper away from Caleb and hanging it on a special rack for repairs before pulling a larger size for me.

The second jacket fits well enough. I don't love the high collar or the way my blouse bunches under the sleeves, but I can deal with it. Sofia checks some tags, scribbles some numbers on another paper, and makes me sign. I move down the line (passing the station where we are the only ones NOT receiving hats with shiny silver triangles on the fronts, sigh), and then we're back to concert arcs just in time to pack up and apply sunscreen for marching practice. Whenever Ms. Schumacher compliments low brass through her megaphone, I look for Sofia on the field. She tosses her hair or rolls her eyes every time. Harsh, but far from indifferent.

I hit the practice rooms feeling more hopeful than hurt.

I'M HAVING A PERFECTLY PEACEFUL LUNCH ON Wednesday—Caleb lost in his headphones, Bloom playing with the ginormous robot pen he uses for all of his home-work, Milo updating me on the saga of Taylor Swift's dating life, and none of us getting our homework done even though we all swore we had to work through lunch—when Elias comes in like a wrecking ball complaining about Jonathan and map tests and mosquito bites and the cafeteria serving the same vegetarian meal three days in a row.

"ELIAS!" Neeraj, half asleep in the doorway of a practice room, wakes up to do his shout-and-point greet-ing before tipping his baseball cap back over his eyes. We scoot to give Elias plenty of space as his airstream of com-plaints slows and he starts to look a bit less ready to burst.

"Sorry, estoy hasta la madre; how're y'all?"

"Como siempre," Caleb says, face neutral. It might be a casual answer to the question or might be a dig at Elias's constant state of agitation.

It's getting to be routine, the lunchtime low brass circle. The boys talking about the same music and video games and freshman teachers, Bloom on his phone but throwing in a devastating observation once in a while just in case you for-got he was there, quietly judging everyone. Neeraj shouting "JOE-NATHAN!" when Jonathan joins halfway through the hour, having just finished his Young Entrepreneurs Club meeting. Milo inviting Caleb to split his earbuds so they can share music is a new development today (and

Caleb accepting the offer is interesting—he's usually too much of an audio-quality snob for that), and it makes Elias jealous because he is a trumpet player with the heart of an infant who can't stand not being the center of attention, so he starts blasting reggaeton on his tinny phone speaker, and I definitely can't revise my Spanish essay under these conditions, so I give in to shimmying and singing along instead, until Drum Minor Hannah has to come out of a practice room to tell us to *please* keep it down.

"HANNAH!" Half-awake Neeraj does not read the room at all.

"She's just mad because she plays the bassoon," Elias whispers when she goes back into her practice room.

"She's just mad because she's responsible for you clowns," Bloom says. "I know her pain."

"She's just mad because she doesn't get to play music this year," Milo guesses. "I would miss it if I were DM. I miss my clarinet."

"She's just mad because y'all are ignoring her actual complaint and speculating about her emotions instead of fixing the problem," I say, reaching for Elias's phone to turn the music down even though the song is ending. A few seconds later, the rhythmic bass line disappears entirely and a pop-y guitar replaces it while a croony voice starts singing something distinctly less dance party-ish about besos.

Caleb grabs the phone. "What is this abuela music, dude? Is this Romeo Santos?"

"Ew, no. In this house we respect women like our king, Prince Royce." Elias takes the phone back and raises the volume past my carefully chosen reasonable level.

Caleb shrugs. "I respect women by stanning Red Velvet." Milo doesn't try to hide his full-on heart eyes at that, and Caleb full-on grins back. Interesting again.

"Let's all respect women by listening to our drum minor," I suggest. But when the music changes to "Chantaje," I go back to dancing because, well, how can I help it?

"I actually know this one." Jonathan beams. "I used to watch the music video in middle school."

Elias's eyebrows shoot up. "Man, nobody needs to know you had a thing for Shakira in middle school."

"That is not what I said, and you're lying if you say you don't have a thing for Shakira *now*. Everyone does."

"Even I do," Caleb says. "I didn't think anything could distract me from Maluma's sexiness, but then Shakira moved her hips and I was like, *Damn, maybe I'm a little bi.*"

Milo snorts and shrugs indifferently, but whispers "Maluma" dreamily under his breath.

"Y'all are so weird." I sigh. I never get it when people look at a picture of a celebrity couple or whatever and declare, "Welp, I'm bi!" Like, people are really seeing photos of strangers and . . . what? Imagining taking off their clothes and touching them? Seems fake.

"Yasmín, don't tell me you're immune to Shakira's charms!" Elias says. "I refuse to believe it!"

"So you do want to hear if *Yasmín* has a thing for Shakira?" Jonathan mutters. "Classy."

"Shakira is the most perfect and beautiful human to ever grace the planet, no one is arguing that," I say. "But I can appreciate that without wanting to sleep with her."

The level of skepticism in the circle of faces staring at me makes my face turn red. "Whatever. Y'all are just gross." That's probably not fair. Sofia would definitely call me judgey and prudish if she were here, even though she's more into Tom Holland's dancing than Shakira's.

"I mean, I'm with you," Bloom says, surprising me because I forgot he was here again. "But that's just, you know, 'cause of . . ." He glances around the circle but doesn't finish his sentence. Everyone does some version of wide, curious emoji eyes at him until he takes a big breath and spills it all out in one long sentence. "You know, 'cause I'm gray ace and gray aro—romance and attraction are both medium to nonexistent, so basically all the stars have to align for me to be into someone."

We all nod, and I try to remember exactly what I know about asexual and aromantic identities, but other than dumb jokes about plant biology, I'm coming up mostly ignorant. It can't just mean that Bloom doesn't talk about touching celebrities, right? That's a perfectly reasonable preference, not an identity. Anyway, I'm glad to have an ally in not wanting to participate.

The boys keep talking Shakira and other celebrity crushes, getting progressively hornier on main until Bloom and I are putting our fingers in our ears and *la-la-la*ing in protest. We're in the middle of a scandalized giggle fit because both Milo and Caleb *like*-liked the fox from *Zootopia* when Sofia walks into the hallway, flute case in hand.

"Can y'all . . . ?" She waves her hands, and we scatter to make a path past the doorway.

Neeraj sits up suddenly, hat flying off. "Oh, uh, hey, Sofia," he says softly. Like, really softly. "What's up?"

Without paying him any attention, Sofia picks her way over our lunch trash and enters the farthest practice room. Neeraj sighs and retrieves his hat.

Interesting.

"Okay, but speaking of hot people . . ." Elias stage-whispers.

"I am begging you to end your train of thought," I say. The last thing I want is to hear the boys objectify Sofia. That's way too weird.

"Seriously, dude, shut up," Neeraj says without lifting his head or his hat.

The conversation continues (luckily off the topic of real people we go to school with), but I'm distracted straining to hear Sofia's flute at the end of the hallway. I just want to know how good she is. I don't hear her play much anymore, so I don't know if I could still give her a run for her first chair position.

Based on the muffled vibrato through the closed door, I think I could. As much as I'm getting used to my new section, I wish I still had the chance to challenge her.

ON THURSDAY, MOM GETS HER FIRST POST-HUMPHREY client. To celebrate, Ellen brings home a bunch of fajita meat she can't eat, and Dad and I do all the dishes while Mom checks out the family's style survey and Pinterest board.

"I'm sure this is just the tip of the iceberg," Dad declares. "Everyone who scrambled to get things livable after the hurricane is going to look around now that the dust has settled and realize they hate their backsplashes." He passes me a glass to dry. "And your mom will swoop in to save the day. She'll be back to normal hours in no time."

Because I don't expect him to be watching me, I don't keep a lid on the hope shining through my expression. Dad lets out a quick, loud laugh when he catches it.

"Stop it!" I laugh. "I didn't say anything!"

"You're a teenager, Mini-meen. You're practically required by law to think your parents are overbearing. It's okay."

I pick up another dish innocently. If Dad wants to get caught making fun of Mom's parenting, he's on his own.

"You've been really patient with her—with everything this year," Dad says eventually. "You're a pretty remarkable kid."

"I've been told I embody the 'spirit of resilience' we're trying to capture this marching season." I giggle and interrupt my Ms. Schumacher impression.

Dad makes a mock awed face. "Impressive. But I miss the days when us old folks thought the kids had it too easy instead of thinking they embodied the spirit of resilience." I snort and he shrugs. "So I guess band is going well?" he asks. "Even with all the new changes your mother is so excited about?"

I giggle again. "I guess . . . yeah. It's fun." The Low Brassholes text thread lights up my phone, probably with another pointless YouTube link, which doesn't disprove my point. "My new section is a bunch of immature boys, but it's fun."

Dad nods thoughtfully. "I try not to touch gender stereotyping with a ten-foot pole these days, but I can see how you, as a unique and un-stereotyped individual, might benefit from a little bit of unique individual immaturity in your life. And it might be good to make some friendships outside of Sofia too, hmm?"

What is that supposed to mean? Why does everybody have something to say about my choice in friends? "Has Ellen been talking to you?" I ask. After Ellen grilled me about the whole situation, she somehow came out with the impression that it's Sofia's fault I'm not a flute. The last thing I need is for her suspicions to get back to Mom, who would just blow everything out of proportion.

Dad shakes his head cryptically. He finishes washing and grabs a dishrag to help me dry.

"Don't you have casework?" I ask him. "I can finish up."

"Don't you have homework?" he shoots back, and keeps drying. "So when do we get to hear you play your tuba?"

CHAPTER 10

Sra. Mendez finally accepts my first essay, just in time to send my second one back for revisions. Happy Friday to me. Ms. Schumacher announces that the forecast for next Friday is starting to look "really promising," because the temperature is supposed to drop ("to something actually resembling fall," she says with a huge born-in-Minnesota smile, which probably means it's going to be arctic). That means instead of khakis and polo shirts, we might get to march our first show in full uniform! So to prepare, and since it's only seventy-five degrees instead of ninety-five outside, she wants us to practice today in our uniforms.

I try to take this news calmly, but my heart pounds fortissimo in my chest. In exactly one week, we'll be lining up at the uniform closet just like this, except the shakos, jackets, instruments, and lyres will all go with us onto buses and into a football stadium, where we'll march not just for the DMs and a bunch of mosquitos, but for our first real audience.

What if it goes horribly? What if it goes well?

Ms. Schumacher takes our dress rehearsal seriously, handing out thin white cotton gloves and emphasizing that only the first pair is free. I put mine on immediately, admiring the crisp seams running down each finger, suddenly relieved that I'm a brass player as I watch the woodwinds pass scissors around to chop the fingertips off. I say, "Treviño," when I reach the front of the line, and the saxophone section leader collects my uniform, and I take the armful of clothes back into the band hall, where Jonathan and Bloom are already pulling their bibs on over their shorts. The space is quickly becoming a sea of blue and green, shiny hats and diagonal slashes of color. The uniforms make the upcoming performance feel more real.

"Too bad Ms. Schumacher didn't tell us to bring our marching shoes," Jonathan says, adjusting the straps of his bib before shrugging on his jacket. "It's going to totally ruin *the effect*." He zips the jacket, pulls out his phone, and swipes open the selfie camera to check himself out.

"I think they want to keep dust off the shoes," Bloom mutters, "for as long as possible." Jonathan doesn't hear or doesn't listen, busy picking filters for his photo. "And today is mostly for getting the feel of the jackets, I think . . ." When it's clear that Jonathan is paying no attention, Bloom shrugs at me.

I move closer, leaving Jonathan to admire his uniform. "I actually am nervous about the shoes," I admit. "They look like they pinch." My marching shoes, mailed to me after I filled out a sizing form over the summer, have been sitting in a shoebox since then, clunky and black and stiff. I didn't think much about it when I knew nothing about marching, but now I know exactly how fast and precise my steps need to be, plus I'm doing it all with a thirty-pound brass dragon wrapped around me! "Have you ever seen anyone wipe out with a sousaphone?"

"It'll be fine," Bloom says. "You march really well." He pulls on his jacket, a little big except for the sleeves coming up short. Once he zips it, though, "the effect" actually works well. He looks significantly less slumped and stringy. "And it could be worse—some bands have to wear spats. Oh, are we supposed to hook this collar thing? I can't make it . . ."

"I got you." Sofia did mine when I was trying the jackets on, and I see everyone around the room partnering up to get theirs fastened, so I don't think it's weird to grab Bloom's collar and notch the metal hook into its clasp above the zipper. It does mean I sort of touch his neck, though, and also smell whatever not-as-bad-as-Elias's body spray or deodorant he uses. We both step apart quickly when I finish, and he tugs the collar to make sure it stays.

"Uh, thanks." His voice is normal amounts of under his breath. "Want me to get yours when you . . . ?"

I hurry to slip on my bibs, only struggling a bit to get the straps to fit right, and then I pull my arms through the sleeves of my new jacket and free my ponytail from the stiff collar. I hike my shoulders a few times. The jacket fits, but it's less comfortable than it felt in the uniform closet. I remember Sofia's dig about my sizing—maybe these jackets just weren't designed to fit over my chest, and now that I have to wear it for hours instead of minutes, I'm more nervous about the tiny spots of discomfort. Bloom hooks my collar closed, which only makes me feel more like I'm being strangled—I guess this is why we have to have a dress rehearsal.

I overlap the bottom of the zipper and pull it about four inches up before it catches on something, so I have to pull it back down and try again slowly. It catches in the same spot, and I check for loose threads and stray pieces of fabric either from the jacket or the bibs, but I can't find anything keeping it in place. On my third try, I pull as hard as I can, which gets the zipper up an extra two inches, but then it absolutely refuses to move any higher. I am officially over these things, effect or no.

I remember that at least one of the jackets had a broken zipper during try-on day. I'm sure I can just go back to the uniform closet and exchange this one for a jacket that works. I wish I had checked the zipper more thoroughly when I tried it on, because it seems like the kind of thing I should have caught. The thing is, I remember zipping the zipper with no problem. And I also remember the jacket fitting better than this, I'm sure of it—even the sleeves don't hit my wrists at the right place. So, okay, maybe there was some totally unintentional mix-up, and this isn't the jacket I signed for, and I can quickly and quietly get it fixed so I'm not too late to the—

I can't get the zipper back down.

I take a long breath and tug it up and down, trying to wiggle the jammed metal back the way it came. Nothing. I start to feel very sweaty where the polyester wraps around my neck and lower torso.

"Bloom?" I ask, my voice coming out squeakier than I want it to. "Can you help?"

Bloom can't get the zipper down either, and now my breath is getting ragged because of the claustrophobia that I definitely have and always forget about since I'm lucky enough to live in the city with the most empty space and the fewest underground tunnels. "Can you just—!" I yelp, making Bloom step back and Jonathan finally come over to see what's up. He hovers for a minute, and then Milo comes to check on me and starts nervously whispering advice that Jonathan ignores. I'm sweating from the way they crowd around me, grateful when Caleb pushes past them and whispers, "Tranquilo, Bobby," before yanking the jacket so hard the zipper pull snaps off—it's only small and plastic. I am tranquilo, thank you very much, and I'm not even panicking about the zipper pull because it's totally fine; it's easy to replace it with a safety pin or something, but I need to get out of this jacket!

And now we've attracted attention from around the band hall, and I'm zeroing in on every hand hiding a curled lip and every rolling pair of eyes, and Neeraj, shoving his usual bottle of blue Gatorade into Elias's hands, says something about opening jars and grabs the two sides of the jacket and pulls on them. I'm feeling light-headed, and I logically know that the jacket isn't tight enough to squeeze me to death, but that doesn't stop me from gasping, and Bloom is somewhere behind me asking if I'm okay, and that makes me inexplicably, incandescently annoyed, so I turn to find him and—

The zipper snaps audibly. Neeraj's hands fly wide and knock the Gatorade out of Elias's grip, and an arc of blue Gatorade splashes across several of my section mates' uniforms. I claw my way out of my finally open jacket front, flailing as something yanks the back of my neck. My section mates are screaming for napkins like a bunch of panicked toddlers, and literally everyone is staring at them, staring at me, and someone clears their throat behind me. I turn to see Bloom spinning around too (holding my broken jacket by the collar), and behind him are Ms. Schumacher and Mr. Green, the percussion director, and even the color guard director, Mrs. Valerie, staring at the scene.

And now I kind of wish the jacket had just strangled me.

THE WORST PART OF THE DAY WASN'T SITTING IN Ms. Schumacher's office hearing how much each jacket costs, and how long we need them to last, and how dry cleaning and repair is setting back the budget. It wasn't staring at the form I had signed swearing that this exact jacket was in good working condition when I tried it on, my own loopy handwritten 7 matching the number 7 inside the broken jacket collar. It wasn't even being forced to go join the rest of the band with half our section in bibs with no jacket, and then me alone having to stay late after practice to choose a new jacket with Ms. Schumacher watching. All of that was embarrassing and horrible.

But the worst part is the special highlight on the Reflections Instagram.

Hurricane Yasmín sweeps across the uniform closet— at least one casualty.

How many fake brass disasters does it take to destroy school property? Actually just one, but she'll drag everyone down with her.

I'm not saying none of those freshmen has ever gotten laid, but I am saying I would hate to see them try to unhook a bra . . .

Maybe we should shut down low brass until we can figure out what the hell is going on.

When I start to feel really bad, I call Sofia. She doesn't answer. I need her to answer, so I call again. She still doesn't answer. Milo told me, in no uncertain terms while we sat in Ms. Schumacher's office waiting to get chewed out, that Sofia sabotaged my jacket on purpose. "She literally filled out your uniform sheet, and it's not like she tries to hide that she's still pissed at you for what Andy brought on himself. You need to say something."

To Sofia or to Ms. Schumacher? I wondered, but it wasn't going to happen either way. "It was an accident," I whispered. He responded with the same twisted "yeah, right" face he uses when Elias promises that *this* will be the last pencil he needs to borrow from one of us.

But Milo is pessimistic. Sometimes Elias keeps hold of a pencil for most of a week. Sometimes a broken jacket is just an absurd, surprising accident.

I need Sofia to answer her phone to prove that's true.

I don't have anyone else to call. I think about calling Laylah, but I've never called her before and it seems rude. Ellen's still at work. I need to do something or else I'm going to start crying and then Mom will notice I've been crying when she comes in to say goodnight. I can't start crying. I try Sofia one more time, and then I scroll my recent texts and see the Low Brassholes chat, and I guess it's worth a shot at least.

I call Bloom because he's less likely to trash-talk Sofia than Milo is, and also because he's the section leader and I guess he has a certain calming presence. He picks up on like the millionth ring, when I'm sure it's going to go to voice mail.

"Yeah?"

"Hi," I say, suddenly not sure this is a good idea. "Sorry for . . . I hate texting."

"Uh, yeah?"

Bloom's voice is so monotone. It's impossible to tell what he's thinking. But I don't have a strategy here anyway, so I don't need to carefully gauge his reaction. I just need . . .

"The Reflections are having a field day."

"The what?"

"The band gossip Instagram. KH . . . BM-whatever Reflections. They're all making fun of me about the jacket."

"Oh." Bloom pauses. "Is Ms. Schumacher going to make you pay for the cleaning? Because it was definitely more Neeraj's fault than yours . . ."

"No, no, it's okay." Bloom, standing behind me, was

shielded from both the Gatorade and the visit to Ms. Schumacher's office. "She just lectured us." I know it could be worse. I do. But . . . "The posts are really wild. People really hate me."

"People are still giving attention to that garbage?" Bloom asks.

I sigh. "Whatever. Never mind."

"No, I just meant . . . People are . . . You didn't do anything . . . It's just a pointless account."

"Well, it had a point when they were all mocking *you* on there with that video," I snap. I don't know if it makes any sense.

"I mean, I never would've seen it, so . . . not really. Those guys were just . . ."

"Oh, so you're also mad that I said anything? You think I'm some hurricane ruining the season?"

"Uh," Bloom says. "No? I'm . . . glad, I guess. I mean, it's more work, but I like . . . It's better than my old section, anyway."

I mean, that makes more sense than whatever I was saying.

"Sorry," I say, less to make sure Bloom isn't mad at me and more because I'm just being difficult for no reason. "They were dicks."

"Yeah, party dares and that stuff really isn't my . . . you know, because of the whole ace thing."

"Oh yeah." My fists clench, thinking again about all of Andy's gross insults. "That's cool. I guess. I don't know much about it, I guess."

"Yeah, nobody does," Bloom says, totally matter-of-fact.

"I mean, is it . . . Do you wish people knew more?"

"Eh. It is what it is."

"I mean, you could . . ." *tell me.* "Never mind." If he wanted to talk about it, he would. No need to pry. "So do you just . . . not care what people think? Or if you're the joke on social media?"

"Nah. I mean, I just don't know. So I can't care."

"That sounds . . . relaxing." And impossible. I know there was a time, a very recent-memory time, when I didn't check Instagram all that often or intently. But it's like trying to remember life before Humphrey.

Bloom snorts. "I guess? I use the internet to follow memes and current events, so it's not that relaxing, just less personal."

I pull my phone away from my ear. I close Instagram. It feels like I can breathe again. "Well," I say into the phone.

"Well," Bloom says back.

"That's a deep subject."

"Huh?"

"Wells." I giggle. "Wells are a deep subject."

Long silence. Then a sudden high note of genuine laughter.

I appreciate being appreciated. "Thanks, it's my dad's joke."

"Deep subject." Bloom laughs again.

I'm feeling better. Weird. "I guess I'd better go finish my homework. Thanks."

"What for?"

"I don't know. Answering."

Bloom snorts. "I almost didn't."

I'm not really sure what to say to that, so I say nothing.

"But I'm glad I did."

I hang up and manage to finish my pre-calc homework and get into bed without checking the Reflections highlights once.

CHAPTER 11

Mom wakes me up early on Saturday morning, which, fine, it's just the only day of the week I get to sleep past eight a.m. She's in my room to complain about something Tía Andrea said in the group chat, and she wants to know why there's an incomplete in my Spanish class online grade book, and she's grumpy that Ellen came home so late last night, and she has questions about the PSAT. She coaxes me out of bed with her nervous energy, and I follow her into the kitchen for green breakfast smoothies.

". . . and I don't see why she keeps calling me about it like I'm supposed to care," Mom huffs, half her rant lost behind the whir of blending kale.

My stomach lurches, not because of the dubious green liquid. It's not hard to imagine Sofia saying the same about me. She still hasn't returned my calls from last night. She hasn't even texted.

It's early. She might not be awake yet. But a voice in my head, the same voice that whispers choice phrases from last night's highlights, tells me that she isn't going to call. That she agrees with what everyone is saying. That she might be saying it herself. I'm horrible; I'm a liability; I'm a disaster.

". . . And she must know what people are saying about her . . ."

Last night's anxiety crawls back into my skin. The more I try to force the thoughts away, the louder they are. I try to remember what Bloom said about not knowing and not caring, but it sounds like nonsense in my brain now.

"Mom?" I ask. "Does—did anybody tell Tía Andrea . . . Maybe she's trying her best."

Mom stops halfway through pouring the smoothie out into two tall glasses and tilts her head at me. "What, mija?"

"I don't know, shouldn't you give her a chance to—I mean, I know you've given her chances, of course. But isn't there something she can do now? Something to make up for everything?"

Mom looks at me with her worried face, like she's about to come feel my forehead and sing "Sana, Sana, Colita de Rana." "What is this all about?"

I shouldn't have said anything. "Nothing. It's nothing."

Mom frowns. "Is everything okay with you?"

"Pretty much," I say, and then quickly change it to "Yes!" when Mom's frown deepens. "I'm good. I'm great. I was just thinking about . . . There's been a lot of drama in band lately. I was thinking about how to defuse it, you know?"

"That's thoughtful." Mom smiles. "I'm sure your friends appreciate that."

I should have enough control to *not* choke on my smoothie laughing, but I don't. "Uh . . . that's not really how drama works, Mom." I've definitely tipped my hand. Mom purses her lips and gives me a piercing stare. "But it's not a big deal," I backtrack. "It will blow over."

She passes me a paper towel with an extremely suspicious expression. "You are my sweet girl." She says it like a threat. "Do you want me to talk to someone at your school?"

Absolutely the last thing I need. "No, Mom, it's okay. I'm fine. Everything's fine."

Mom stares at me for another long moment. "You're sure, mija?"

Something Mom and Ellen share, though neither of them will admit it, is the wild-eyed intensity they get when they have a cause. They're both willing to scream and rage and make a scene—Ellen for justice and politics and changing the cultural narrative, Mom for tradition and family and loyalty and, well, for me. That's why I have to be careful, so I don't set her off on a path of destruction. That's why I can't tell her the truth.

I finish my smoothie, but I don't relax until Mom is back to complaining about Tía Andrea and I'm back to talking her down from making a big dramatic gesture. That's what I'm good at. That's the thing that's supposed to make people appreciate me.

I send Sofia one more text, apologizing for calling so much last night, telling her that it was nothing and that I'll see her at church or school. Blessed are the peacemakers, right?

AFTER A WHOLE SATURDAY AFTERNOON OF STREAMING cartoons and catching up on homework and wrangling the Low Brassholes group chat into actually picking a time for sectionals, I feel mostly ready to face Laylah at Sunday school. But when I walk into the tiny colorful classroom, Mr. Frederick and a couple of my classmates are setting the desks in a big semicircle while three strange adults stand around a box of doughnuts with GILBERTO REYES, WHO IS ALSO EATING DOUGHNUTS, WHAT IS GOING ON?

Why is Gilberto Reyes in my Sunday school classroom? Why is Gilberto Reyes smiling and waving at me?

WHY is GILBERTO REYES walking this way? Why is my brain incapable of anything but asking why?

"Morning," Gilberto Reyes says. To me. To wish me a good morning. In Mr. Frederick's Sunday school/Continuing Catholic Education classroom. "So this is your parish?"

I nod?

"Cool. We're doing talks from different Catholic organizations today. I'm here to speak about this shelter, Casa San Julián, where I work sometimes."

"I didn't know you work there!" I say, which comes out a lot louder and more stalker-y than I meant, but in my defense, I am excited to hear that my crush instincts are so good that they picked out a boy who volunteers at a shelter in his free time. "Uh, I mean, my sibling works with them. I've gone with her a couple times for, like, the backpack distribution and Christmas toy drive."

"Oh, awesome. Who's your sister?"

"Uh. Sibling. My sibling is Ellen. Lopez-Rourke."

"Oh yeah! Ellen, with the . . ." Gilberto gestures to illustrate Ellen's topknot. "I had no idea she—they?—were your sibling."

"Yeah, she is." I smile. "She likes the Catholic Worker Movement because they're all communist and everything."

Gilberto laughs. "The movement is actually against

any kind of political . . . but yeah, they come across basically communist."

"Not unlike the actual teachings of Jesus," I half whisper.

"I mean, I've *been* saying." Gilberto laughs again. Wow, he's actually cool. Oh no. This is ruining my ability to crush on him. I can't have a crush on him if I actually want to talk to him! "No, yeah, Ellen is awesome. And sorry about misgendering. I don't know if I should've known already or if she's stealth on purpose and I should go back to not knowing now or . . . ?"

"I think she's just kind of low-key? Like she uses they pronouns sometimes online, but she asked us to stick with she and her in real life so random people don't end up in her business."

"Yeah, I get that. Well, I'll follow her lead."

For a second I forget that I'm awed by Gilberto Reyes being *Gilberto Reyes* and just really appreciate that he's a decent person and I feel comfortable talking to him.

"Oh, and hey. I missed you in the practice rooms on Friday," he says, and all my comfort evaporates. Friday. He was there. He probably saw everything. He definitely knows that I ran home and nearly had a nervous breakdown. He's being kind, but only because he knows exactly how much of a mess I am!

I have to act normal. "Oh yeah. Friday was . . . a lot."
I try to shrug. I try to look normal.

"I'm sorry Ms. Schumacher went off on y'all. She
didn't have to take her stress out that way."

"No, no, it was fine."

"Debatable." Gilberto frowns. "But, uh." He looks at
Mr. Frederick and all the desks that have filled up around
the room. "I guess I have to go give this talk. Wish me
luck."

"Good luck," I answer dutifully, though I'm not sure
any luck I can offer will do him any good; I seem to at-
tract the worst kind. "You're going to be great." I scramble
away before anyone can notice that the compliment was
over the top. I find two free seats for me and Laylah, who
runs in late halfway through the Charismatic Catholic's
speech.

"Is that . . . ?" she whispers, and I nod frantically as
Gilberto takes the front of the room.

At least, I think while we sit through two and a half
more talks, this will give us something to talk about besides my humiliation.

"I feel like convents must've been badass back in the
day," Laylah says when the speeches are over and Mr.
Frederick sets us free to chat about our impressions of the
different organizations. "I mean, that nun made it sound

kind of cool even now, but imagine back when it was fully a communal dorm for all the presumed ladies who refused to marry men? Where is the HBO show about *that*?"

"Yeah, old-timey nuns were probably cool . . . when they weren't complicit or active forces of colonization and indoctrination." I sigh. Laylah nods wearily and grimaces. We know the history of the church is fraught. "Anyway, I'm still trying to get my head around every altar at every church having a dead saint's relic." The Charismatic Catholic speech had a lot of surprises.

"Oh yeah," Laylah says, "at my old parish they brought in like a hundred relics one week, and you could walk around and find which one called to you and then learn about that saint. It was like a museum."

"That's wild. I've been Catholic for sixteen years and I've never heard about any of this, much less the speaking-in-tongues thing!"

Laylah nods. "I mean, I already knew my Catholicism looked different from, like, my homophobic aunts and uncles in Georgia," she says. "I think there are just a lot of ways to be Catholic."

"That's smart." I nod. "They should have you teach this class."

"I think Mr. Frederick's doing a good job!" Laylah protests, which makes me laugh, and then I try to bully her into raising her hand and sharing her smart observation with the class and she tries to get me to leave her alone.

We never end up discussing my awful jacket at all. Maybe Bloom is onto something about ignoring the Reflections.

Sofia calls me Sunday night. I slam my history book shut (I was way over the Ottoman Empire, much like the rest of the world) to answer.

"Hi." I'm not sure what to expect or what to hope for. I'm weirdly nervous that she didn't text first.

"Hey." The word hangs in the air for a long time before Sofia continues. "I couldn't answer your calls on Friday because I was hanging out with Andy."

"Oh yeah, that's okay," I say. Even though it wasn't really an apology, I heard the hint of one peeking through. "How is he doing?"

"Great." Sofia spits the word out. "Just great."

"Uh . . . ?"

"We broke up," she says. "On Friday. And he's doing great because he's a huge fucking jackass."

Do not say, "I told you so." Do not say, "¿Ya ves?" Do not say, "Took you long enough to figure that one out."

"Oh, I'm sorry."

"No, you're not," Sofia snaps.

No, I'm not. "I'm sorry he's a jackass. How are you doing?"

"I'm great!" Sofia lies. "I just love this. Especially the week before our first game when my garbage section can't play their music and Ms. Schumacher is going to blame me when she realizes her whole flute section is just for show!"

Look . . . I loved being a flute. I cared a lot about playing my part well. I took pride in it . . . But now that I spend almost the whole show more than halfway across the football field from the flutes, I can say for sure that they're just for show anyway. Nobody is hearing those parts from the top of the bleachers.

But that's not what Sofia needs to hear. "Wow, I can imagine. It seems really hard to be a section leader." She huffs, but not as angrily as she could. "If it makes you feel better, you're definitely doing a better job than Bloom. I have to keep setting up schedule polls for him because he doesn't know how. He's never even tested us on our music individually." I feel a twinge of guilt at the disloyalty, but Sofia's pain is more immediate.

Sofia gives a shaky laugh. "Wow, no wonder y'all sound like crap."

She's lucky I'm too full of the Holy Spirit to kick her while she's down. "My point is that you're awesome. And I'm sorry that anything is making you feel like you aren't."

Sofia sighs, the sound soft in my ear. "Yeah, I'm . . . I'm sorry too, I guess."

Oh wow. Unlike me, Sofia doesn't apologize every

time she breathes wrong. I think the last time I heard her make a sincere apology was at her ice-skating birthday party when she knocked a line of parents over.

"What for?"

Sofia sighs again. "I don't know, Yasmín. Am I not allowed to pity my tragically meme-ified friend? I didn't realize it would be so . . . Well, you know how people jump on things." She rushes to continue before I can say anything about Instagram. "There's just been a lot going on. And I've also been stressed out planning this silly flute sleepover; it's traditional after the first football game. Um, speaking of which . . . you should come. You're basically still an honorary flute, right?"

I wonder if I can count this as one more miracle to attribute to the saint relic the Charismatic Catholic brought in this morning. Freeing Sofia from Andy's jackass clutches *and* changing her heart to forgive me. I shoot up a prayer of thanks just in case.

"Excuse you," I say. "I'm an honorary tuba. I'm always a flute. Count me in."

THE WEEK FLIES BY FASTER THAN MS. SCHUMACHER wants, but by Thursday she finally stops holding her decision over our head and officially commits to fielding the whole show on Friday. I'm a little giddy when Sofia drives me home after my practice-room time and her flute

sectionals. I don't even mind Mom asking a million questions about the bus we're taking to the game and why she
can't just take me to the stadium herself since she and Dad
and Ellen are all coming to see the show (and sit through
the football, which is a pretty big sacrifice all around).

I pull my marching shoes out of the closet Friday
morning. They came with long black socks so that no one
has any excuse to show off bare ankles or polka dots when
taking giant steps across the field. I run through my mental checklist—shoes, lunch, after-school snack, nail polish
remover, two frozen water bottles, overnight bag for
Sofia's sleepover, and, of course, my secret weapon—and
then text a reminder to the section.

We are not forgetting shoes! And snacks.

Did that sound weird? I hate texting. But at least I get
a thumbs-up emoji from Elias, who, let's face it, was most
likely to forget something. I steal one of Ellen's granola
bars and then let Mom know I'm ready to head out.

"This is nice," Mom says as we pull out of the driveway. "I feel like you never let me drive you anymore."

"Well, it's been such a busy schedule, and I have Ellen
and Sofia," I say guiltily. "And you're busy too! How's it
going with the new client?"

"It's going okay, I think," Mom says. "They haven't
recommended me to anyone yet . . . but don't worry about

that. Is your English class getting you ready for the PSAT? And did you turn in your Spanish essay? And are you ready for world history today? You really need to bring that quiz average up."

Luckily we make it to school before I have to talk too much about the part of my life I spend the most time on and form the least memories about. I jiggle my leg through my morning classes, forming almost no memories, which might not do much to help my quiz average. I ask Neeraj a million questions about football games over lunch (95 percent of which he answers with "I forgot" or a shrug) and then finally get to sixth period feeling more or less ready to combust. I've been humming my (slow, boring) part of the show music all day, stepping in time down the hallway, imagining each marching set on the field . . . I'm ready. I have to be ready.

We all get our uniforms from the closet. My stomach drops as mine is handed over, but Lee catches my eye and wordlessly nods to the empty practice rooms. We each claim one and change in privacy, and when I come out he hooks the collar of my perfectly normally zipped jacket, and I do the same for him.

"You ready?" I ask him. "You have everything?"

"Nah, I forgot to bring my shoes because nobody re-minded me— *Oh wait.*" He smirks at my temporarily alarmed face.

"Not funny!" I squeal as we join the rest of the low brass. "And, look, did anyone forget their shoes? No? You're welcome! Now let's plan bus buddies so that no *loners* have to hold everyone up trying to find seats." Lee smirks at me and accepts Neeraj's high five that solidifies them as bus buddies.

"Oh, good idea," Bloom says. "Everyone do what Yasmín . . . you know."

"Bloom," I whisper a little later. "Did you plan a treat for everyone? Candy to eat on the bleachers, or paper plate awards, or something to celebrate making it to the first game?"

Bloom's eyes go wide. "Fuck. Was I supposed to?"

I mean, not officially, no. It's a nonrequired bonding opportunity, like the flutes' postgame sleepover. But I have a secret weapon up my sleeve to make sure we don't miss out on our own bonding.

"Okay, sorry, I'm not trying to be rude, but . . . I kind of figured you wouldn't have, so I brought some homemade cookies. Well, Pillsbury, but still. So you can announce those when we get our third-quarter break, okay?"

"Oh," he says. "Thanks. You're full of good ideas today."

"And every day." I give an exaggerated flounce on my way past him to the cubby closet.

I have to be full of good ideas. I have to have a checklist.

This performance has to go well, so I can't afford to do any unplanned or poorly thought-out thing that might mess it all up. Not if I want the Reflections account to find a new target of the week. Not if I want to save the season from Hurricane Yasmín.

I push the Reflections out of my brain by stuffing my headphones in my ears and humming along to "Driver's License" until my section has paired off.

"Section leaders, get everyone in line for uniform inspection, please!" Gilberto calls from Ms. Schumacher's office. The band hall gets even more chaotic for a minute before finally starting to settle into a blue-and-green order, a slow-moving sea of diagonally color-blocked jackets and mirrored hats.

I wipe my palms on my jacket, even though I'm about to slide gloves over them anyway. God, please don't let me slip, or drop the Dragon, or lose a glove on the bus. I'm going to throw up. I run through my uniform checklist— earrings out, nail polish removed. "Milo, your collar," I hiss, prompting Caleb to help the baffled clarinet fix his clasp. Ms. Schumacher and the other adult staff call us to attention. I stand frozen (feet together, shoulders back, chin up, chest out, eyes with pride), listening as people get scolded for rogue jewelry or makeup choices or wonky hat angles.

"Okay," Ms. Schumacher says finally. "Looking good,

low brass. You can bring your instruments over to the bus now, percussion should be almost finished loading up."

Out in the parking lot, I follow Hannah's shouted instructions and slide the Dragon into the storage compartment under the designated bus. When I go back inside, Ms. Schumacher is giving the tail end of another set of instructions, sounding even more stressed than she did five minutes ago.

"What'd we miss?" I catch Laylah and Mia near the cubby closet.

"Something wrong with the third bus. They're trying to fix it."

"Oh crap."

"Yeah." Laylah sighs. "We're all supposed to hang tight for fifteen minutes."

"Hey, at least it's not anything you did this time, right?" Mia teases, then frowns when Laylah elbows her. "Okay, I'm joking."

"Remember, no eating in your jackets—and NO COLORED LIQUIDS!" Ms. Schumacher calls before disappearing into her office with her phone clutched to her ear.

"Hey, band!" Gilberto says loudly a minute later. "Let's get this place cleaned up while we wait. The more we do now, the sooner we can get home tonight!"

It's busywork, but I'll take it. I grab some empty chip

bags in a corner and take them to the trash can. When I turn back to search for more trash, Bloom is standing behind me with his hand halfway out but not quite committed enough to reach my shoulder.

I raise my eyebrows.

"Uh, yeah, hey." Bloom shoves his hands into his bib pockets and rocks on his heels. "That was really good, all the stuff today . . . The reminder texts, and the cookies, and the bus buddies idea . . ."

"Oh, thanks." My shoulders relax; I guess I was half expecting to be in trouble again. "I just wanted to be sure we're doing everything we should be doing."

Bloom rocks again, frowning slightly. "Yeah, that's . . . I'm not good at . . . Everyone sort of thought Neeraj would do it, you know?"

I do not know. "You thought Neeraj would do what?"

"Oh, uh, be section leader. I thought he would do it, since he's older and I'm not very . . . you know." He pauses and glances at me. "I don't really know what I'm doing."

"I guess." I take a few steps to the side and lean against the wall, gesturing for Bloom to follow me since this is a weird conversation to be having while blocking the trash can. "First of all, Neeraj would be a terrible section leader. Like, among other things, he just skipped our last sectionals entirely."

"He still plays better . . ." Bloom trails off and shrugs.

"Right, but a section leader has to care if everyone plays well. And, *by the way*, a section leader should care if someone skips sectionals entirely!"

Bloom hangs his head. "Heh, yeah, see, that's what I'm—that's my bad."

It's funny. I know exactly what I could say to make Bloom feel comforted and justified and better about himself. It's probably even what he wants me to say, and I'm usually all about telling people what they want to hear. But I guess I'm not in the habit of giving Bloom calculated lies. Maybe it's because I don't care if this one inarticulate freshman likes me, or maybe it's because I genuinely suspect that he won't like me any less for not boosting his ego. Either way, I let his apology hang in the air without rushing to reassure him that he's a good—no, a *great* section leader, really.

"So . . . yeah." He rubs the back of his neck. "I originally tried to get Neeraj to do it, but . . . you seem like you would be, um, better. And I don't think Ms. Schumacher cares—our section's such a mess anyway. So you can if you want to. Co–section lead. With me. And help keep things organized."

Padre nuestro, protect me from inarticulate freshmen who COMPLETELY BURY THE LEDE! "You want to make me section leader?"

My total shock makes Bloom shrink into his baggy

jacket. "Co? You don't have to. Just seemed like maybe . . ."

"Yes, obviously I want to!"

Bloom blinks, then smiles. "Really?"

"Really!" I'm heating up in this jacket, too excited about too many things, ideas swirling through my head. "I really . . . Thank you!" I take a breath. "Seriously, thank you. You could have easily just said nothing and kept letting me do things."

"Oh, but that wouldn't . . ." Bloom shakes his head. "Well, I'm really glad and relieved. And I'll talk to Ms. Schumacher."

"Cool."

We stand there for another minute, both grinning, until Gilberto's voice makes me jump. "Hey, band! Buses are sorted. Head out to the parking lot, please! First football game in T-minus one hour!"

There's a general cheer, but I'm too bemused to join in. This is happening. I'm going to my first performance.

And I'm going as a section leader.

CHAPTER 12

I kind of forgot there would be football at a football game. We arrive well before the game starts, but it's weird to see the student athletes warming up on the field, probably just as stressed out about their performance as we are (or, to put it less nicely, as indifferent to our performance as we are to theirs). And it's not just the football players. The cheerleaders mill around the bottom of the bleachers, stretching or adjusting their costumes or practicing the crisp arm movements they'll be doing in unison soon. The dance squad, like the cheerleaders but even sparklier, practice playing their routine music on the loudspeaker. The yearbook and newspaper kids approach with cameras and notebooks, idly asking random band members for quotes. I recognize a few kids in nearly every group, faces I've only seen glazed over and slack now vibrant and electric like they never are in class.

We settle in a block that more or less mirrors concert arcs as the fans start trickling in. I know this is very Texan of me, but I get a little caught up in the excitement of the whole event. Up near the top of the bleachers, the Dragon leaned carefully against the bench next to me, I feel like the whole semester has been leading up to this moment for so many of us, and all that hope and stress mixes with the late-afternoon chill (thanks, unseasonable cold front!) to create an atmosphere of possibilities.

Then Gilberto and Hannah lead us through a warm-up, and I realize that the slight chill has made half the band tooth-achingly flat and that sitting right behind the drumline is going to be a headache, and some of the magic dissipates as performance anxiety creeps back in. But I'm still excited.

We start playing some stand tunes as more fans enter the stadium, and the other band shows up and plays some of their music, and there are a bunch of announcements and pregame dances and cheer routines and ROTC marches. As the home team, the other band gets to play the anthem, and then the sports part starts and we can mostly relax until halftime.

Mostly. Gilberto or Hannah will shout a song title every so often, using secret wisdom (or awareness of the game) to know when it's our turn to play. Then we all scramble to hoist our horns off the bench and over our heads while flipping our lyres to the correct music in time for their count-off, since no one in this section has anything but the show music memorized (and even that is iffy). I don't know how football works, but when the players are playing, we have time to chill and talk and dream about our third-quarter snack break as the sky darkens and the floodlights come on.

Bloom catches my eye from the opposite end of the row during some downtime. "Should I . . . ?"

I shrug, not sure what he's asking, but I guess he takes it as a go-ahead because he gets his knees up on the bleacher so he's sitting higher and waves his hand for everyone's attention.

"So, uh, we have kind of an announcement, pending Ms. Schumacher approving and everything . . . Yasmín agreed to be co–section leader. Uh, also she brought cookies." Bloom ducks his head and gestures to me.

"Whaaaaat?" Neeraj, eternal hype man, runs from his seat on the opposite end of the row all the way down to give me a high five. "That's awesome, dude. You're, like, so on top of things."

"About time we officially recognized all her work as section mom," Elias says from the middle of the row.

"Uh . . ." I grimace, not sure how to respond to what

sort of should have been a compliment, and not sure why exactly I hate it so much.

Luckily, Lee elbows Elias. "Don't say that shit; it's sexist." His face turns bright red as he says it, but he holds Elias's guilty and confused gaze.

"She's section leader," Bloom explains. "She's in charge of getting shit done, not cleaning up after you. Nobody calls me the section mom. Or dad. Or anything."

"To be fair, you're not as nurturing *or* as authoritative as Yasmín," Elias says. "And you don't bring snacks. But sorry. It's about time we officially recognized all her work as a motherfucking boss."

This, I can accept.

"I'm happy to take on the responsibility of section mom if y'all don't want to." Jonathan raises his hand. "Can I send Elias to time-out, indefinitely?"

"Dibs on being the section fun uncle." Neeraj raises his hand.

"Bro"—Caleb shakes his head—"you are without a doubt the section bio parent who picked adoption as the best choice for your life situation."

"And loving it." Neeraj winks.

"I feel like we've gotten off track," Milo says, lifting his water bottle and clapping my shoulder. "Congrats to Yasmín!"

"Yasmín!"

"Hooray!"

"Cookies!"

I catch Sofia, at least ten rows down, turning to look at us, and I realize with satisfaction that we're being the rowdy bro-y stereotype of a low brass section.

"Speech!" Caleb calls, using the cheering as an excuse to sling one arm over a suddenly pink-faced Milo's shoulder.

I raise my water bottle and take the opportunity to give the rowdiest, bro-iest shout I can muster. "Low BRASS!"

WE'RE GIDDY AND GIGGLY ALL THE WAY UP UNTIL THE middle of the second quarter, when Ms. Schumacher leads us down off the bleachers in a long line to set up for the halftime show. We've practiced this, sort of, on the gravel track and the practice field, without the fuzzy noise of the bleachers or the sticky-sweet fried smell of the concession stand or the dark of the tunnel where we wait, standing to one side so the football team can file past us. We've practiced without the announcer's enthusiastic disembodied voice announcing, "Kingwood High's Marching Band performing 'New Directions: Three Movements of Growth and Change.'"

I follow the line, matching Lee in front of me, step

for step. The Dragon unfurls above my head, heavy and ready to roar. We're buzzing with bridled energy, eyes with pride and with terror and with anticipation.

Gilberto climbs to the top of his metal podium, and Hannah climbs onto her slightly lower one a few yards away. They raise their hands, and across the field our horns follow in a quick snap of movement. Then, in four short motions, he counts us off.

On *four* we breathe. On *one* we step.

Halfway through the opener, our arc turns out flat at the park and play, and I know we're going to hear about it later. During the drumline's solo, I catch my foot weirdly on the Astroturf (why can't we have real grass??) and have to hop to get back in step. Our playing is weak through the entire third movement, but all I can do is grit my teeth (metaphorically) and play as many notes as I can in time with Gilberto's constantly moving hands.

Last note, eight counts. Last rest, four counts. Step and close. Horns snap down (more relevant for Bloom, Neeraj, and Elias than for me and the Dragon and the other sousaphones). I hear Ms. Schumacher's voice in my head, telling me to keep this intensity, to hold this closing moment, while the echo of the trumpets fades.

I love it. It's better than rehearsal, better than the silence of a practice room, better than the perfect acoustics of a concert hall. My lips ache from buzzing, and my arms and legs ache from carrying the Dragon, and my heart pounds in my ears as we file off the field in a triumphant semi-chaos of synched steps. I love it. I want to do it again.

We have the whole third quarter off, free to shed our jackets and eat or buy snacks and visit friends and family in the stands. Bloom and I give our notes on the show over cookies, break up a near food fight between Jonathan and Elias, and collapse with relief when the rest of the section isn't looking.

"We could've done a lot worse," Bloom says while I lie sideways across the bleacher and text Ellen to see where she and Mom and Dad are sitting. I beam because he's right, and because I had some part in it, and I plan to have even more of a part in our improvement.

THE BUS RIDE BACK TO THE BAND HALL IS RAUCOUS, AND the rush to turn in uniforms and head to the buffet pizza place down the block is chaotic. Then I pile into Sofia's car and text Mom a photo of the whole flute section crowded into the familiar Palacios living room, with Sofia's abuela putting the finishing touches on the abundance of snack foods before retreating to her bedroom with her noise-canceling headphones and sleep mask.

Mom texts me back, Is there a BOY there? and I reply, He's a flute and Ms. Palacios OKd it. There's a good chance Mom will call Ms. Palacios for the scoop on that, but luckily it's officially not my problem because I've done my duty of proving that I am exactly where I said I'd be.

Ms. Palacios shows up then, with her nightdress and her perfumed hand lotion, and fusses over everyone (but especially me). "I haven't seen you in so long," she says. "If you girls aren't going to have sleepovers anymore, then your mom and I need to organize a swap one weekend. I want to hear about the tuba! And all those boys! How are you managing?"

Sofia rolls her eyes at me, and I crinkle mine back. She's told her mom about me.

"Your mom says you're doing great with AP classes, of course," Ms. Palacios continues. "Sofia had so much trouble with them last year." She reaches to smooth Sofia's hair as she passes with an armful of sodas. Sofia ducks and scowls.

"Well, you know, last year . . . with Humphrey . . ." I say. Ms. Palacios is so nice, but the comparisons are uncomfortable. "Everything was really overwhelming." Ms. Palacios waves that off and goes back to complaining about Sofia's grades. Sometimes I do appreciate Mom's overly intense loyalty—yeah, it means that she'll yell at me about my grades while telling Ms. Palacios how well I'm doing, but at least she's not in the habit of scolding me in front of my friends. Ms. Palacios gives me one more big hug and makes me promise to visit more, and then retires, probably to hop on the phone with Mom.

Even though we all just ate pizza and talked through the whole performance at band dinner, our sleepover starts with more snacks and more discussions about the game and the new round of chair tests and band-couple gossip. Felpudo gets overexcited begging for chips and licking faces until he finally sprawls in front of the TV with his paws in the air. Everyone's on a sugar high and an adrenaline high, and Katrina might just be high in addition to passing around sips from her Coke bottle that turns out to be at least 60 percent rum.

"Somebody confiscate Yasmín's phone," Sofia comments dryly before taking a swig from the bottle. I stick my tongue out and remind myself that she invited me here, so she must not be that worried about my snitching.

I feel a tiny twinge of regret that we missed this type of bonding last year and that I can't fully participate this year. I never got to find my feet in the section—that's part of the reason I liked third-wheeling with Mia and Laylah, or trailing behind Sofia. I try to believe it's not too late, even if I feel more like a guest among the flutes than the low brass.

We vote to put on *High School Musical* (ultimate comfort movie), and Laylah and Mia cuddle up on the love seat while the freshmen ask me to dish about the low brass boys (who I guess they see as viable dating options rather than weird youngsters).

"Do not date low brass," Sofia warns, barging into our conversation with a mouthful of mini marshmallows and a mournful look in her eyes. "They're all jackasses, cien porciento. And they will all leave you for some ugly piano player in AP Music Theory."

Oh, damn.

I pat her back and trash-talk Andy until she feels better, and then Katrina suggests Truth or Dare and Han counters with Never Have I Ever.

"But I have a bunch of bleach and hair dye," Sofia complains. "I wanted to do a group dare."

"We can still do it!" Han shouts. "We can all dye our hair! Pinkie swear we will!"

"Sorry, my hair is delicate, and I'm trying to grow it," Laylah says. Mia covers her buns with her arms and mutters, "Not today, Satan." The freshmen look uncertain but don't seem able to stand up to the peer pressure of Yuki and Devin's excitement.

I raise my eyebrows at Sofia. "My mom would utterly freak."

"Where's your spirit of adventure?" she asks. "Where's the bold Yasmín who took the low brass section by storm? Hey, did I hear right that they made you section leader?"

"Yes!" I squeal. "Well, Ms. Schumacher has to approve it, but I think she will."

"Wow," Sofia says. "Congrats."

"It's so cool." I pick another green M&M out of the bowl on the coffee table, bouncing along to "Bop to the Top." I'm excited and sugar-high and not thinking very carefully. "Who would have ever guessed that this whole low brass thing would turn out so perfectly?"

Which, I realize as soon as Sofia's face falls, was kind of an insensitive thing to say. I mean, I don't think Andy was an exemplary boyfriend until he joined AP Music Theory, but, you know . . .

"Uh," I try to say, "I didn't mean . . ."

Sofia grabs Katrina's mostly empty Coke bottle and takes a swig. "So, Never Have I Ever?" she asks, cutting me off.

We get in a circle, and since there's hardly any alcohol left, everyone gets an energy drink so that the more things you've done, the greater your chance of pulling a caffeine-induced all-nighter. Sofia starts us off with a band theme: "Never have I ever played a brass instrument."

I sip my (gross) drink without complaint, feeling like this is a reasonable petty response to my comment. The freshmen follow the theme by getting the upperclassmen to drink with "Never have I ever been to UIL" and "Never have I ever been to Homecoming." Han makes herself drink with "Never have I ever marched a whole show without playing," and then it's my turn.

"Uh . . ." I don't want to target anyone, and the band

theme seems played out. "Uh, I guess, never have I ever gotten drunk."

I was trying to pick a general mid-level rebellious thing. I was not prepared for every single person—even the freshmen—to drink, leaving me alone twirling my can between my fingers awkwardly.

"Mia's cousins sneak wine away from family gatherings," Laylah explains with a little shrug in my direction. "I went for the Fourth of July."

"Seder," Devin says. "And Purim."

"You really haven't, Yasmín?" Katrina asks.

I was trying to be middle-of-the-road! Where is everyone even getting enough alcohol to get drunk? "I . . . guess I'm pretty straightedge," I say. Sheltered, more like. Sheltered and even more sheltered for not realizing how sheltered I am.

"I guess that explains why you were so freaked about the low brass party," Han says.

"No," I protest, "that wasn't about alcohol. I'm totally fine if people want to . . ." I'm losing the thread of what I'm saying. Too many eyes on me. "I mean, it's your decision."

Katrina raises her Coke bottle to that and takes a swig.

"Oh, thanks, Saint Yasmín." Sofia rolls her eyes. "For granting us your pardon. Who's next?"

"That's not what I . . ." Okay. Forget it. I take a sip of my drink before remembering how bad it is.

"Let's get to the juicy parts!" Katrina says. "Never have I ever had sex!" She tips her bottle back and drains the last drops, then points around the circle one at a time. The freshmen giggle. Han tilts her head back and forth like she's considering, but ultimately leaves her can in her lap. "No, not Saint Yasmín, obviously," Katrina says as she skips over me (which, cool, that's another nickname I would very much prefer not to stick). She turns to her other side, where Mia, half in Laylah's lap, whispers some quiet debate. "Whatever question y'all have going on there, I'm going to say it's probably a yes."

Mia grins and Laylah ducks her head, but they both drink. Yuki and Devin shake their heads, and then we're back at the beginning of the circle.

Sofia drinks.

What?

WHAT?

"What?" I ask, and by ask I mean screech, and Katrina puts her chin in her hands and leans forward and may as well be eating popcorn for how much she's enjoying the show, but I can't help asking anyway, "When? Who? What?"

How did I not know this? Why didn't you tell me?

"That's not how the game works," Sofia says.

"Was it Andy?" I have a sinking feeling in my stomach that only gets worse when Sofia freezes. "What the fuck?" They only started dating in May. That's barely four months. This had to be recent, and then he just . . .

I should have gotten him expelled for real. I should find him now and kick his ass. "Why didn't you tell me?"

"Oh, I have no idea. Maybe because I knew you would be exactly like this about it!"

Nothing is making any sense. Sofia had sex and she didn't even tell me and she got her heart broken and I've barely spoken to her in weeks. I know she was mad at me, but I thought I was fixing it. I thought our friendship was stronger than a poorly thought-out mistake and a jackass boy. She should have kept me in the loop. She should have let me threaten her horrible ex with bodily harm. "You shouldn't have . . ."

"Don't you dare," Sofia interrupts, voice low.

I don't know what she means. But I guess I don't know anything. I shake my head.

"Never have I ever finished a game of Never Have I Ever without a dramatic reveal?" Mia jokes into the silence. With a couple of awkward laughs and coughs, everybody drinks.

"*High School Musical 2*?" Laylah suggests. "And I think some of y'all said you were going to dye your hair?"

Blessed are you, Laylah, for getting us out of this awkward situation. The circle scatters as folks swap their energy drinks for water or soda, run to the restroom, or grab more snacks. I don't feel hungry. I feel weird. I'm sad and I'm angry and I want to punch Andy. I think Sofia thinks I'm mad at her, or judging her, but that's not it at all. I want better for her, and I'm furious that she didn't get it. I feel left out, insulted, an afterthought to my best friend, my only friend. What's wrong with me? I pull a blanket over my feet and lean back on the couch, head still spinning. *High School Musical 2* is a relaxing soundtrack while I try to pinpoint why I feel like shit.

There was one time over the summer, sometime before the Fourth of July, when Sofia came over unexpectedly with Whataburger milkshakes. She was, I don't know, she was complaining about having her abuela and her mom bickering all the time, and saying that the summer was too long and boring. And I think I said something about Andy—shouldn't she be entertained by her boyfriend? She had been hanging out with him so much. It felt like she didn't have time for me. I didn't love it. And she said something about how actually he was *plenty* entertaining, and then I got grossed out and told her I didn't want to hear it. And then she got quiet and finished her milkshake and left. And barely answered my texts after that.

Why do I hate hearing about her and Andy so much? I think it's cute when Laylah and Mia are all over each other. I don't even really mind Elias and Jonathan fantasizing about Shakira, as long as they don't make me participate and don't get too specific about the details. It's just because I hate Andy, I guess? What else could it be?

Before I can figure anything out, my swirling thoughts crash into my exhaustion like two eighteen-wheelers. My eyes droop, and my head sinks deeper into the couch cushions.

"Yasmín?" A voice speaks in my ear. I think it's Laylah. "Yasmín, they're all dyeing their hair now. Do you want to join?"

"I . . . My mom . . ." I say, trying to turn my face toward the voice but lacking the strength. I was up so early. It's so late.

"Told you she's not one of us anymore." Sofia's voice, and Sofia's footsteps walking away.

"Wait!" I say. "I can . . . just the bottom? Like an inch or two?"

Sofia's laugh sounds closer now, and soft, like she's trying not to wake me up. Like one of our million middle school sleepovers, like years of being best friends, practically primas, like all of that stuff that doesn't go away over one bad summer.

"You can do it," I tell her, and I don't know if she hears me, because I fall asleep waiting for an answer.

"SHITSHITSHIT!"

"Calm down!"

"I'm calm! Shit! No, Yasmín, *don't move!*"

I snap awake with an unpleasant level of adrenaline, absolutely positive that I just closed my eyes except that I know *High School Musical 2* well enough to recognize the finale. I sit up, and there are more screams, and there's resistance on the back of my head, an extra weight dragging at my ponytail when I try to pull it over the back of the couch.

"Who was supposed to set the timer?"

"Don't move, just— It's getting on the couch!"

I'm dragging my brain back to functionality the best I can. "Qué—the fuck is going on?"

Laylah plops onto the couch, one hand on my shoulder. "Okay," she says, voice dangerously chill. "It's going to be fine. No one is hurt. But you have every right to be mad."

I scan the room and see most of the flutes crowded around the back of the couch behind me.

"We were trying to dye your hair like you said, but we sort of lost track of time, and the bleach—be careful."

I reach for the top of my ponytail and follow it down until I hit a second scrunchie holding a washcloth around the bottom half of my hair. I pull the whole thing forward, causing a ripple of squeaks and footsteps as everyone races around the couch to watch. The washcloth-wrapped bundle has a pungent smell and . . . does it feel warm? I pull the scrunchie down and unfold the cloth to reveal tinfoil that definitely feels warm, with white liquid leaking out of the corners.

"Maybe go to the bathroom?" one of the freshmen suggests, but I can't consider the wisdom of that advice until I see what has been done to my hair. I unwrap the tinfoil to more squealing and Laylah holding up the washcloth to catch the drips.

A wad of orangey-yellow hair—more than an inch, more than a few inches—tangles inside the foil, looking very strange and kind of slimy.

"You need to wash it," Katrina says. *"Carefully."*

I stand up, disoriented and still full of bad adrenaline. I stumble to the kitchen sink. I wish everyone wouldn't follow me. Where is Sofia? Where is Ms. Palacios?

The bleach is on at least six inches of my hair. I stick it under the water and start to work out the bleach and . . . "Y'all. Y'all! This does not feel normal!"

Everyone screams again, and Katrina says, "Don't pull it!" but it doesn't matter because my hair has turned into a gummy substance that stretches and snaps when I run my fingers through it.

What. The. Fuck.

"Okay," Katrina says, "stop pulling it. Your hair is fried. Do you want to try to save some of the end, or should we just . . . ?"

Just what? Chop it all off? I ignore Katrina and keep pulling my fried hair out in clumps ranging from copper to platinum. How high up does it go? How short will my hair be? And *where* is Sofia?

Like a switch flipping, or like a clump of hair snapping somewhere in my chest, my tear ducts suddenly activate, and I do not want to be crying over my hair at a flute sleepover but I definitely am, and it's too late to do anything about it now. Laylah pats my back, and Katrina offers her own version of comfort ("At least your roots are safe! I've seen so much worse on YouTube!"), and Mia nearly bodychecks one of the freshmen who tries to come in, screaming, "Get that camera away from her!"

It's not the end of the world. It's just an unexpected haircut, and nobody's hurt, and everything's fine.

Except me. I'm hurt. I'm not fine.

I flip my soaking wet hair over my shoulder and stomp into the living room.

Sofia hangs back, away from the doorway, nibbling on a Twizzler. She looks surprised when I come at her, water and tears streaking down my face.

"Where were you?" I ask.

She hesitates. Shrugs. "You said it was okay. Someone didn't set the timer like she was supposed to. I wasn't even involved."

That's the whole problem. She should have been involved. She should have watched out for me.

Eventually Sofia tosses her hair. "Whatever, Yasmín." I notice the delicate green stripe she's added to her right temple.

I lock myself in the bathroom until Ellen comes to pick me up. I never remember if this literary thing is irony or coincidence or poetic justice or what, but whatever it is, it isn't lost on me that this all started with someone else locked in a bathroom. I take the time to type out a text to Bloom, asking why every band party is shitty. He answers (it's surprisingly early, only one in the morning) and asks if everything is okay, but I don't have the energy to explain everything, so I just say yes.

Ellen takes me home, and when I tell her to please not ask, she doesn't, and that makes me pretty grateful to have a sibling like her.

"I'm glad you moved home," I say.

"Oh, thanks. It's been . . . Well, there have been some upsides. Maybe when I finally get a real job I'll stick around and save up, at least until you graduate." She smiles, only a little pained at the idea. When we stop at a stoplight, she reaches for the end of my ponytail. "It's going to look totally normal once you cut it," she says. "I'm almost disappointed. A little higher and you could've justified an undercut or a really dramatic bob. Don't tell your mom I said that."

I snort. "Do you ever . . ." I start to ask, not sure how to say what I'm thinking in the few blocks we have left of this car ride. "Do you ever fall out of friendship with people?"

"Oof. Yeah, sometimes. It hurts. But I've found that a lot of friendships can survive more than you think they can."

"Yeah," I say. Maybe I'm being super dramatic about this whole thing. Maybe Sofia was busy with hosting, and I was asleep, and nobody set the timer like they were supposed to. Maybe that's all it is, even though it feels like so much more.

"Friend drama is rough," Ellen says, pulling into the driveway. She stays at the wheel for a moment and looks me over. "Are you okay?"

"I'm okay," I say, testing the words out. "Like you said, it's survivable. I'll survive."

"Okay. Good, I think." Ellen frowns a little but takes the keys out of the car and opens the door. She stands in front of the door to her garage apartment while I head for the back door to the house. "Oh, word of advice?" Ellen calls softly. "Maybe finalize the haircut before you show your mom."

. . .

Mom and Ms. Palacios thwart that plan by talking to each other, so Mom barges into my room to see the full fried-hair horror show first thing in the morning. With the edges dry and brittle and standing on end, it kind of looks like someone added an orange tutu border to my hair. Mom, with the light highlighted streaks of her dark hair already slicked back in a neat bun, shakes her head in horror.

"I don't understand what you were thinking," Mom yell-lectures as she sits me down in front of her bathroom mirror and takes a spray bottle to my head like I'm six years old.

"I told you, it was an accident— Ay, Mami, enough." Mom meets my eyes in the mirror and smiles, probably because I haven't called her Mami since I was six years old, and she used to drip water into my eyes then too. "I wasn't trying to do it. Just cut it off, please."

"You have such nice hair," Mom says. "And if you want to lighten it, you can go to my salon."

"It was just a bad idea. It was a sleepover thing."

"You really shouldn't consider any ridiculous colors," Mom says. "They don't look good at all, and colleges will look at your social media and your photos, you know."

"I *know*."

I imagine, for a second, that I told my mom how Sofia let it happen, how she's the one who made me leave the flutes in the first place. I imagine how she would freak out, how she would call Ms. Palacios in a rage, and how the two of them would either clash on opposite sides of our fight or, more likely, mesh into one punitive force against Sofia. I imagine Ellen lecturing to no one about consent and body autonomy. Even Dad, who's usually laid-back, would get on board if he thought Sofia wasn't a friend to me, the way he once drove my friend Samantha home and told her mom she wasn't welcome at our home anymore because she wouldn't stop calling me an alien.

Sofia would be banned from the house. She would be steamrolled by the protective bulldozers in my life. Even if I'm pissed right now, I don't want that. Knowing how my family loves me, and how they hold grudges, it's just better to keep my fights to myself.

CHAPTER 13

"What the—" Neeraj and I meet by the vending machine Monday morning, bright and way too early since we somehow voted on morning *and* lunchtime sectionals. I don't know which of us does a bigger double take. He's shaved his head. I mean, more like a buzz cut, not totally bald, but definitely a big chop.

"You have hair!" he says.

"Yeah. You don't."

"Well, I thought it was in solidarity!" He claps his hands to his head. "Why do you have hair?"

It's too early to make sense of Neeraj. "What are you talking about?"

So . . . it turns out I'm KHMB Reflections famous *again*. While I spent the weekend letting my boiling hurt simmer and cool—not telling my mom anything about my semi-fight with Sofia, letting Laylah compliment my fix-it cut at Sunday school and tell me how bad she and Mia feel about everything, generally working toward getting over it or at least not making it a big deal—Instagram has gone in the opposite direction.

No one has posted the actual video from the party, but everybody seems to know someone who knows someone who watched it, and the rumors have gotten out of control. I would've thought the mean-spirited gossip couldn't surprise me anymore, but I underestimated how much glee some of these anonymous posters would get from my misfortune.

Justice is a dish best served bleached.

The flute section playing the long con of pettiness is the energy I'm trying to bring to this school year.

Someone should really tell Hurricane Yasmín that parties aren't her thing.

I have the video in my possession. If you guess who I am, I'll DM it to you. Good luck.

Neeraj leads me out to the parking lot so I can avoid walking through the band hall. I spent the weekend talking myself down, but now I'm shaking and angry all over again. We had our first halftime performance. Our season is coming together. What more penance can I do?

What do people want from me other than a periodic punching bag?

We pass the dumpsters. It seems ironic or poetic or whatever since life is garbage.

"She has hair!" Neeraj announces when we enter the back hallway. He goes straight for Elias and socks him on the shoulder. "She has hair, Einstein."

Elias, whose eyebrows look extra huge on his hairless forehead, claps his hands to his buzz cut. "Why do you have hair?"

"Oh my God . . ." I cover my mouth to hide a very unsympathetic laugh. Elias, Neeraj, and Lee stand together with matching fresh buzz cuts, punching and bickering with each other. "Did y'all . . . coordinate this?" The giggles burst past my attempt to hide them. "That is— Thank you. Y'all are the sweetest. Not the brightest, but the sweetest."

"I don't get it," Elias says. "How did you get your hair to look normal?"

"I cut like eight inches. It's not exactly normal." I flap my tiny ponytail to prove my point.

Elias shrugs. "Looks the same to me. Man, whose half-baked idea was this? Don't answer that," he warns Neeraj. "Now who wants breakfast tacos? I brought them to comfort Yasmín, but I think we deserve them more."

So morning sectionals was a (very nice) trap all along.

Milo, Caleb, and Jonathan all arrive later with

apologies or excuses about their lack of haircuts, ranging from "My mom would've killed me" to Jonathan's "I figured it was safest to ignore Elias." But Milo has a bunch of YouTube links about how to style bobs and pixie cuts ("I didn't know how short we were talking. Honestly this is a cute look."), and Caleb brought Shipley's kolaches to go with the tacos.

"Y'all . . ." My mouth is full of potato-and-egg taco, and my eyes are full of tears I'm desperately trying to keep from spilling over. Why am I an emotional wreck lately? "This was so nice. I can't believe you did this."

At first I think nobody's listening, but then Lee bumps my elbow. "What are sections for?" he asks with a smile while everyone else fights over the last ham-and-cheese kolache.

The food is long gone by the time Bloom shows up, late with Starbucks. The bell's about to ring, so Neeraj and Jonathan and Lee have already left for homeroom, and Caleb and Milo are lingering in the doorway before they have to split in different directions.

"You missed the party," I tell him.

"Yeah." He shrugs. "Good thing it wasn't a *real* sectionals or I'd be a bad co–section leader. You didn't answer my texts."

I didn't? Crap. "Sorry, I'm really bad at texting. I hate it. Phone calls are so much better."

Bloom looks legitimately shocked, possibly the most emotion I've ever seen on his face. "Oookay, boomer. Sounds fake, but I guess I'll keep that in mind."

"What was so important that you missed my buzz-cut party?"

"Honestly? Sleep." He shrugs. "I did get you this, though." He passes me the Starbucks cup. "Didn't know what you like, but it has lots of sugar."

"Aw, you do care."

"Debatable," he deadpans. "Anyway, see you." He turns to leave the band hall.

"Bloom?"

He stops. "Mhmm?"

"Nice haircut." It's not a buzz, but his curls have distinctly less volume, and his ears are actually visible now. I see the tips of them turn pink.

"I was overdue for one."

"Sure you were."

I practically skip to pre-calc, sipping my Starbucks and swinging my short ponytail as I go.

AS THE DAY GOES ON, THE REFLECTIONS ACCOUNT SHIFTS from posting about me to posting about the low brass buzz cuts, then to comments about the first game, and finally back to random "I can't, I have rehearsal" memes. I guess the bright side of the internet is its short attention span.

And outside of band, my haircut is just a haircut, which my classmates either compliment or ignore.

My weekend of moping and drowning my sorrows in textbooks pays off when I ace my pre-calc pop "exploration" (it's a quiz grade, just call it a quiz!) and earn bonus points for outlining the WHAP chapter.

I *knew* it would be okay, but it's still a little surprising how okay it is. Maybe September is going to be my month? Or maybe I just jinxed myself yet again.

I make it through lunchtime sectionals without having to see any flutes, but when sixth period rolls around, I'm stuck staring at the back of Sofia's and Yuki's heads with their matching green streaks, Han's green tips, and Katrina's Billie Eilish–style green roots. Even though half the section didn't participate, something about the matching badges of flute honor pisses me off, and the Dragon honks and growls and splutters to match my rage. Bloom shoots me a look when I stick a wrong note loudly in a rest measure, but I can't make myself focus any better.

Everything is fine. Why am I still so angry?

It's easier on the field, when we're more isolated and I can focus on staying in step with Lee. I'm not surprised when rehearsal ends and the flutes pack up and leave one by one without ever saying a word to me. Other than Laylah, who already checked on me at Sunday school, I don't expect anything else. What would they say? Their actions at the sleepover (and then, undoubtedly, online) already said everything.

Sofia didn't try to call or text all weekend, so why would she care now? Maybe she's mad about my shock at the Andy sex reveal, and maybe she has a right to be, but I'm so tired of trying to apologize to her and only getting further from her good graces.

The bitterness burns a pit in my stomach. It's uncomfortable and unpleasant, and I want to get rid of it. I stare into the abyss of my giant cubby, breathing slowly until the urge to cry disappears.

This is all okay.

Maybe this was the penance I needed to finally get public opinion back on my side. Maybe when I don't run crying to Ms. Schumacher this time, people will start to realize that I've learned from my mistake.

Maybe even Sofia will realize that I've suffered enough.

No, that's too much to hope for. Sofia isn't just mad about what happened during band camp. I don't know if I can fix what's wrong between me and Sofia. I don't know if I even understand it.

Gilberto sits by the whiteboard scribbling in a composition notebook when I drag the Dragon toward the practice rooms. "Hey," he says. "Good work today."

I wonder if he means it in general or if he actually thinks I did well.

"And section leader too," he continues with a smile. "Bloom told Ms. Schumacher about that, so we'll make an official announcement tomorrow."

"Oh, you don't have to . . ."

"Sure we do," he says. "It's a cool thing. Y'all have done really well with the situation. It's impressive."

The smiling, the compliments, the way Gilberto Reyes not only knows who I am but also wants to celebrate me—it's all a little much for my poor emotions. I can't enjoy his smile when Sofia's blank stare is haunting me. So much of the fun of even having a crush was dissecting the impossibility of the crush with her. Whispering about boys was a favorite pastime all through middle school, tucked up in Sofia's bed with Felpudo pinning down the covers between us. We told each other every minute detail of what our crushes said and did . . . pretty much all the way up until Andy.

My fists clench thinking about Andy, but it's more than anger at him. I'm mad at my reaction. I'm mad that I'm so mad. Sofia thought I was mad at her about Andy when really I'm mad at her for so many other reasons.

Gilberto is still standing there, being nice and friendly, and instead of saying thank you, I spit out a desperate non sequitur.

"So you're Catholic, right?"

Gilberto laughs. "Uh, yep. Which part of the Sunday school speech tipped you off?"

I probably flush. The weird question that's been weighing on me since the sleepover takes advantage of my awkwardness to sneak out of my mouth. "What do you do about the whole . . . 'don't have sex until we say you can and only the way we say you can' thing?" I definitely flush. What exactly possessed me to say the word "sex" to my unattainable but also surprisingly approachable crush? "I'm not . . . I just . . . I don't want to be judgmental." I didn't think I was judgmental! But everything that happened at the sleepover still feels confusing and raw. Everyone thought I was—*Sofia* thought I was on some high horse of piety, like I buy into Mom's hype about being "a good girl." She thought I was judging everyone— judging *her*.

Gilberto's eyebrows jump, and for a second I panic that *he's* judgmental and that he now thinks I'm some kind of sex fiend. My stomach shrivels in discomfort, in shame. I'm normally on the other side of this kind of thing, like when the boys were sexualizing celebrities and Bloom and I weren't. Did they think I was judgmental then? Bloom did a good job of explaining his feelings without judgment. I wonder what he would say about this.

But then Gilberto heaves a huge sigh and says, "Yeah, that's the question, isn't it?" and the relief I feel is probably a gift of the Holy Spirit. "I just work on, you know, prioritizing my ideologies. Love everyone first, and then follow the rules second, or not at all. It's annoying that the rules can't be more . . . but oh well." I nod, probably way too hard, and Gilberto smiles. "Also one of my friends—well, an internet friend—teaches sex ed at a hippie school, so I'm not solely bombarded with the church's and Texas's messaging, which probably helps."

I laugh. I almost wish it were simpler, that the church's messaging was perfect and complete all the time for everything, but I'm glad that I'm not the only one trying to piece myself together from fragmented beliefs. I'm glad Gilberto didn't say it was simple when I know it's not.

I hate that I was so afraid he wouldn't answer that way. I also hate realizing that I probably made Sofia feel small and ashamed when I reacted to her confession. I wasn't mad at her! I was mad at Andy . . . but maybe she didn't hear it that way.

Gilberto clears his throat. "I won't lie and say this is what I thought student leadership would be about, but, uh, I can link you to some of my friend's resources if you need . . . ?"

I yelp and shake my head violently. Gilberto shrugs, and I give some kind of laugh-thanks-apology and then disengage and make a break for the practice room.

"Hey, one more thing." Gilberto pops to his feet and follows me so that we're walking into the back hallway together. "Unrelated, I promise."

"Yeah?" I ask. I feel sweaty about this whole conversation. Gilberto is kind and thoughtful, and I would like a break from him now, please.

"Obviously I don't officially know anything about any unauthorized gossip 'grams . . ." Gilberto says. "But . . ."

He leans forward, reaches his hand toward my face . . .

And almost gives me a heart attack until he catches the end of my ponytail and tweaks it.

"I think this is very You, and you're clearly leaving the haters behind in the dust. Keep it up."

He goes back to the band hall, and I proceed to hyperventilate in the practice room because OF COURSE Gilberto Reyes wasn't trying to KISS me and also THANK GOODNESS, because that would have been extremely weird, and does that mean I don't have a crush on him anymore?

It takes a long time to regain my practice-room calm, and honestly, I'm not sure the Dragon ever fully recovers.

INSTEAD OF ELLEN, MOM SHOWS UP TO DRIVE ME HOME.

Which isn't necessarily unusual, except then I get into the car and immediately know that Mom's here because she's mad. I can't not notice the tightness of her lips pressed together and her fingers gripping the steering wheel, or the way she greets me without meeting my eyes and zooms a little too fast out of the parking lot.

Every other part of my day—Gilberto, Sofia, the Spanish essay I need to revise—becomes background noise, pushed away to focus on this new crisis. Why is Mom mad? How can I fix it?

I'm flipping through my mental index of things I could be in trouble for. My grades are improving, but my Spanish essays aren't, and I feel like Sra. Mendez is losing patience with me. I left my room kind of a mess this morning. I stay too late in the practice rooms. My heart jumps. Did Mom somehow find out that I've been staying late alone with Gilberto Reyes? And talking about sex?

"Thanks for picking me up," I say, trying to sound polite without coming across as brown-nosing. "Did Ellen work late?"

"No. She's at home," Mom says, and my amorphous anxiety settles into concrete dread. She's been fighting with Ellen again.

I wait for her to launch into a list of complaints so I can assess the damage. They've been getting along so well, relatively, especially now that Mom's been in a better mood with a client to focus on. What changed?

But Mom doesn't say anything, and the longer we drive in silence, the more uneasy I feel. When we pull into the driveway, Mom idles the car without unbuckling her seat belt.

"I guess you don't need me to ask if you have home-work to finish?"

I inspect that minefield of a question for clues, coming up mostly empty-handed. "I finished almost everything, but . . . thanks for asking."

"I know you're getting older," Mom says. "I know you want to control your own life. But I still have things to teach you."

"I know! I know, Mom."

Mom inhales slowly, then finally turns off the car. Her hair has been straightened *and* curled, her blouse is crisp and jewel-toned, all of which probably means she saw clients today. Before the interior lights shut off, she reaches to smooth the top of my hair and brush my short pony-tail. "I think this looks good," she says.

"Thanks."

"But you won't go too much shorter, will you? You need to be able to pull it back so it doesn't get wild."

"Okay, Mom." I check the rearview mirror for out-of-control frizz. "I won't cut it shorter."

Mom seems satisfied with that, finally heading inside. I eat my leftover dinner while she shuts off all the lights in the house and retreats to her upstairs workroom. I wait until she's gone before turning the kitchen light back on (I'm still here) and putting water in the electric kettle Ellen brought home from college.

Ellen peeks her head through the back door just in time to accept her cup of Sleepytime.

"Thanks." She hangs her head into the steam. "Did I get you yelled at?"

"No, I just wanted to see if you were okay." And I want to know what the fight was about. It's rare for Mom not to lay out the whole drama for me. It makes me nervous not to know how to track the undercurrent of anger in the house. It makes me feel like the wave is behind me, ready to crash.

Ellen tilts her head at me. "I'm fine, kiddo. I'm just worried about you."

Me? Again? Was this fight about me? My heart rate spikes. "Don't worry," I say quickly. "I'm great."

"Oh yeah?" Ellen *hmms*. "How is Sunday school going? A very invested birdie told me that you haven't picked your confirmation sponsor yet."

Ah, shit. "Crap. Uh, I guess I'm still thinking about it."

"Sofia said no?"

"Yeah, uh, she and I have been a little . . . off." It's hard to admit even that understatement, but I don't think I can really avoid it. It's been going on for a long time now, and it isn't getting better.

Ellen nods. "I picked up on that," she says. "When I picked you up. From her sleepover. In the middle of the night. Do you want to talk about it?"

Wait a second, how did she curve this so that we're analyzing *my* problems? Sneaky older-sibling powers!

"No, it's . . . it's okay. I don't think it's a huge deal or anything."

Ellen sips her tea with both eyebrows arched.

"What?"

"Okay, so maybe I was slow to put it all together, but as your mom made clear during our discussion today, you're not exactly the type to just randomly decide to fuck with your hair. Uh, mess with."

I suddenly get very interested in my mug. So they were fighting about me. And Ellen figured out . . . whatever she thinks she figured out. That Sofia was involved in my hair. But it isn't a big deal like Ellen's trying to make it. I'm fine. I've been working hard to be fine.

Ellen waits quietly, which I do not like at all.

"On Friday you said friendships could survive a lot," I remind her. I want that to be true. I want to believe that even if it takes longer, even if it gets messier, eventually Sofia will figure out that I'm not her enemy.

"And today I'm saying that you don't have to coddle bullies. Or make tea for people who get in silly fights that make you uncomfortable. Or put everyone's feelings above your own."

Whatever. Ellen thinks that three months working at a crisis line makes her an expert in self-care and boundaries, but she doesn't actually know what she's talking about. "Sunday school taught me that we're supposed to forgive. Seventy times seven times."

Ellen snorts. "I know I'm a Bad Catholic or whatever, but when I hear that Jesus said that, I just want to start tallying so I can see exactly when people run out of chances."

I roll my eyes. "That's the opposite of the point. It's supposedly like, back then that was so high that it was basically like saying infinity."

Ellen tilts her head at me again. "Come on, you expect me to believe he could walk on water but he couldn't count to four hundred ninety?"

"Not the point!" I giggle. I forget what the point is, exactly. Something about not wanting to give up on Sofia, even if it feels like she gave up on me.

We sit in silence for another couple of minutes before I decide to stop beating around the bush. "Did you and Mom get in a fight about my hair?"

Ellen sighs and looks at the ceiling. "I would say that we had a lively discussion about body autonomy and how teenagers need to be supported in, not discouraged from, taking control of their lives, including their physical appearance."

Ugh. Ellen thinks she knows everything about everything.

But I am feeling a little better somehow.

"You're a good listener," I say.

Ellen's eyebrows rise dramatically. "I've been called a lot of things, but that's a new one," she jokes. "Uh, but thanks. I think waiting tables is helping me improve, actually. And the volunteer stuff also—I've been talking people at the house through some of the immigration stuff and connecting them with lawyers. It's a lot of . . . customer service, really. I'm getting better, in English *or* Spanish. Now if only I could turn any of these new skills into an actual job . . ."

"Hey, soft skills are very valuable," I say confidently, because I researched the qualities of a good leader when Bloom made me co–section leader. "Good that you're developing yours."

Ellen laughs. "About time. But I'll never catch up to you; you're a natural at all this."

My smile falters a little. I want to be a natural leader, a people person, someone who always knows how to smooth things over. I thought I was. But . . . "I'm not good enough," I grumble.

"Hey," Ellen says sharply. "Forget that. Nobody has hired you for your soft skills yet, which means it's all just free emotional labor, and you don't have to do it. Okay? It is literally not your job. I mean it."

Ellen thinks she knows everything, but I'm not feeling that annoyed about it. Just because she goes overboard appreciating her own wisdom doesn't mean I can't occasionally appreciate her wisdom too.

For example, she made a good point earlier; I should be taking more control of my life.

"Do you want to be my confirmation sponsor?"

Mom won't approve, but I can make her see the benefits. Maybe I can spin it as a way to get Ellen to come to mass more.

"Oh." Ellen swirls her tea for a second. "Uh, thanks. But . . . nah. You don't want a Bad Catholic sponsor."

"You're not bad! You volunteer at an immigrant shelter!"

"That's just social justice stuff."

"Liberation theology!" I half shout. "It's an important form of Catholicism! It got Oscar Romero sainthood!"

"I feel like the assassination got him sainthood," Ellen points out. She drains the rest of her tea. "Thanks for asking. I guess if you really can't find anyone, I could do it. But . . . to be totally honest, I'm not sure how I feel about the church these days, and it seems like you could find someone better."

Great. So now I have two "emergency-only" sponsors and no one actually wanting to do it. I know it's not like I'm inviting people to a Schlitterbahn trip, but is it really so awful to consider talking about God for a couple of hours with me?

I get another flashback to the awful game of Never Have I Ever. Does Ellen think I'm judgmental too? Is that why no one wants to be my confirmation sponsor?

"I think you're a great Catholic," I tell Ellen, just in case she doesn't know. "I want to be more like you."

Ellen's eyes widen in alarm. "Oh God, don't say *that*. Maybe just focus on being yourself. Seems easier."

I TRY TO TAKE ELLEN'S ADVICE THROUGH THE NEXT WEEK. I focus on scheduling sectionals, making Bloom run music tests (and then making Neeraj show up for his), and generally getting us ready for our second football game. Ms. Schumacher chooses the flutes as section of the week, citing their spirit, and I refuse to let it faze me. I create a formula for Spanish literary analysis essays that seems to reduce my number of required revisions, and I get rides with Mom instead of Sofia, even if it means extra lectures about my breakfast choices and my PSAT prep. I keep practicing in the afternoons, and Gilberto keeps being normal and not kissing me (which is perfect).

The third Saturday of September is the PSAT weekend workshop. I'm used to showing up to school at odd hours, but it's weird to file into the cafeteria instead of the band hall. I see a lot of familiar faces as I scope out the tables: acquaintances from class, a group from my middle school that improbably stayed friends in high school, a clump of slouching percussionists that I'm almost brave enough to go say hi to—until I'm distracted by a wildly waving hand at the back corner table. What is Elias doing here? I immediately head toward him, but he keeps waving until practically the moment I sit down across from him and Jonathan, who's also here, looking preppy as usual but acting a lot more subdued than Elias, and nursing a ceramic coffee thermos.

"Yay, we have a whole low brass contingent!" Elias says after I sit down.

"Yeah, uh, I guess so." I try to think of a polite way to ask what they're doing here. Freshmen don't have to worry about the PSAT, do they? I look around again, but it's hard to tell how many of the unfamiliar faces are actually freshmen versus sophomores I haven't met. "What brings y'all here?"

"Same as you, probably," Jonathan says. "Trying to elbow my way to the top of the class so I can get into an Ivy League college so my helicopter parents don't think I wasted my potential."

I laugh. I'm not exactly Ivy League or bust, but I get the sentiment. "They're starting you early, aren't they?"

Jonathan rolls his eyes. This is the first time I've ever seen him express anything resembling rebellion. "You know the 'on time is late' band mentality? My parents apply that to every academic and extracurricular milestone as well. If I'm not practicing the PSAT this year, how will I be able to ace it next year? And if I don't do that, how will I ace the SAT the first time I take it? And if I don't do that, how will I be a competitive Early Decision candidate? It's the same way I have to be three years ahead in my math courses and already working on my Eagle Scout service project."

I nod, but I also cringe. Mom puts pressure on me, but she generally wants me to hit all the expected academic markers, not leap out in front of them while juggling burning bowling pins. I guess I'm lucky in that, and lucky that last year we didn't have as much of a chance to fully get into college-prep mode.

"See, this is the stuff I never know about." Elias shifts his body on the tiny cafeteria stool like he's looking for the quickest and most unique way to fall off. "My parents didn't get their degrees in this backward country, so we're missing all the secret info. I'm just trying to get into *a* college. I had no idea that the school had classes to learn how to take these backward tests. They should really advertise it better." He finally swings his legs out under the table and rests his feet on the seat next to me. "But then Jonathan told me about it because he has that secret info."

I raise my eyebrows and nod at Jonathan. Tipping off your classmates to your study plans doesn't exactly scream "elbow my way to the top of the class." Besides, I would've thought, the way these two are always at each other's throats, that he wouldn't want to spend an extra Saturday with Elias.

Jonathan sits up a little straighter as Mr. Dansey comes by with an attendance checklist and a stack of practice packets. "Just make sure you pay attention," Jonathan says to Elias once the AP moves on. "We can't be rivals if you're not on my level."

Elias socks Jonathan's shoulder, somehow upsetting his own balance and crashing his feet back to the floor. "Wait a second, our rivalry is supposed to be musical only!" he says. "Is this why you started studying for geography? Ha, I didn't know we were rivaling, and I still beat you at that map quiz."

They start bickering in earnest, which makes me laugh but also squeezes something sour out of the aching part of my chest. I can't remember the last time I actually enjoyed the "playful" rivalry I thought I had with Sofia. And when she had the chance to compete with me on a level field, she chose to get rid of me instead.

One of the PE coaches/history teachers gets up at the front of the cafeteria and starts a PowerPoint of overly basic info ("What is the PSAT?") and eventually sets us to work on our packets. Elias and Jonathan spend the whole time happily boasting and trash-talking, and it reminds me just enough of how Sofia and I used to be. How we aren't anymore.

When did we go from being rivals to being enemies?

I THINK ABOUT CALLING SOFIA ALL AFTERNOON, MORE than I think about my Personal Order of Difficulty on the PSAT reading passages. But I don't call. I don't know what I want to say yet.

Laylah misses Sunday school. Mr. Frederick asks me where she is and acts surprised when I say I don't know, so I end up texting her just because I'm embarrassed that we're not as close as our teacher thought we were, which is a weird reason to start texting someone, but oh well.

Oh yeah, Mia's parents invited me to Black Baptist church this week, she texts. The Holy Spirit is having a great time here and so am I. 😊🕊

I tell her to have a good time and then stress about whether I should say something else, but Laylah asks me about the pre-calc test, and we end up replying back and forth (thanks to me paying close attention to my phone). By the time she says she'd better go, I'm comfortable enough to say, It was cool talking outside of CCE. We should do it more.

I know, Laylah texts back almost immediately. Like, how have we never texted?

I'm bad at texting! I type back. It's consistent. I'm the worst.

Ha, no worries, Laylah says. I'm not great at it either. And I guess we were always—well, I was always kind of preoccupied with Mia.

She types and deletes for a while, and I take a guess at what she's debating saying. Yeah, and I was always busy with Sofia. I send the text and then wonder if it's a weird thing to say? It's true. Is that weird?

Be friends with me now, Laylah says, and I wish I could hear her tone of voice because there are a lot of ways to interpret that, but I'm pretty sure she means the one where I stop being friends with Sofia. Except I am even more preoccupied with Mia these days, and it is a (very excellent) problem. Why does being happy leave so little time for, like, responsibilities and homework and everything else?

I send back several laugh-sob emojis. I wouldn't know.

WE PUT IN SO MUCH WORK THE WEEK BEFORE OUR SEC-ond football game. Which is great, but the problem with absolutely drilling music is that we all start getting cocky about our playing. And the problem with playing a sousaphone confidently on a football field is that it's loud. Which becomes a really big problem when you play in the middle of a rest at a dramatic standstill moment of the second movement, which is what happens during the second football game.

"This fucking instrument," Milo stress-whispers

through clenched teeth as we march off the field. "All I want is to keep a low profile—why did they give me a foghorn to broadcast my mistakes?"

"Shh." I gesture at him to relax, then shift over so I'm close behind a couple of trumpets. "God, I'm sure Instagram is going to blow up over Hurricane Yasmín smashing through the park and play," I groan loudly. I hear at least one trumpet snicker and catch a nearby color guard twirler whisper to a pit percussionist. I shift back to Milo. "That should do it."

Milo cocks his head at me. "Do section leaders have to be martyrs, or do you just like getting roasted?"

"Neither, I just owed you one from band camp." Milo continues to frown, like maybe he doesn't remember our crash or Andy's jackassery. "It's not a big deal," I say. "It's a drop in the bucket of internet hate." Milo's frown deepens. He looks almost sad, almost worried, and I don't like that at all, so I quickly change the subject. "Besides, Ms. Schumacher is going to make the whole section do pushups either way."

Milo groans. "This fucking instrument."

I *almost* make it through the whole weekend without checking how bad the posts are.

BLOOM TEXTS SUNDAY MORNING, AND THEN SUNDAY afternoon he texts to ask why I haven't answered, and then Sunday evening he sends me a series of question marks.

I'm sorry, I type one-handed under the dinner table so Mom doesn't get annoyed. Family stuff. It's more excuse than truth, but in my defense, it sounds a lot better than "I couldn't read your texts because I hate them."

Oh, well, except that apparently, I sent "Family stiff," which sounds vaguely sinister. But within seconds Bloom's replied: I need help with Neeraj.

?

I text that to mean "be more specific, please," not "why?"—Neeraj makes himself one enormous problem in a section full of what should be bigger problems. Just this week he scored almost the lowest on his music quiz AND was twenty minutes late to sectionals.

He refuses to step up. He acts like it's a big joke every time I try to talk to him. And you said as section leaders we shouldn't let that slide . . .

It's true, I did say that. But that was before I realized how much work it takes leading a section: all the staff emails and extra meetings and keeping everyone updated on scheduling and music and uniform plans each week.

Yeah, I send. Not sure what to do either. Maybe some touch love?

. . . ?

TOUGH** TOUGH LOVE!

😂 😂 **but still question mark**

??

sigh I meant, can you elaborate on what you mean by "tough love"?

Okay, seriously, who texts the word "elaborate"?
Like bros and personal trainers, I type. Or like boot camp.
Yelling at someone to make them do something harder.

. . . does that work?

Like Sofia used to tell Han she was worse than 2nd graders
playing recorders.

I have totally forgotten to keep my phone hidden, so
Mom clears her throat and I unbury my face from the
screen and take a couple of enthusiastic bites of the keto
mac and cheese. When Dad gets Mom excitedly talking about the lighting options for her new client, I read
Bloom's latest text.

So I should tell him that, like, the shofar at Rosh Hashanah
last week had a fuller tone than he does?

Maybe? Maybe pick something he'll get.

Oh right, so more like telling him that even Yasmín has a better tone than he does.

Ha ha, very funny. I send a cute smile emoji to prove that I'm only taking the compliment out of that tease. Then I add, But yes, that might work. I put my phone in my lap while Mom asks about school. Then I return to it, semi-rethinking my advice. You have to check your delivery, thouhg. Thin line. I finish my "mac and cheese." Also make it sound natural.

So do you always strategically plan your seemingly natural motivational insults?

I can picture Bloom's face, half teasing smile and half sincere curiosity. I decide to give him a true answer.

I always plan everything I say. Don't you?

Uh, that would be a good idea, but . . . Bloom keeps typing after that message, so I wait to see what's next. Wait is *that* why you take so long to type??

I snort into my glass of water. Don't be mean! I'm doing my best, I hate typing!

"Yasmín," Mom says with a slight warning in her voice.

"Sorry." I clean the last of the arugula off my plate

and bring it to the sink. Before I can sit back down, my phone rings. "Oh, I have to get this; it's band stuff."

Mom and Dad look at me with neutral raised eyebrows. I can tell they want to ask details, so I make a beeline for my room and shut the door behind me.

"Hello."

"Hey," Bloom says. "So this is really how you prefer to . . . ?"

"Yes, a thousand percent." I know it's weird, because Sofia tells me all the time how weird it is. She's the only one I call, though, so it's probably fair that she makes fun of me.

Bloom makes a noncommittal grunt, probably accompanied by a shrug.

I feel a little selfish, making him speak out loud when he clearly hates it. "I mean, we can stick to texting if you really want."

"No, it's cool." I wait for him to say something else, something about how weird it is, but he doesn't. "So when should I talk to Neeraj?"

"Oh, I was trying to say that, like, maybe trying to confront him privately is part of the problem. Neeraj doesn't take personal stuff seriously, but he cares about looking cool. So calling him out publicly might be the right call. Using the *gentle* tough love technique consistently in practice and sectionals might motivate him to work harder to avoid the gentle embarrassment. But if you still want to do a serious talk, we can. You don't have to do it alone. We're co–section leaders, remember?"

There's a long pause.

"I can see why you prefer the phone."

MOM CORNERS ME AT THE END OF THE WEEK TO ASK about my sudden increase in phone calls. I have to explain that it's just band stuff, that I'm a section leader now and I have more responsibilities. Mom says that my responsibilities are making me laugh a lot, so I quickly change the subject to her paint samples.

Bloom does make me laugh. He's taken to calling just to practice his tough love insults, which are usually bad, but they seem to be having an effect. After a week, Neeraj has started playing his horn even when we're marching. It might also have something to do with me casually mentioning that Sofia hates people who don't take their parts seriously, or it might all be attributable to Bloom telling Neeraj he's going to start calling him Sleepy every time he lags behind the arc when marching.

Tough love works surprisingly well on Milo too. His playing is still weak, but Bloom and I put a little pressure on everyone, and suddenly I see Milo staying late in the practice rooms with me several times a week. Or maybe he just does it because Caleb stays too and gives Milo a ride home. But they haven't said anything about whether they're an official thing or not.

I float the idea of asking them about it, but Bloom vetoes that as outside the duties of a section leader, because he is a killjoy.

He can't stop me from chatting with my section mates, though. Especially when Caleb and Milo, who have sat on either side of me in concert arcs since our very first sectionals, start to pull their chairs next to each other instead.

"I think I'm a natural matchmaker," I take the opportunity to joke over one lunch when a bunch of the boys are retaking a geography quiz and Milo and I are left more or less alone with sleeping Neeraj. "Last year I sat between Laylah and Mia, and we all know how that turned out."

Milo sticks his tongue out over a very pink face. "Maybe you just have an abnormally high tolerance for third-wheeling, did you ever think of it that way? Also, I don't know what you're talking about."

Instead of quipping back, I consider his suggestion seriously. I really don't mind being a third wheel—didn't with Laylah and Mia, don't with Milo and Caleb. "Is it abnormal to love love?"

Milo grimaces. "Gross and yes. The usual response to couples or flirting is annoyance? I have to pretend to be happy for people while secretly burning with envy?"

I shrug, not sure if I'm weird or Milo is. It's fun and cute when people start dating, and, like, isn't that what we all love about romance stories? Getting to see people find a nice match and be happy? I don't get where jealousy comes in.

"Hey, you're supposed to agree with me so I don't feel like a petty person." Milo bites his nail and laughs.

If this were the beginning of the year, I wouldn't hesitate to agree with whatever Milo wanted, just to make him more likely to befriend me. But I'm actually curious, and I think we're already friends enough that Milo will answer honestly. I think he trusts me, and I trust him not to make fun when I ask, "So, like . . . when you see Mia and Laylah making out . . . are you thinking . . . that you want to be doing that?"

Milo mirrors my cautious face back at me. ". . . Yes? Are you . . . not?"

Not really, no. I mean, I would like to have a *person* the way I would like to have, you know, a car and a closet full of fluffy ballgowns and quality eye shadow palettes, and sometimes I watch cute rom-coms and do some light yearning. But . . . "I don't know. This stuff is all so weird." Milo still looks uncomfortable, so I quickly add, "And subjective. You're a very valid person who is only occasionally petty in a lovable way." Milo smiles and nods the affirmation back at me, and it's nice to know my trust wasn't misplaced. I was half expecting him to laugh at me. Sofia would have. "And I will love your love if and when it comes to fruition."

"Gross." Milo tries to cover his smile with his Capri Sun but utterly fails. "Can we go back to silence? The silence was nice."

So of course that's the moment that the geography quiz group comes loudly into the hallway, yelling and screaming and generally sending our lunchtime into the increasingly familiar chaos.

OUR THIRD FOOTBALL GAME (ALSO OUR FIRST HOME game) goes well. The bleachers are crowded and our uniforms are boiling, but the thrill of flying through every movement as seamlessly as we do at our very best rehearsals can't be dampened. The upperclassmen snark that we should've been performing at this level since game one, and to that I respectfully think (but don't say out loud): shut the hell up. The low brass crew spends our third-quarter break sweating in our bibs and chomping on the slightly burnt oatmeal cookies Bloom brought. The trombones get together and play "Prince Ali," the song they arranged as their own personal stand tune.

"We should play something like that," I say, reaching for another cookie.

Elias flails so hard into my elbow that he sends my

newly selected cookie flying down toward an unsuspecting saxophone player. "Aaaaah, can we please? Can I have a solo?"

"We could play the Avengers theme," Neeraj suggests.

"Meh. Make it 'The Imperial March' and I'm listening," Jonathan says.

"We're obviously playing 'Despacito,'" Elias scoffs.

"There are some really cool low brass ensemble songs on YouTube." Lee shrugs. "We could see what already works."

I choose a new cookie and chew it slowly. I didn't expect such an enthusiastic response. "Are y'all actually ready to learn a whole new thing?"

There's a general chorus of yes-shaped sentiments. Bloom shrugs at me. I shrug back.

"If y'all can pick a song—ONE song—I can take a stab at arranging it," he says. "Or, I guess, easier to ask Ms. Schumacher for old arrangements and pick one. I've never arranged anything ever, so that's probably . . ."

"We'll look into it," I suggest over Elias's loud, lonely chant of "'Despacito'!" "Either picking something that exists or trying to make something new. I don't know how to arrange either, but I'm sure it can be done."

Bloom laughs. "This is what I get for teaming up with a go-getter, huh?"

We plan to stick around after the game to ask Ms.

Schumacher about old arrangements, but she beats us to it by inviting us to her office, which only makes me a little nervous.

"You've been doing great with your section," she tells us, making me do a tiny happy dance in my seat. "And the show looks solid, but not spectacular. I was wondering how you would all feel about adding back some of the more complicated marching we cut out, giving you guys a little more to do."

The way she says it kills my happy dance, reminding me how easy our part of the show is and how often the band moves around us while we stand in place or make relatively tiny adjustments. I feel silly for being so proud of our unspectacular achievement. But I look at Bloom. This is going to require a lot more tough love, probably. I'm a go-getter, but this isn't something I can go get on my own.

He shrugs. I raise my eyebrows. He rolls his eyes and slumps a little lower in his chair. "Yeah, I guess we can . . ."

"We'd be happy to!" I finish for him. "I'll text the Low Brassho—the section group chat to warn them right now!"

"Great!" Ms. Schumacher beams. "We can feel it out together and see how complicated we want to make it, but I think this will really elevate the show in a way that the UIL judges will respond to. Thank you both."

She nods a dismissal, and I pop to my feet. Bloom doesn't.

"Uh, also . . ."

Huh?

"We wanted to work on an ensemble piece for the stands . . ." Bloom starts to explain his request for Ms. Schumacher while I gape at him. We just got a huge amount of work added to our plate. Does he really want to take this on too?

"Now who's the go-getter?" I ask when we leave the office.

Bloom shrugs up to his ears, teeth bared and eyes wide like the "eek" emoji. "I learn from the best."

CHAPTER 14

October's first week hits me hard with allergies, a ran-dom cold snap (below fifty degrees! Why would it do that?), and a slew of major tests and projects just in case I wasn't busy enough with band season. Laylah and I start a running text thread where we mostly just yell at each other to spend more time studying and then share baby animal GIFs when we actually study. There is no before school, or lunch hour, or after school, or weekend anymore. There is only rehearsal, and the time between rehearsal when I frantically try to stay afloat.

I'm treading water and eating jicama slices in the back hallway, laughing at Laylah's utter lack of venom as she texts me super-nice encouraging statements to keep going, with "OR ELSE" tacked on like an afterthought, when Elias spills Capri Sun all over my latest draft of another Spanish essay.

"Leave it," I groan as he tries to sop up the mess with a tiny Lunchables napkin. "It was bad anyway." I drop my head against the wall behind me with a clunk. I thought I was improving my essay skills, but we switched from opinion papers to this different one, and now I'm back to square one.

"Ay, pobrecita." Elias pats me on the shoulder. "Do you need tutoring? I thought you said you speak Spanish."

I groan again, not even proud enough to defend my bilingualism.

"Here, dámelo." Caleb reaches over Bloom and grabs my shitty, sopping draft. "What's it about?"

"Like, telling a meaningful experience through place; I don't know."

"Okay, okay, a descriptive essay." Elias nods sagely. "You gotta use your five senses and shit. That's cool."

"Descripción," Neeraj adds unhelpfully. Bloom whacks his ear with his weird (and apparently hefty) robot pen.

"Yeah, but I can't." I point to my (pointless) paper and read a particularly drab sensory sentence: "La carretera es gris."

"Wow, I could have written that," Neeraj says. "And I haven't been in a language class since elementary school."

"It does sound a little Spanish 1." Caleb shrugs sympathetically.

"Well, what am I supposed to say?" I ask. "Que la carretera fluye como una corriente en el mar de tierra plana?" I gesture dramatically as I say it.

"Wh—yes! Yes, write that!" Elias steals my pen and starts scribbling on the one dry spot left on the paper.

"But nobody talks like that," I grumble.

"Poets talk like that," Caleb says.

"Writers talk like that," Elias agrees. "Do some more like that and you'll be golden. Metaphorically."

I shake my head. They don't get it. I've tried this before, with Mom and Ellen and Sofia. It never works when I try to put pen to paper. I get tangled up in the word I'm writing, and all the words I was thinking of saying disappear, and I end up with "The highway is gray." I'm equally bad in English; I've just been lucky with easy teachers.

"I can't write like that," I tell them. "I can never write what I want to say."

"Fine," Elias says. "Then tell us: ¿Qué quieres decir?"

It's easy when he puts it like that. I've had my topic picked out for weeks, and I've already written the essay once and a half. I tell them about the times Mom and I would make the endless-seeming trips down from Houston to Monterrey. "En las noches, cuando el cielo se unía con los llanos y el tiempo no tenía sentido . . ." I tell them how Mom always drives in silence, too stressed about whatever we're leaving behind or driving toward (like my tía's hospital stay) to talk. "Pero en el coche, no existían los problemas; los escapábamos." I repeat what I already said about the total lack of scenery and then talk about finally stretching my legs under the carport of Abuela's boxy one-story house, "el centro y el corazón de la familia Treviño."

Elias looks at me, down at my half-written paper, up at Caleb. "Why didn't you write any of that?" he demands.

"I thought I did!"

"No way!" He points at my opening line. "This makes it seem so boring! Why didn't you add any of the cool parts?"

"I just can't write," I whine. "Talking is different."

"You should do what you just did, then," Bloom says. "Speak everything out loud. Then you don't even have to think of it as writing."

"But I already forgot what I said." I wish everyone would leave me alone to fail in peace instead of trying to help me with ideas I know don't work.

"Not to be creepy," Bloom says, holding up his rocket ship–looking pen, "but . . . it seemed like you needed help so . . . sorry, but I recorded it. I can text it to you, and that way you can just transcribe it."

I blink. "You can do that?"

"Yeah, it's a recorder pen."

"Dude, do you record everything we say?" Elias asks.

"Obviously not." Bloom hunches his shoulders. "I just record classes while I take notes. And then I recorded this because it . . . Never mind." Bloom ducks his head and shoves his pen into his pocket.

I click my tongue at Elias. "I meant more like *can* I do that? It feels like cheating."

Bloom shrugs. "I was almost failing all my classes in middle school because my brain refuses to process audio that doesn't provide an instant dopamine hit. So I record class lectures, and now I'm not failing. It's not cheating to work with what your brain gives you."

I must look skeptical, because Bloom keeps going. Now that we spend more time talking, I'm more used to the way he either doesn't talk at all or dumps all his ideas at once. "The way I had it explained to me is, like, if you want to keep knocking down walls with your head, you're welcome to, but it's just a big unnecessary headache. The door is right there, and you don't get extra points for style."

Everyone kind of laughs at that, but I just blink. I have basically lived my whole life with the assumption that I do get extra points for trying harder than anyone else. I don't think that's necessarily a bad thing.

But I also didn't think I had a choice.

"I . . . Yeah, I guess so." I shrug. Honestly, if you'd asked me at the beginning of the year, I probably would have said that anyone who didn't beat their head against the wall trying to do everything "normally" was doing it wrong . . . Including Bloom. Which was super unfair of me. "I'd like that recording. I can try it, at least. Thanks."

"Fine, but no more recording without permission, Bezos Junior," Neeraj tells Bloom. "Also, how're you a musician with audio-processing issues?"

Bloom rolls his eyes. "Music is an instant dopamine hit."

I mean, I can agree with that.

I almost ask him why he puts up with my phone calls if his brain hates listening so much, but at the last second I decide it's kind of an awkward question. Plus, what if he agrees with me and then I have to switch back to reading long paragraphs of text?

But I resolve to try to be better about answering his texts. It's the least I can do.

"Check it out," I tell Caleb and Elias when I get to the band hall on Friday. "I got my essay back!" I hold out the paper with the big A– on top. "Spelling and accents are still garbage, but she liked my poetic descriptions!"

"Spelling?" Elias asks. "How can you mess up spelling in Spanish?"

"Nice." Caleb high-fives me. "So what time do we meet tomorrow?"

Our first Saturday-morning game is tomorrow. Because of that and round two of chair tests next week (low brass is doing ours as a group because Ms. Schumacher decided she'd rather test how well we blend together than waste time ranking us, which is a relief), Ms. Schumacher has given us the afternoon off from rehearsal. I try to propose an impromptu sectionals—we really aren't great at blending together—but everyone mutinies.

"I haven't had a Friday off in so long," Neeraj says. "I'm going to watch my embarrassing reality shows live with commercials, and you can't take that from me."

"I'm going to see a movie," Milo says, his face inexplicably red until Caleb elbows him lightly and says, "What a coincidence; I'm also going to see a movie. Maybe I'll run into you there."

"Y'all are using your one day off of band to hook up with people you see every day in band?" Jonathan shakes his head. "You hate to see it. You *expect* to see it, but you hate it." I'm not sure where he gets the superiority complex; other than a few polo-shirted kids from the Young Entrepreneurs Club, I don't know of Jonathan hanging out with many outside-of-band people. None of us do, because the school is big and clique-y and band kids tend to stick together.

"Why aren't we having a party?" Elias mopes. "I want to play *Mario Kart*!"

"Oh, I would actually kill for a round of *Mario Kart*." Lee sighs wistfully.

"Come over, man." Elias brightens up immediately. "We can order pizza. Anyone want in?"

"I feel like my track record with band parties speaks for itself." I sigh. Anyway, Bloom and I already planned to use the time to finally do a deep dive of the archived music closet to see what tuba ensemble pieces we can find. Jonathan groans again about everyone needing to get a life outside of band.

We rush through sixth period, getting increasingly giddy until Ms. Schumacher dismisses us. Almost everyone clears out immediately, excited to leave the band hall while the sun is still out.

Except the flutes don't clear out. They have sectionals, apparently.

"Have they always been this shrill?" I ask Bloom as we retreat into the archives and the flutes warm up. "Surely we weren't this shrill when I was there."

"Dunno how to answer that . . ." Bloom makes a mock scared face.

I'm weirdly mad that Sofia got her section to rehearse today when I couldn't. As if she did it specifically to bug me. We haven't talked in ages, but she's still always hovering in the back of my consciousness, because she's always hovering somewhere near me at rehearsal, at lunch, at mass. Now her voice carries into the room, a reminder that she's working hard while I'm getting caught up in unnecessary section hijinks.

I open one of the file cabinets from 2009. Ancient history in the form of old band music stares up at me. "It's going to be fine tomorrow, right?" I ask. We added a few new sets to our show, nothing completely groundbreaking, but I now have nightmares about accidentally running the old version on instinct.

"It's going to be fine," Bloom echoes back.

"Do you believe that, or did you not process what I said?"

"Hmm?"

I whack his arm, which only earns me an even more confused look because I guess he wasn't faking.

"Sorry," he mutters, "I can't hear."

The way he says it, hunching his shoulders apologetically, reminds me a lot of the way I sometimes say "I can't read" when Sofia gives me her patented look of impatience because I'm failing to interact with text the way she expects. Bloom told us he doesn't do audio processing great. I'm making him feel bad about the way his brain works, and that's shitty and I shouldn't do it. Nobody should do that.

"Sorry," I say, but Bloom has already turned back to his own file cabinet.

"Here," he says. "Take a look through these." He holds up a stack of music books.

The closet is small but packed densely. About one of every four years is missing, thanks to the bottom shelves flooding out last year, but it's still wild how many copies and original music books fit.

The flutes are loud. Closing the door on this tiny space would give me claustrophobia sweats, but I wish I could block their chipper twittering. It makes me think of the disastrous sleepover, which makes me think of Sofia, which makes me think about how weird it is that we're not talking.

Bloom, searching more efficiently than I am, starts a pile of potential music between us.

"Do you think they know we're here?" I ask.

"Mmm." Bloom is engrossed in a file cabinet.

"The flutes. Do you think they know we're here?"

"Not sure."

I'm tired of wondering what Sofia is thinking. She probably isn't thinking about me at all. "Do you have big plans tonight?" I ask Bloom. "Pizza parties? Movie dates? Reality TV marathons?"

Bloom snorts.

"Okay, fine. Video game levels to beat? Magic: The Gathering tournaments?"

"Not this week." Bloom smirks. "Uh, no, we're probably going to do Shabbat dinner with my aunt and uncle. They're a lot more observant than we are, so it's weird but cool."

"Cool." I don't really know what that means. "So are you not observant?"

"Oh, uh, I mean, I go to temple, but it's reform and really, like, liberal and guitar music, so my aunt and uncle wouldn't find the way we do things 'correct.'"

I've heard some of those words? It's weird to realize how much background I'm missing about other people's religions. Like, at some point last week Neeraj mentioned having a family shrine at his house, and I just had no context for that knowledge. I want to ask Bloom for more details, but I'm self-conscious about my ignorance (and privilege, since I don't think people are this lost when I talk about church or Christmas or whatever).

"And obviously I'm not going this week," Bloom adds. "To temple. Because the game."

Oh, wait, Saturday morning is Bloom's church time? "That's not fair. Ms. Schumacher won't let you miss?"

Bloom tilts his head. "Uh, I don't know. I usually just skip whenever there's school stuff."

There's a lot of school stuff on Saturday mornings. Even the PSAT prep classes. That's not fair.

I finally find some tuba arrangements. A lot of them

are out-of-date pop culture that I don't recognize or care about, but I pull out a few that sound cool and add them to the pile.

"Hello?" Gilberto Reyes looks in through the half-open door. "Oh! Hey, Yasmín. Jonathan."

Heh. Jonathan. I forgot that was Bloom's first name too.

"Are y'all planning to be very long?" Gilberto asks. "The flutes are wrapping up at four."

"Uh . . ." Bloom looks at the rows of cabinets we haven't touched yet.

"I sort of wanted to get some practice-room time later?" I say. "But if you need us to clear out . . ." I wonder if Gilberto Reyes has a movie date. I wonder how I feel about *that*.

"Mmm, no, it's . . ." Gilberto taps his chin. "I mean, you're both staff now. Would y'all mind locking up if you're staying? I'll text you the checklist, and you don't need keys. Just don't leave anything you can't live without."

"No, yeah, I mean, sure," Bloom mumbles. I almost forgot how quiet he is sometimes—how quiet he used to be *all* the time. I guess he's not as awkward around the section anymore. I echo his agreement to make sure Gilberto hears it.

"Cool, thanks so much. I'm going to head out, then. But I'll miss my practice-room bud." He winks at me and then swings out the doorway and walks away.

I think my face turns very pink. What was that?

"Uh," Bloom says.

"Nothing!"

He raises his eyebrows high. "I was going to ask how you feel about Selena, but now I think I should ask if you're hiding something . . ."

"I'm not hiding anything! And I love Selena, obviously!" Bloom keeps staring at me. "Really, it's nothing. It's just . . . Gilberto . . . I sort of had a crush on him at the beginning of the year, that's all."

Bloom tilts his head. "But now you don't?"

Excellent question. Bloom waits patiently while I consider. "I don't know, I guess I sort of realized that I, like, liked him like a celebrity." Wow, I sound like I can't string a sentence together. "Like the way that celebrity crushes are, I don't know, harmless?" That sounds weird, but the only other word I can think of is "toothless," and that sounds even weirder. "Because you're never going to meet them anyway?" Bloom stares, probably because I'm not making any sense. "I mean, obviously I've met Gilberto. But . . . Anyway, so now I don't know if it really counts, like, as a crush because . . . because people normally want to *do things* with their crushes, right?"

"Probably asking the wrong person for 'normal.'" Bloom shrugs. I feel like I should either correct him or apologize, but I can't decide which, so I don't say anything.

"But actually," he says, "I think I know what you mean. Or at least it sounds consistent with things I've heard people say before. You can totally have infatuation that, like, wears off as you get to know the person and realize you don't click or whatever. I don't really get that, but . . ." He does the little shrug again, retreating into his shoulders, implying (again) that he's not normal.

"That's not it, though." I'm a tiny bit annoyed both that Bloom is being self-deprecating and that he's gotten my feelings so wrong. "I still like all the things I liked about Gilberto. If anything, we clicked more than I expected! It's just, I want him to like me, but I don't want . . . I wouldn't want him to ask me out, you know?" Now that I've said it, it seems silly and obvious. People want to go out with their crushes. Like Milo and Caleb going to their movie, presumably so that they can sit side by side in the dark and think about kissing each other. People want to kiss their crushes. "That's proof that I don't like him, isn't it?"

Bloom tilts his head, sets the music folder he was holding down on the carpet, and stares into the space in front of him for a long time.

"Uh," I say. "Now I think I should ask if you're hiding something."

Bloom's eyes shift back to me, then down to the floor. "No," he says, "I was just thinking." He picks the folder back up and shoves it into the nearest file. When he glances back at me again, I raise my eyebrows. "I don't know." He sighs. "I don't want to tell you how you're feeling."

"I kind of asked," I point out. "And if you're wrong, I'll just laugh at you and tell you you're wrong."

Bloom snorts. "Okay, well, then it sort of sounds like you're describing interest, just maybe not an . . . allo crush." He looks away from his file cabinet long enough to judge my response. I'm not sure what my response is. "'Allo' is the opposite of 'ace' or 'aro,'" he clarifies. "Like, the typical attraction experience."

"I know!" I say quickly. I do know. I looked it up at one point after Bloom was talking about it. I got some of the basic vocabulary, but I didn't really get much further than that. I think I had a pre-calc quiz to study for, plus everything the website was saying seemed so subjective. What even is "primary sexual attraction"? How would anyone even know if they experience it?

It's my turn to stare at the wall for a minute.

"So yeah," Bloom continues, interrupting my slow realization that maybe I should go check out that website again. "Gilberto is cool and impressive, and his style is extremely good. You're allowed to feel drawn to him platonically or even aesthetically without wanting to 'do things.' But, you know, that's the ace and aro discourse talking. You could also just say you're not into him."

Wow, okay. Yeah. I like all of that.

"Sorry, I think about this stuff probably too much." Bloom's voice and head drop back into that self-conscious posture. "Sometimes I go down the ADHD hyperfocus rabbit hole and . . . overcomplicate . . ."

"No, wait, it's really interesting!" I didn't mean to embarrass him with my lack of reaction. "I was . . . processing. I appreciate you talking about it."

"Oh. Cool." Bloom nods. "Yeah. Uh, I used to worry a lot about being normal. Allo dude culture is not subtle, you know?" He puts on a deep bro-y voice (that honestly sounds like he's mimicking Neeraj). "Are you a *boobs* man or a *butt* man? Or are you a *gay* man because you want to have sex with dudes and look at *their* butts?" He returns to his normal voice. "And I'm over here like, shrug emoji, no thoughts, head empty, Mii waiting-room music playing on loop."

I laugh, and Bloom buries his smile in a new stack of music. "My cousin's had a girlfriend for like two years now, and they haven't kissed because of religious things, and one time he was telling me about it and how all his secular friends think it's a fate worse than death, and I was thinking how it sounded nice! But not because I want to be closer to the Lord or anything. It just seems like less pressure."

"Are crushes anything but pressure?" I ask. I sort of thought that's how you identified a crush—by the crushing feeling in your gut. How have I been hitting my head against so many walls and Bloom just knows how to avoid them?

"I don't know, I've only had like one and a half in my life," Bloom says. He pulls his knees up and locks his elbows around them, looking a little less withdrawn than usual, taking up a little more space. "But my extremely personal experience is that all the types of attraction have the same emotions at their core. Maybe people want different things from different people, but if you care about someone, you don't care about them romantically or platonically or sexually, you just care. So I try not to stress out too much about what I'm feeling exactly and just hang with the people I want to hang with." He ducks his head again. "I guess that would be harder if you were, like, dying to kiss or confess to someone, though."

"Yeah, no, that makes sense . . ." I'm being such a bad conversation partner, nodding along while holding on to about a million things I could say. I could say that Bloom has the "good girl" trait too, pious behavior lining up with what he wanted to do anyway. I could say that I'm nervous to learn more about these identities he's so comfortable with, and that I really admire how sure he is of himself, even if he hides it behind a boatload of awkwardness. But I'm too busy trying to both process and remember Bloom's words. I need time to think.

Luckily, Bloom isn't one to push or talk over my

thoughts. He goes back to his search with no indication that my silence has offended him. It's unfamiliar. It's relaxing.

It's confusing! I like Gilberto, and I think he's cool and he has a nice face. But why did I decide he was the person I had a crush on? It wasn't because I wanted him so badly. I mostly wanted, well, I wanted an answer to give when people asked me who I liked. And I guess I wanted some kind of acknowledgment from him, but I want that from lots of people. Like, I spend just as much (okay, a lot more) time thinking about Sofia as I do Gilberto Reyes. If Bloom's right, then are those the same type of caring? What does that mean? Why did I label the one I'm still mostly afraid to talk to "crush" and the one I feel like I'm dying without "friend"?

We keep sorting through music. The flutes digging into each individual stanza of the show music is a perfect soundtrack to my repetitive thoughts. It's a relief when they pack up and leave, if only so I'll stop straining to hear Sofia laugh. She hasn't sounded this relaxed all year—not when I'm around, at least. The realization aches.

Bloom doesn't force me to talk, but he lets me start a pointless conversation when I get tired of my trilling brain. We talk about the new marching sets and UIL and the all-state audition étude. Bloom's voice is low, and my thoughts finally match the band hall's quiet.

"I think we have more than enough options to look

through, if you want to stop," Bloom says at 5:30. When did it get so late? "I'll play through them to weed out any that sound bad, and then start a vote for which one to learn."

"It might have to be a bracket." I look down at our pile of more than twenty strong possibilities. "But that could be fun bonding." I stand up and stretch. "I really did want to use the practice rooms, and my sibling usually picks me up closer to seven, so I can lock up if you need to go." I don't love the idea of being all alone in the band hall, because it feels like the opening of a horror movie, but it's fine.

"No, I'll practice too," Bloom says. "I can get started checking out some of these and also work on show music."

"Cool." I head for the cubby closet, a little relieved. The band hall is just too quiet when it's totally empty.

Ellen texts me when her shift ends, so I pack up and knock on Bloom's practice-room door to see if he wants anything from the vending machine. We snack on Honey Bun cakes while we make sure the music closet is in order and start working our way through Gilberto's lockup list. The flutes left the place pretty neat, so we mostly turn off lights and appliances.

Most of the band hall doesn't have exterior windows, so when we have to turn off the main fluorescent lights, we use the switch in the back hallway near the door that is our only source of natural light. The band hall goes dark, except for one yellow-orange glow illuminating a bunch of blue posters.

"Damn," Bloom grumbles. "Ms. Schumacher's office."

We left a light on in there, apparently. I flip the fluorescent switch back up, but nothing happens.

"They take forever to turn back on," Bloom says. "I'll go get it."

I turn the useless lights back off and follow him anyway, because now it's dark and creepy and silent, and I have strong pack animal instincts. We follow the light to the office, where both a lamp and a computer are still on. Bloom texts Gilberto in the dim office and gets confirmation that we should turn the monitor off, then puts his hand on the lamp switch.

"Ready?"

He clicks the lamp off. The dark is instant and total. In spite of the clear warning, I get that jolt of adrenaline that comes with fear, the same one I used to get when I had to cross a dark hallway to use the bathroom in the middle of the night. I know logically that if I take one step out of the office doorway, I should be able to see the back hall, but I can't see it now. I can't see anything.

"Where—?" I whisper, and my hand finds Bloom's hand, and we both latch on.

Before a full second has passed, we step out of the

office and my eyes adjust enough to make out the shape of the walls around us in the dim light. Bloom drops my hand and turns on his phone flashlight.

"Sorry, should've done that first."

My heart is still pounding, which seems silly since it was only a brief moment of "it's pretty dark" and not, like, a sprint through a murderer-infested forest, but adrenaline's weird like that. "I guess this is a good ramp-up to Halloween." I giggle. "Why is this place so creepy in the dark?"

"Heh, yeah." Bloom shrugs and sweeps his light around the empty room. "Probably because it's usually so busy."

"Let's go," I say, hurrying to the back hall. The thin windows on the back doors let in a blue-tinged light from the parking lot that makes sharp shadows on the floor. Still kind of creepy, but more noir than horror.

"Sorry I grabbed you," I say. I definitely didn't mean to be weird about it.

"No, it's fine. I did it too." Bloom keeps his eyes on the window.

"Yeah, it was really dark."

"That's a thing, isn't it?" Bloom asks. "Reaching out in the dark . . . It's one of those arguments in favor of religion."

I don't know what he's talking about, so I just shrug.

301

"I used to see it online when I was thirteen and considering going through an atheist phase," he says. "I would look up talking points on both sides. So if someone argues that religion is just made up as a tool to control others—which, unfortunately, lots of evidence for that one—one of the counterarguments is that, like, humans everywhere across all cultures come up with their own forms of religion. It's, like, basic instinct. We're always reaching for a higher power, the way we always reach out for a wall if the lights go out. And that's supposed to prove . . . uh, I don't know what, exactly. But I didn't end up becoming a full atheist."

"But we didn't reach for a wall," I point out. I like what he's saying, though. I've never heard it before. Why is Bloom so full of interesting facts and stories and research?

"Well, yeah," he says. "I guess that fits even better with how I see religion, though. We're always reaching out for connection."

"Whoa." I feel like I sound bad at talking again, but I guess Bloom should understand that at least.

"Uh, sorry. I didn't mean to get really . . ." I am going to have to smack this kid if he keeps apologizing for talking. I like it when he talks! "Do you, uh, even like religion?"

"No, yeah! I do." Weird that Bloom didn't know that.

I guess I don't talk about it much, because who wants to be that Christian kid? But he asked, so . . . "I'm Catholic."

"Oh." Bloom pauses. "So that's, like . . . Orthodox Christianity?"

Ellen texts me that she's here. "Maybe. I have to go. Is your ride coming?"

"Yeah, I'm good." Bloom rocks on his heels and pulls his phone out of his pocket, which is when I realize that he hasn't been staring at it at all in the past twenty minutes. That's got to be a record. And instead of getting lost immediately in the screen, he keeps his eyes on me for an extra second. "See you."

"See you." I'm weirdly reluctant to leave him, probably just because I wouldn't want to be the one left in the dark. "Text me about the songs you tried out?"

Bloom smiles. "I'll call."

CHAPTER 15

Neeraj is fifteen minutes late on Saturday, and the only reason I don't strangle him is because I don't have time. I can't say that I love morning games. Everything feels doubly hectic since I'm not awake, and even the Starbucks Bloom brought me is not cracking the exhaustion.

"Hey, Yasmín." Elias bounces up like the excited puppy dog he is. "Look what Lee did for me last night."

I spin around, irrationally nervous that the boys have done something reckless or juvenile. But when I face Elias, he looks normal, his hair still short and his grin still way too pleased with himself. "What?"

He tilts his head back and forth until I spot the shine of a small silver stud in each of his earlobes, surrounded by a slight redness.

"I learned how to pierce ears at horse camp," Lee

says proudly. "And I won our *Mario Kart* bet, so . . ."

"And my sister let me steal these." Elias beams. "Do I look cool? Wait, but you have to imagine them bigger, like Bad Bunny." He poses with his arms crossed and his lip pouty.

"Oh yes, very cool," I say. "Take them off."

"What?" Both boys gasp.

"You can't wear any jewelry in uniform," I remind them. "That's been the rule forever. Why do you think I don't wear earrings on game days?"

"He can't take them out now!" Lee grumbles. "The holes will close up."

"Oh well." I sigh, wanting to rub my eyes and maybe go sneak a fifteen-second nap leaning against the Dragon's case. "Maybe he'll lose to you in *Mario Kart* again someday. For now, bet's off."

"Bloom!" Elias cries, cupping his ears protectively. "Yasmín's being mean to me!"

"I am not! I thought you would be happy to—ugh, fine." I hold up my hands in defeat. "Does it mean a lot to you to keep them in?"

Elias nods pitifully.

I sigh again. "I'll see if I can track down some Band-Aids."

I stomp away from the now beaming Elias, wanting to grumble but mostly annoyed that I didn't think to pack

Band-Aids in my section leader situation-preparedness kit (safety pins, valve oil, ChapStick, ponytail holder, rubber bands for broken lyres, etc.).

I check with the saxes and the clarinets out of foolish optimism, but they both point me in the same direction. Why do sections have to be so stereotypical? Why are the flutes the only ones who have the necessary supplies to deal with earrings?

"Sorry." Mia shrugs, blinking sleepily from where she's leaning against Laylah's shoulder. As the flute with the most piercings, I decided it was worth a shot to check with her. "I don't bother with them anymore since none of my piercings are new and all of my jewelry is cheap. Your best bet is . . ."

I know, I know. Sofia.

"I can ask," Laylah offers, but she glances guiltily at Mia's head on her band polo. I don't want to ruin their moment, especially since I know Laylah's been sad about having to spend more time actually studying and less time "studying" in Mia's room. So I turn her down. I'm not *afraid* of Sofia.

Hey, I text Sofia like you might approach a wild animal: slowly and making my presence known. Not because I'm afraid, just because it's a necessary precaution. Do you have any Band-Aids? I look around the band hall, but I can't find her anywhere. One of my clowns pierced another one of my clown's ears. I'm surrounded by clowns.

"I'm right here." Sofia's voice behind my ear makes me jump. "You couldn't just come ask me?"

I spin around. "Didn't see you," I say defensively. "Haven't seen you much." I try to make this sound joking, but it comes out with an accusatory bite.

Sofia looks so annoyed, even though I've done nothing but stay out of her way for weeks. My slight smile tightens. "So can I have some—?"

Sofia holds out a pair of Band-Aids without comment.

I snatch them with a frustrated sigh. I don't want us to be like this. I want to apologize for the sleepover, and I want her to apologize too. I want to figure things out. But I can't do it if Sofia keeps icing me out. "Great," I snap, matching her utter lack of warmth. "Thanks. See you."

I head back to Elias, confused and annoyed and grumpier than ever. Why is she acting like this? Why are we like this? I don't like it.

We never talked about the party. Maybe that's part of what's rotting between us. Space isn't working. I should do something. I should get her to talk to me.

But first I should get my section through this performance.

It wasn't even that bad.

It really wasn't that bad. It was just one, admittedly

glaring, admittedly section-wide, admittedly hard-to-recover-from, single mistake.

It was just that almost exactly half of us, sleepy and running on autopilot, didn't step off for the new glorified jazz square around the fifty-yard-line we've been learning for a few weeks now, and the other half did, and so our whole line collided with itself and then we didn't know whether to try to complete the square or scrap it and stay in place.

Okay, okay. It was a disaster.

Bloom tries to do a pep talk under the bleachers during the third quarter, but the effect is reversed by some jerk percussionists pelting us with popcorn and booing when we go back to our seats.

Elias keeps screenshotting mean posts from Instagram (we're sitting two rows above some of the posters, so it's not exactly discreet or anonymous!) and sending them to Low Brassholes, which kind of makes me want to rip the Band-Aids (and the studs) off his ears. Above and below our row, people are loudly discussing our chances for UIL and how our Homecoming performance will look (consensus seems to be either "disaster" or "boring").

Low brass considering stepping up: "Ew."
Low brass considering fucking up: "Eyyy!"

TIL what it sounds like when a sousaphone gets crushed under pressure.

You: "low brass cracked."

Me, an intellectual: "profound alloy experienced fission."

"Elias, enough!" I stuff my phone deep in the pocket of my bib. "Why do we even have this Insta? Can't someone report it?"

"You already tried that." Jonathan scowls at me, face red. "You might notice it didn't work out well for you. Or us. Or anyone. So rather than yell at Elias, you could just admit that this is all *your* fault."

There's about five seconds of silence after he speaks, during which my tear ducts start working double, triple, quadruple capacity. I know Jonathan is a little vain, a little self-important, and a lot competitive. But I didn't think he would turn on me. Is this how the whole section feels? Do they resent that I'm dragging them down?

Then Elias shoves Jonathan so hard he almost falls backward off his bench. "Dude, shut the fuck up."

"We're not going to do this." Caleb points a finger at Jonathan.

"Stop living up to your jackass low brass ancestors," Milo snaps.

"Also, the account is bad. It's mean-spirited and out of hand, and it shouldn't exist," Lee adds.

"Okay, okay." Jonathan rolls his eyes guiltily and nods at me. "Sorry. I just meant—"

"Don't talk to her," Bloom snaps, voice firmer than I think I've ever heard it. "Go talk to the trombones who I can see on their phones posting right now. Go on, make yourself useful since you want to pick a fight so badly."

Jonathan hesitates. The rest of the section waits, tensely silent. Bloom has been practicing his tough love, landing on something like jokey teasing. Nobody seems quite sure what to do with his seriousness. When Bloom points firmly down the bleachers, Jonathan slowly stands up and takes one faltering step toward the aisle.

"Sit down." I hold up one hand to stop him and one to make Bloom stop pointing. "It's not my fault or Elias's fault. We're all having a bad day." It doesn't help that the midday sun is brutal as we sit here, watching our football team lose and wishing we had gotten several extra hours of sleep.

"I am sorry," Jonathan tells me, chin tucked and mouth twisted sheepishly. "I'm pissed. Shouldn't have taken it out on you."

"I know. We're good." I gesture again for Jonathan to sit. Bloom makes a half-choking snort noise, and I shake my head at him. *Let it go*. He frowns but presses his lips together.

Jonathan doesn't let it go, though. "I think you're a good section leader or whatever. I just really don't like being the section to hate."

"Yeah, me neither." I shrug.

"The rest of the band can go eat a bag of their least preferred body part," Lee says. I feel like I should correct that attitude, but honestly, I'm too busy laughing.

"Oh, that's the energy we should bring to our ensemble stand tune," Milo says. "That gives me an idea . . ."

"CeeLo—'Fuck You'?" Caleb asks.

"Mmm, that might not get approved, but I like the way you think." Milo smiles. "I feel like Taylor Swift has some good anti-hater songs."

"Why is it always back to Taylor Swift with you?"

"Why are we even discussing this? We already decided on 'Despacito'—Bloom! Yasmín! Tell them!"

"Nobody agreed to that, Elias, shut up!"

So, you know, at the end of the day it wasn't really that bad of a game.

I SPEND MOST OF SATURDAY AFTERNOON LISTENING TO angsty Olivia Rodrigo music and composing a text to Sofia. I even try Bloom's technique of speaking the things I want to write. It's worked surprisingly well with my past two Spanish assignments. Sra. Mendez thinks she finally got through to me, and Mom is thrilled that my online gradebook is less of a mess these days.

Hi. I recently realized that some people have different communication styles, so I'm trying to respect your style by texting you. Do you want to grab lunch after church tomorrow? I feel like we need to sit down and talk about everything. I want to get things back to normal. Let me know, thanks.

Does it make sense? Does it sound weird? I kept trying to add in something like "I care about you," but that absolutely sounded weird, so I took it out.

Sofia answers pretty quickly: Not particularly.

Even without voice or body language, the text radiates the same energy as our last conversation before the football game. It hurts all over again. I know everything is messed up right now, but how am I supposed to fix it if Sofia won't even talk to me?

So, I call her.

"What?" Sofia's voice in my ear is venomous. My relief that she picked up flashes into irritation.

"What is your problem?"

"I don't have a problem except the one harassing me with phone calls right now."

"Sofia, what is happening?" My voice sounds desperate in my ears, which makes me angrier. "You've been mad at me for like two months. I apologized about the report. I'm trying to make up for it. I've tried hanging around like normal, and I've tried giving you space. I don't know what you want from me!"

"I don't want anything from you," Sofia says, but it's hate, not indifference, when she says it. "And news flash, Yasmín: you're not as great of a friend as you think you are. You're not as great of a musician as you think you are. And you're not as great of a person as you think you are."

Conflicting reactions hit me in slow-mo. Hurt, obviously; indignant protest that I don't think I'm so great; indignant insistence that I am *so* a good person; frustration that Sofia doesn't care if I'm a good person or not, she's just trying to hurt me. And it worked. It's been working. I'm hurt.

My brain, always so preoccupied with calculating and recalculating the quickest route to reconciliation, suddenly suspends guidance. I'm tired of caring about Sofia. I'm tired of reaching out for the person who was always there and finding nothing but cold air and burning humiliation.

Why do we have to reconcile?

I don't need her.

I take a shaky breath, my chest expanding big with the freedom of owning my anger. And it's like as soon as I give it permission to stop walking on eggshells, my brain pulls out a chainsaw and goes absolutely, calculatedly apeshit.

"Great," I say. "Thanks. This was perfect." I've tried to mimic Sofia's stinging attitude before, but this is the first time I've heard myself match the cruelty of her tone. "Now I know that you're a bitter, jealous, ugly person who's done nothing but hold me back since middle school. Because guess what? I have a lot more and better friends now than I ever did before you tried to dump me. Enjoy your reign of terror over a section that doesn't even like you, and I hope you know you're only on top because you didn't dare compete with me."

I hang up.

And for the second time this year, I feel the sinking and drowning sensation of total, immediate regret.

I pull my knees to my chest, perch on the edge of my bed. I don't feel good about lashing out. I feel empty and nauseous, my eyes skirting around the room, finding signs of Sofia everywhere. The stuffed neon green hedgehog she brought me back from her eighth-grade field trip to Six Flags. The nice photo of us from a middle school concert that Mom framed and put on my desk, and all the goofy selfies that she printed on my fifteenth birthday card, taped crookedly to the wall behind it. I debate calling back. Why did I do that? Why did Sofia do it? Why did we say the meanest things we could think of?

My stomach aches. I drop my feet to the floor and my head into my lap. What happened to Bloom's theory that whatever kind of relationship you have, it's supposed to be based on caring for the other person? What does it mean when it's based on hurting them? What label do you put on that?

Mom knocks on my bedroom door, then opens it before I can do anything about my posture or my tears.

"Your tías do not know what it means to— Mija? Are you okay?"

"I'm fine." I scramble to sit up straight. The blankets are rumpled, my desk cluttered, my laundry basket over-full, but none of it is as much of a mess as I am. "It's fine."

Mom looks frozen in place, like she has no idea what to make of the situation. "Are you sure?"

I have to hold in a semi-hysterical laugh. "Mhmm. Fine."

Mom's face passes through confusion and into annoyance. "Don't lie," she says. "Just tell me what's wrong!"

I click my tongue. "Calm down. Don't worry about it."

That was the wrong thing to say. I feel like I knew it was the wrong thing to say as I said it.

"Don't tell me to calm down!" Mom yells. "Why are you crying?"

"Can you stop? It's not a big deal."

"Why are you being so rude then?" Mom asks. She

sounds so bewildered. "Why are you trying to fight with me?" I can practically hear the unspoken cry of "I expect this kind of thing from Ellen, not you."

I'm the one who holds things together. I can't be the one who gets upset and breaks them.

"I didn't mean to fight," I say, taking a breath, pushing down the turmoil my conversation with Sofia left in my stomach. I need to tell Mom something simple, so much simpler than the truth. "I had a problem with . . . this boy I like. The drum major. He doesn't know I exist. But it's okay; I'm over it."

"Oh . . ." Mom's face softens immediately, like I knew it would. "Well, of course you could've just told me that. It's for the best, mijita linda, you don't need to worry about boys until you finish college."

"I know," I say. Those have always been the rules. I've even seen how the switch flips on some of my older cousins, from "No boys!" to "You're not getting any younger, why don't you ever bring anyone to Christmas?" The good girl path is so impossibly narrow, and I might not naturally follow it forever. But I can't live my life trying not to fall off.

Mom pats my head, a hint of confusion resurfacing on her face. "You know you can tell me anything, right?"

"I know," I lie, and just like I expect, Mom smiles. I don't feel my usual triumph or even relief as she leaves my room, even though I coaxed that smile out of a near disaster. I swallow hard, tears still swelling behind my brittle calm. I put in my headphones and scroll Spotify for something soft and soothing, settling on Natalia Lafourcade. I can't tell if I wish I had kept my cool with Sofia or if I wish I hadn't with Mom. I can't tell if I'm ready for the consequences either way.

I'M ALMOST AFRAID TO GO TO THE BAND HALL ON Monday, paranoid that Sofia will take spectacular revenge, but she walks past me without so much as blinking, and I guess she's choosing to end this in ice rather than reciprocating my fiery bang. *You didn't dare compete with me*, I told her. Maybe I was actually right?

Lunch feels mostly normal, and our rowdy section cracking jokes in the back hall helps to let down my guard and my guilt and my fear that Sofia will suddenly pounce. If I'm a little slower to laugh at jokes or a little less excited about following the conversation, the boys don't mind.

With mid-October chair tests done and posted, we turn our rehearsal attention dutifully to Homecoming. The Friday night game and Saturday night dance are coming up at the end of the week, and the whole school is getting excited, the kids who haven't been to a football game all year suddenly knowing the schedule and planning to buy or decorate their mums, couples forming or splitting up as this pivotal romantic moment looms. We have to focus on learning a new song and a new formation to cover the long stretch of halftime announcements and awards. It will probably be easy (boring), but my nerves jangle at the possibility of a thoughtless misstep like last game.

"This should not take long," Ms. Schumacher warns as she passes out the music. Milo groans at the prospect of learning another new piece, but we hack through the simple bass line decently by the end of the hour. Then we go outside, knock out the new drill, and then we can finally go back to rehearsing our actual show.

Without exactly admitting that she's proud of us, Ms. Schumacher cancels morning rehearsal for the rest of the week and gives us the last half hour of practice to clean the band hall, practice rooms, and cubbies. It's a fun and easy task compared to more run-throughs, getting eaten by mosquitos, and doing push-ups when our lines aren't up to her standards.

"Yasmín, let me use your phone?" Elias begs. "Mine is out of battery, and Caleb says I'll mess up his recommended music." He hooks my Spotify up to Ms. Schumacher's giant speaker so he can blast Bad Bunny and Maluma for the whole band's listening pleasure. A few upperclassmen, mostly trumpets, try to grumble about it, but it peters out amid the general acceptance that Elias will care more about being a good DJ than anyone else.

We fill trash bags with empty breakfast bar wrappers and Gatorade bottles and old crumpled papers pushed into the back corners of the low brass cubbies (and we do it without pushing anyone into a cubby . . . against their will, at least). I take the bag out to the dumpster in the parking lot and come back to see the boys having a mouthpiece-buzzing contest. What a bunch of dorks.

Bloom, who's trying to convince Neeraj to stop egging on Elias and Jonathan's rivalry and instead grab the other broom from the clarinets, looks up when I approach. His exasperated scowl slips.

"What are you smiling about?" Neeraj asks.

Bloom shrugs. "Yasmín's back. I'm smiling because I don't have to keep y'all under control by myself anymore."

"I went outside for like twenty seconds." I laugh. "I assumed you would be fine."

Elias elbows Bloom, lower lip protruding while his eyes flash with mischief. "Why don't I ever elicit smiles like that?" he asks.

"You do," Bloom assures him. "Whenever you leave."

Elias fake wails at the insult as everyone *ooh*s and teases and fails to sweep our corner. What a bunch of dorks.

CHAPTER 16

I get a mysterious email on Tuesday morning. It looks like a Reflections account announcement, and it opens on a link to a new post, so I don't expect it to be anything good, but I open it casually because it's a random Tuesday and you just don't expect a Tuesday to betray you.

But sometimes Tuesday does.

EXCLUSIVE: TEXTS FROM A HURRICANE LINK IN BIO to see what our favorite natural disaster really thinks of us!

Liked by thatbandkid09, buttfartzzzz, and 12 others.

View all 19 comments

Beatoftehdrum06: Should we maybe worry about who hacked the phone? I know Hurricane Yasmín has enemies but . . . not actually cool, y'all.

I blink at the post. I read the one visible comment under it. I see there's a new highlight that's just labeled "reactions."

> Look! Up in the sky! It's a flute! It's a tuba! No, it's a self-important harpy incapable of compassion. 😵

> ***Thots and prayers to the low brass boys who seem like they've been doing their best and don't deserve this.***

It's not exactly confusing—I'm almost too familiar with the gut punch of anonymous hate at this point—but in the seconds it takes me to find the link everyone is reacting to, my brain fills with static and gives me absolutely no idea, not even a catastrophic thought, about what to expect. Texts? A hacked phone? Is it supposed to be my phone and my texts? How would that have even . . . ? I'm the center of this storm again, but I can't think of any horrifying secrets that I have to reveal. For a second I even think, *How bad could it be?*

The page loads. It's a series of screenshots taken from my phone, presented without context except who they were sent to, mostly Sofia and Bloom, some to the group chat. Some I remember sending, plenty I don't.

To: Sofia

Don't worry, if Hannah keeps teaching us in the slowest and most inefficient way possible, I'll never learn to march anyway.

To: Sofia

You've gone soft taking your chair tests against slacker upperclassmen for two years. I'm here now, so you should be more nervous.

To: Sofia

First off, my new section leader is antisocial and awkward. Who heard that mumbling and thought "leadership material"??

And Neeraj is a waste of an upperclassman—worse than Han, even. No doubt!

The whole section is kind of a clown-car crash. At least I get why you were all kicked out of your old sections, but can you try to be less terrible?

To: Bloom

Neeraj? dragging down the section? Shocking.

To: Sofia

It's hard to believe in an omniscient, omnipotent, and benevolent God when you hear our former clarinet play. Or our section leader speak.

To: Sofia

I'm surrounded by clowns.

To: Bloom

Obviously Milo needs the most work, but Caleb too. Like, stop flirting with mediocrety and each other!

To: Milo

Getting Andy expelled? Did you mean best decision I ever made?

To: Sofia

And now I can creep on Gilberto Reyes all the time, so that's a plus.

To: Bloom

Lee can't do Wednesday or Thursday for sectionals (does he have a social life? How??).

To: Low Brassholes

Elias, shut up, nobody cares.

To: Low Brassholes

If (when) someone murders Elias they can just frame Jonathan, we all know he would do it for one corn chip and the chance to claim that he's a better player.

To: Low Brassholes

NOBODY LIKES YOU, ELIAS.

To: Low Brassholes

All in favor of bullying Elias out of the section?

The thing is . . .

This all looks really bad.

Like, way worse than I thought it could be. Like maybe I sound really harsh, really needlessly mean. Like maybe I've said some things I wouldn't—didn't—want everyone to read.

Like maybe the Reflections account finally found a way to make my friends hate me.

Or, I guess, I did.

I try to call Bloom as I get dressed and packed, but he doesn't pick up. I try to text him, but he doesn't answer. The boy has his head buried in his phone 24/7, and his normal response time is so freakishly fast that it gives me typing anxiety, so this silence is a lot worse than any answer.

The Low Brassholes thread is silent too, which isn't

unheard of, but it still feels ominous. I would really love a series of pointless Elias GIF-spams right now.

I always really love a series of pointless Elias GIF-spams.

I have to tell him. I have to tell Elias, right now, this second, how much I appreciate his random eyebrow-wiggling, arm-flailing, spam-spewing presence in my life. I have to set the record straight. I can't let him believe those things on Instagram . . .

The things I *said* . . .

What the fuck is wrong with me?

I can't think of a single thing to write in a message to Elias that wouldn't make everything worse. I can't imagine Lee wants to be reminded that he trusted me with his phone number, or that Milo and Caleb and Neeraj want to hear my excuses. There's no excuse for this, no spin, no way to dodge or defuse or delay the fact that I said hurtful things about my friends, and now they are undoubtedly hurt.

I'm a bad friend. This is what bad friends do.

I clutch my phone tightly, waiting for Bloom to call back, but it stays stubbornly still and silent. Mom talks about her client's frustrating painters, how long it's taking them to work and how that affects something else she's planned. She asks if I need coffee. "You look sluggish."

I say I'm tired.

I don't know what to do when I get to school. I stand in

the parking lot for a while, but I get nervous that someone will pass by and see me.

I decide that hiding in the library is more dignified than hiding in the bathroom. I don't know if I deserve the dignity. I stay until I'm sure the hallways are clear, arriving late to first period. The color guard girls in pre-calc give me major stink-eye the second I enter, and I shrink into my seat and try to avoid eye contact with any band kids for the rest of the day. I want to say that it isn't fair, that I would never say those things. But I did, and everyone saw, and I can't even blame them for hating me, because I kind of hate the person who said those things about my friends.

At first I'm waiting for someone to confront me, but soon it's obvious that everyone who knows is giving me cold shoulders, empty glances, and the absolute silent treatment. I might as well be locked behind a wall of glass. I keep my phone in my lap through the whole morning, staring down at the bitten-apple logo, willing it to buzz with a text from Low Brassholes, or Bloom, or Laylah, or anyone.

Well, not anyone.

I'm not completely oblivious. I know who the most likely suspect is here. And I know, logically, she's been the most likely suspect all year. The one who brought me to the sleepover and dyed my hair, the one who wrote down the wrong jacket number and then swore I had done it myself. Maybe the one running the Reflections Instagram all along, I don't know, I wouldn't put it past her. Everyone tried to tell me—Milo, Laylah, Ellen (Ellen's going to be so annoyingly "told you so" if she finds out, God).

I told Sofia I could make friends without her.

She told me I wasn't as good of a friend as I thought.

I shouldn't be surprised that she would go this hard to prove I was wrong and she was right.

THE THING IS, YOU CAN'T SKIP MARCHING REHEARSAL. Not for anything, and especially not this late in the season, and especially if you don't want your band director to get annoyed and reinstate morning rehearsals for everyone. We're trying to field a new routine and new music for Homecoming, and we're still adding new sets to the halftime show—for my section specifically, the section I'm supposed to be leading. Missing rehearsal today . . . I might as well beg Ms. Schumacher to write me a letter of recommendation that says "irresponsible drama queen" in red Sharpie.

So in spite of how desperately I want to do literally anything else, I force my feet to carry me (slowly, reluctantly) toward the band hall for sixth period. I don't have a choice. I agreed to the schedule and absence policy way back in August in the info packet.

The warning bell sounds, and I'm not even in the right wing yet. I don't speed up. One minute later the tardy bell beeps, and I turn the corner to see the vending machines. My lunch—Hot Cheetos and an apple cinnamon cashew bar, scarfed standing outside the library—churns in my stomach.

The hallway is empty. I'm late. I open the band hall door.

A bunch of heads turn toward me and then immediately turn away, like a double-layer domino line. The handful of people still looking have grim expressions and drop their gaze when I meet their eyes. I look farther back, to my section. Seven pairs of eyes stare straight at me, and there's too much distance and depth to the emotions for me to sort out whether I'm seeing disappointment or anger or confusion or what.

Bloom is the first to look away, burying his head in his music stand, and that small dismissal shatters my last hope that somehow I could come out of this okay.

"Miss Treviño?" Ms. Schumacher asks. "Is there a problem?"

I know it's a rhetorical question, but I turn to her anyway, sweat gathering up and down my torso, stomach churning with guilt and pain and half-digested cashews, and I open my mouth to explain, but—

Instead my stomach tries to crawl up my esophagus. I heave, fighting tears because I can't do this in front of everyone. This is only going to make the memes worse, but now that the bile is creeping up my throat, I have no way to stop it.

Gilberto Reyes vaults past Ms. Schumacher and spins me to face the trash can as I barf apple cinnamon and red Cheeto dust. He stands between me and the rest of the band, and I'm grateful for the protection from the phones that are undoubtedly pointed my way, ready to capture my worst moment and pin it like a rare butterfly behind the glass of their screens. Gilberto pats my back softly, and I'm grateful for him, and I wonder if he's the only person in band who doesn't know what I did.

IT TURNS OUT THERE IS ONE WAY TO ACCEPTABLY SKIP today's rehearsal. I spend sixth period in the nurse's office until Mom gets me, and then she grills me for details and scolds me for eating spicy junk instead of a real meal.

I let her find fault with my nutritional choices without comment. When we get home, I crawl into bed. Instagram has some shaky videos, so I can hear myself throwing up from multiple angles around the room, but Gilberto made a good human shield, at least.

Reading the comments makes me want to barf all over again.

Mom comes in and sits on the edge of my bed when I don't budge for dinner.

"You're really sick, huh?" she asks. I nod. Mom *hmms*

softly and pats my forehead, which would be more soothing if I deserved it. As it is, I fake sleep until Mom tiptoes
away, and then I'm free to get back on my phone and see
all the ways I'm hated.

ELLEN GETS OFF LATE, AND I GUESS MOM OR DAD MUST
have told her what was up, because she comes knocking
on my door.

I try pretending to be asleep, but Ellen keeps knocking until it becomes awkward, and I'm forced to sit up. I
don't want to talk, but Ellen doesn't budge until I invite
her in. She has green sauce smeared down half her shirt
and apron, so I hope she'll make this quick, but she sits
down at the edge of my bed and asks, "So is this completely a stomach bug? Or does it have to do with your
friendship struggles?"

I don't want to talk about this. I don't want to see Ellen's
knowing half smile appear as she interprets my silence.
"Yeah, I thought so. I used to babysit you; I remember the
emotional vomiting." She pulls her feet up onto the bed—
gross even without shoes—and settles like she thinks we're
going to have some long heart-to-heart. Like my heart isn't
a jagged pile of burning rubble right now.

"Just . . ." "Go away" is what I want to say, but I use
my last bit of restraint to change it to "forget it. And don't
tell Mom, please. I don't want to add drama."

Ellen purses her lips in wise-sibling disapproval—as if she has any positive track record of handling Mom. I cringe back into my blankets to avoid her stare.

"Who are we beating up, then?" she asks. "I'm in a problem-solving mood today."

"What? Nobody!" She's pissing me off, perched all weird on the bed with knees at odd angles, probably not bothering to keep her stains away from my blankets. She's too intense as always, too ready to comfort and console and protect me when I'm the one doing all the damage. Ellen thinks her sweet baby sister is getting bullied, and I don't have the energy to explain how wrong she is.

I know she's trying to help. I know I'm being unfair. But I already feel horrible, and Ellen being here is making it worse. I feel exposed by the well-meaning force of my sibling, even with the blanket pulled up to my chin. My stomach hurts. It makes me want to hurt her back.

"Well, we have to do something," Ellen continues. "Bottling up all your emotions for the benefit of others is hardly the sustainable or healthy route." She smiles with infuriating sympathy. The undeserved warmth burns my face.

"More sustainable than always making my problems and my opinions everyone else's problem," I snap, striking from my blanket nest like a viper, straight for Ellen's smile. I get a direct hit, crumpling Ellen's "big sibling knows best" look. Her haphazard posture straightens, a sure sign of stress.

I try to soften—I will myself to soften—but I didn't want to have this conversation anyway. "Look, you don't know what you're talking about. Even if Sofia did—" I catch myself, but not before Ellen raises her eyebrows at my slipped admission. "It doesn't matter. I just need to make it right with everyone, and eventually it will all . . ." *be okay*. But will it? This year, with Sofia . . . every time I think we're good, some other problem crops up until it feels like I'm chopping heads off a hydra of hurt feelings and insecurities, and they just keep growing back meaner. "I can make everything okay." I say it like a prayer because it has to be true.

Ellen wears a twisted frown that I think might be pity, but with a heavy dose of condescension. "You know that's a literal recipe for disaster, right? You can't make everyone happy all the time."

Her words knock the breath from my lungs. The blanket is hot and heavy and suffocating, and I can't free my arms because Ellen is still *sitting on my bed* telling me that the only thing I've ever been naturally good at is impossible and wrong. The shreds of softness I was trying to gather burn away. Fuck. Her.

"No, *you* can't," I say. "You can't make anyone happy, because you refuse to try." I claw my way free of the covers, upsetting Ellen's seat and putting her off balance as she half falls, half hops onto the carpet. Why would I even take advice from her anymore? She thinks my life is a recipe for disaster? She's a walking disaster herself. "Mom's right about your attitude," I hiss, like a fountain spraying out every bad thought I've had since Ellen moved home, even the ones I don't believe, even the ones I really, really don't want to say. "Maybe if you tried a little harder to get along, you wouldn't be here bothering everyone, because you'd actually be less of a failure."

My voice drops through the speech, hitting the last word on a whisper, but I know Ellen hears it all. I couldn't stop it.

Any last doubt I had, any hope that the mean texts unfairly represented me, vanishes with Ellen's cleared throat and rapid blinks. I stare at my blanket, hanging down onto the ground, and at the accent wall, and at the photos and old crayon drawings on the wall, and at anything but Ellen's face. I am a mean, judgmental person.

Ellen smooths her apron and clears her throat again. "Anyway, feel better, kid." She leaves the room without looking at me. I wait to hear the back door open and close, and then a few seconds later the garage apartment door *slams*.

"Yasmín?" My door opens and Mom walks in, and I absolutely cannot right now. Can't pretend that everything's fine, can't listen to Mom blame Ellen for the fight I just caused, can't tell her what's happening with Sofia, can't, can't, can't.

"GO AWAY!" I screech, and Mom's sleepy face evaporates into shock and confusion and then disbelief and then anger. I pull the blankets back up to my chin, but they don't stop the outburst. "Leave me alone! Get your own life!"

"Mija, are you—?" She takes another step into the room.

"NO!" My voice hits piccolo range, my throat tight as I try to tell Mom to leave before—but it's already way too late.

"Yasmín, that's enough. Tell me what's wrong." She means, *Tell me what's right. Tell me you're okay. Be the good girl.*

I shake my head and close my eyes so I can't see Mom's reaction.

"What are you doing? Don't be ridiculous. Yasmín! Do you need to go to the hospital? Look at me!" Her hand lands on my shoulder and shakes me, and I bury my head in my hands.

"Connie." Dad's voice is in the doorway now. "I think she's just . . . upset."

Mom's hand drops away. "She's acting possessed!"

Weight settles at the foot of my bed. Mom huffs. My shoulders tense, but Dad doesn't say anything.

And doesn't say anything.

And still doesn't say anything.

I open my eyes. "What?"

Mom and Dad are both looking at me like I'm someone who needs to be handled. Mom opens her mouth, but then closes it and looks at Dad, who stays silent.

"I'm not sorry," I say.

"Okay," Dad says.

My heart pounds loud and guilty in the silence. I pull the covers over my head and curl up under them. "And you're all really annoying."

"Okay."

My hands and chest shake in the dark. Mom must be dying to scream at me. Dad probably just thinks he has to be calm while I'm having a breakdown, and tomorrow he'll come up with an elaborate punishment to fit my crime. Ellen hates me. My friends hate me. Nothing is okay.

At some point I fall asleep, and when I wake up, the weight on my bed is gone and I'm alone.

CHAPTER 17

Nobody wakes me up for school, so I stay in bed. Ellen definitely isn't awake yet, and Mom's car isn't in the driveway, so there's no way for me to assess how bad the damage is. I'm afraid it's bad.

I'm sure everyone in band knows why I'm staying home. I just hope that nobody wants to explain social media to Ms. Schumacher, so they won't turn me in for my fake illness.

I feel bad about faking sick, but it's not hard to play the part by blasting sad music, dozing fitfully, and feeling miserable. I'm trying to hear when Ellen gets up. I'm trying to draft an apology text to her and to the Low Brassholes chat, but I keep losing track of what I'm typing either because I think I hear Mom's car pull up or because I find myself back on Instagram, seeing the new updates that don't have anything to do with me and the ones that do.

At eleven, Ellen slams through the back door. I try to reach the kitchen, but I barely catch the back of her head as she tosses a banana peel into the compost bucket and heads off to work. She doesn't so much as wave at me.

I go back to bed. A text comes in from Laylah: Hey, are you feeling any better? That was rough . . . But I can't open it. I can't listen to a well-deserved lecture about how rough my texts were. Laylah is always trying to save me from my own missteps. She's a good person. She doesn't need one extra terrible friend.

Mom comes home around noon. She's . . . nice. She asks how I'm feeling, offers me Maruchan and Sprite, chats about her trip to the hardware store. I keep remembering the way I screamed last night, like some kind of wild vortex. I keep waiting for Mom to bring it up, for the other shoe to drop.

By three o'clock, the dread of having to go to school tomorrow is making me want to barf again. How am I supposed to just show up now? But how can I stay in band—and lead a section!—if I miss another rehearsal? They'll kick me out if I don't go back . . . but what will happen if I do?

Nothing. Nothing will happen. Everyone will just quietly hate me, and I'll deserve it, and I'll just have to keep marching. I'm not doing this to win a popularity contest.

I'm doing it for my college applications, for my leadership experience, for proving myself as a musician—all the reasons I was so focused on in August.

Why don't they seem like enough anymore? Why does it seem unbearable to rehearse without Milo's snark or Neeraj's goofy hype? Why can't I imagine staying in band if Bloom stops calling me?

Footsteps outside, and a doorbell, but it's not Ellen coming home yet, so I stay under my blanket. Mom answers the door, says something indistinct but surprised, and then her heels click down the hall and she opens my door.

"Yasmín?" she says. "How are you feeling? There's someone asking to speak to you."

I'm so pathetic, my first hopeful thought is that it's Sofia. But Mom wouldn't leave her standing outside, wouldn't say "someone" like that. It's not Sofia. Why would it be?

My heart doesn't quite dare to make a second guess.

"I guess . . . I'll be there in a sec?" I stand up, wishing I had eaten more than one bowl of instant ramen all day. Mom goes back to the door while I quickly change out of my pajamas and smooth my ponytail. I debate makeup, but I probably want to look sick rather than good, in case someone's hoping to catch me in my lie.

I get to the door, and my body starts throwing out panic signals that make me sweat and shake, because I can't imagine why the hell Gilberto Reyes would be standing in my front yard or how this could mean anything good for me.

"Hey," he says. Gilberto Reyes is standing in my front yard saying "hey." Gilberto Reyes is standing in my front yard saying "hey" during rehearsal time, and he's sort of slightly smiling about it.

"I didn't throw up today," I say, guilty conscience pushing its way out of my mouth. "I should have . . . I didn't want to miss rehearsal, but . . ."

"It's fine." Gilberto holds up his hands. "I mean, you know, not fine, but . . . it's not the end of the world or whatever. Are you okay?"

I'm okay.

Of course I'm okay.

It's just a stomach bug; I'm okay.

I keep repeating responses in my head, but none of them come out of my mouth.

I'm fine.

Don't worry about me.

Why are you here?

The silence stretches longer and longer, and Gilberto scratches the back of his neck. "Look," he says, "I didn't want to . . . Officially, I wasn't supposed to know about the Instagram, right? That kind of thing is really dependent on plausible deniability."

Oh God. He saw it. I cringe into myself. "Yeah, you don't have to—"

"No, I do," Gilberto says. "I . . . I did the wrong thing. I thought that it would all blow over faster if leadership stayed out of it. I thought investigating would give more ammo for the bullies to attack you."

"It would," I say. "It definitely would. It's not bullying. It's not . . . I can handle . . ." My mouth refuses to finish my sentences. All my normal lies stick in my throat, choking me.

Gilberto shakes his head. "I reported it to Ms. Schumacher today. It was way past time."

He reported the Reflections account? My heart rate spikes. What happens now? Will Ms. Schumacher read all my texts? I pull out my phone. Everyone must be freaking out. Everyone must be blaming me. I have to see what they're saying.

The eyesore aesthetic doesn't load. The account doesn't exist.

"That was fast," I whisper. My chest feels squeezed too tight. Without the Instagram, how can I know what everyone thinks about me? Knowing hurts, but not knowing is so much worse. What are people saying in their group chats right now? What are they calling me? My shoulders hunch as my brain offers suggestions. My lungs strain. I take a gasping breath, then another one.

"Yasmín?" Gilberto puts a hand on my arm. "Uh, can you look at me for a sec? And just . . . breathe on the count of four?"

Anxiety. I'm having an anxiety attack in front of Gilberto Reyes, in my front yard, wearing my SUMMER SUMS MATH CAMP T-shirt. I kind of start to laugh, which doesn't help my breathing get any calmer.

"Is—" I cough out the word. "Is Ms. Schumacher going to expel me from band?"

"What?" Gilberto looks really alarmed, more than feels appropriate in response to my question. Maybe it's because I feel and probably look like I'm choking to death. "Why would she do that?"

"My texts," I say, laughter dying in my throat. "All the stuff I said."

"That's not . . . No. Those were your private messages," Gilberto says. "They shouldn't have been shared to the whole—and of course, it would be different if it was targeted harassment or hate speech or . . . But Elias was the only person we had to check with since you were actually sending the texts where he could see them, and he swore he never felt unsafe. I think he actually said he deserved worse."

"He . . ." My lungs fill more easily. "He said that?"

"I mean, yeah. Those guys have all been, uh, threatening to fight other sections today." Gilberto sighs. "That's what I'm talking about. It shouldn't have gotten this bad."

I'm staring at Gilberto Reyes, the boy I thought I was in love with, and I can't imagine anything he could say or do that would make me happier than this. My section, those ridiculous clowns, don't hate me. Or maybe they do, but not enough to stop fighting for me. I pull out my phone and try to send a text to the thread, but my eyes are watering too much to see.

"Anyway," Gilberto says, "I, uh, wanted you to know that I'm going to talk to everyone about why I reported. So there are no rumors or speculations that you were involved. And I think Ms. Schumacher will probably make us do some kind of bullying workshop, maybe next semester. It will probably be awful, but I take full responsibility for that. The point is that I'm sorry it took me so long. I'm sorry I wasn't as fearless as you were about standing up to shitty behavior."

If I were thinking straighter, I might remember that I'm supposed to be sick or that I haven't showered today or that my recently exposed texts sort of revealed my crush on Gilberto, and any one of those thoughts might stop me from what I'm about to do. But since I'm not thinking straight, I throw myself thoughtlessly at Gilberto Reyes and wrap him in an unembarrassed hug.

Gilberto makes a slight *oof* and laughs and pats my back, then pulls away and says, "Uh . . . so listen . . ."

"It's okay!" I say quickly. "I used to think I had a crush on you, but now I think it was just platonic attraction plus being nervous about band. Or aesthetic attraction. Or something. I just think you're a cool person." I kind of get now why Bloom seemed so awkward talking about this kind of thing. Feelings are weird and hard to explain, and it's just as scary to tell someone your feelings about them even if you're not confessing love or lust. I'm afraid I've weirded Gilberto out even more by blurting this than if I had just let him assume I had a crush.

"Oh." Gilberto nods. "Uh, cool? Good. Because I . . . am going to college soon, so I'm hoping I'll be able to be a little more . . . *out* once I'm there."

Ah. Past comments slot together like puzzle pieces into that context. Gilberto never wants to go home.

It's not fair. Here we are, two people who don't want to kiss each other, but Gilberto hides out in the band hall for the way his attraction manifests, and I'm the pinnacle of good girl–ness because of mine. None of it is fair, and it's not equal, not even for me and Bloom, because the world holds the two of us to totally different standards. God, can we just stop pretending like there's only one right way to feel, one right category for every person to fall into?

"But"—Gilberto slightly tosses his head, easing the tension of the moment—"thanks for appreciating my aesthetic. Yours is cute too."

"Thanks." I look down at my buzzing phone. Apparently I accidentally sent the first half of my text— You guys with no follow-up—to the Low Brassholes. The boys are replying with guesses to complete my sentence, from . . . suck? to . . . have all been exposed to the barf virus, please self-isolate for the next two weeks and send the names of anyone you've had close contact with in the last week.

I beam at my phone. Then I beam up at Gilberto Reyes. "Thanks for coming," I say.

"Yeah, no problem," he says. "Uh, and I just wanted to check . . . We figured we would just, as long as the IG account doesn't come back, we would just leave it. Unless you want us to investigate . . ."

"No! No, that's okay. We don't need to . . . Lots of people were using it." I don't want to know who ran the Reflections. I don't think it would make me feel any better to know if it was Sofia or some random percussionist. And if it was Sofia . . . "I don't want to expel anyone else."

Gilberto nods. "That's what we were thinking. Okay. So, I'll see you tomorrow?"

"You will." I wave as he climbs back into his truck and drives away, and then I go back inside and see Mom not even trying to look inconspicuous in front of the window.

"So that's what you were so upset about," she says, worry lines between her eyebrows and lips pursed. "How old is that boy? I'm not so sure I want you to be seeing him. Especially if he makes you cry."

"That's not what I was . . ." My phone buzzes again. I don't actually need Mom to understand, so I don't explain. I leave her with her pinched face and her low hum of disapproval and close my door behind me.

In the safety of my room, I work on my real apology text. You guys are about to get an uncomfortable display of emotion: I love y'all. I'm sorry about the texts, and even if you're out there fighting other sections, you're also allowed to be mad at me, because I was kind of shitty esp at the beginning of the year. No more mean gossip, I promise. Sometimes I do get frustrated so I might still complain, but I'll do it to your face. Also I appreciate you all. Also Elias adds a lot to this group chat.

I shower and catch up on homework, finding it easier to stay focused in spite of (or because of) the constant stream of Low Brassholes texts, most of which are fiercely supportive and only a few of which ask me to grovel a bit more. I finally text Laylah back, and she gives me a well-deserved (but gentle) lecture for thinking her "that was rough" referred to my behavior instead of the whole vomiting-on-camera situation.

Why would I have texted to make you feel worse? Laylah asks, and I don't answer her immediately because there are so many answers to that question and all of them make me sound like a very sad person who is more used to toxic than genuine friendship.

Well, maybe that's exactly what I am. But I'm building up my genuine-friendship portfolio these days. So I keep texting Laylah and the Low Brassholes chat.

I also keep catching myself trying to pull up the Reflections account on Instagram, and I feel a tiny prick of anxiety and a stronger wave of relief every time I realize I can't.

Mom and Dad never talk about last night or hand down any punishments, too busy over dinner talking excitedly about Mom's two(!) new clients. It's not until I'm washing dishes with Dad that he asks how I'm doing.

"Fine," I tell him. "Much better."

"That's good," he says. "We were worried about you. Some of us—not me, of course, but some people—still are."

"Sorry." I move a stack of plates from the drying rack to the cabinet, feeling a twinge of guilt but also . . . relief? I did everything wrong. I lost my temper, I made a scene. And I still have people who love me.

"Don't be sorry. It's our job to worry. It's not your job to keep us from it."

I wonder if he and Ellen compare notes.

I BASICALLY LIE IN WAIT IN THE KITCHEN AFTER MOM and Dad go to bed, ready to catch Ellen the second she gets home. I already have tea made and everything.

"Oh, hi," Ellen says, looking worn out and wary. "How are you feeling?"

I slide a mug of hierba buena to her and gesture for her to sit down. She does, her fingers nervously tracing the blue flowers and orange butterflies on her cup.

"I'm not brave," I say, and Ellen immediately cocks her head to the side in confusion. "I mean, I'm not brave about saying what I mean. I like to say what people want to hear." The kitchen is still and quiet, and I wince at how my words fill the space with awkwardness.

"You put up with a lot of things I couldn't put up with," Ellen argues. "And you do a lot of things—social things—that I couldn't do in high school. You're brave."

I shake my head. "I got mad yesterday, and I was horrible about it." I remember Ellen's teary face, the pain of it twisting under my ribs. "But I didn't mean it. I'm really sorry I said it. I'd rather be like you."

Ellen laughs and sighs, staring at the microwave light reflected in the window next to us. "I keep telling you that no one wants that! Keep being the awesome, patient, caring peacemaker you are. Just . . . make sure nobody takes advantage of that."

"And stop saying mean things to people I love," I add.

The quiet stretches out a moment too long. "You could avoid the mean things, yeah," Ellen finally admits, sipping her still-hot tea and wincing. "But you'd have to try a lot harder to offend me, kiddo. I'm basically doomed to keep liking you even when you're acting like a brat."

"Now you get how I feel about everyone!"

Ellen groans. "Listen, I know your mom and I . . . have a lot of conflict, and I know you're really good at smoothing it over, but I promise we don't actually need or expect you to do it. We'll work it out. Or, you know, I'll find somewhere else to live, and that's fine too and is probably going to be better for me anyway. I have been feeling . . . a little stuck. Something tells me you picked up on that." I duck my head, but Ellen doesn't twist the knife any more. "Anyway, that's my stuff. You focus on keeping toxic people out of your circle, will you please? As a personal favor to the people who love you?"

I get what she's saying, I do. But I also know myself well enough to say, "No promises, but I'll try."

Ellen sighs and tips her mug at me in resignation.

CHAPTER 18

I shouldn't feel like barfing again when I get to sixth period on Thursday, but I sort of do. The Low Brassholes chat has been catching me up about the last two days of band, Gilberto talking with Ms. Schumacher and then ditching rehearsal mysteriously, and all of the interviews with the APs to make sure that my section didn't feel that my released texts had created an unsafe environment. I've said my apologies, tried hard not to give explanations or excuses, and endured the teasing and pouting it took before Elias let me off the hook. I feel like, as far as the section is concerned, I'm well on the road to forgiveness.

And bringing Crave cupcakes for everyone at lunch didn't hurt. I made them meet me in the parking lot to eat them, because I was afraid to venture into the band hall until I absolutely had to, but it's nice out, so I don't think anyone minded. Lee only made one wry comment about being too busy with his thriving social life to spend lunch with me.

"I really am sorry," I tell him. "And this isn't an excuse, but I didn't mean it . . . I was mostly impressed."

Lee nods. "I realized that. Eventually. I'm sorry for kind of encouraging everyone not to text you those days after the email."

My eyebrows shoot up as my stomach drops down to the floor. So he was mad at first. Everyone has glossed over it now, but I suspected that they must have felt that way. Even if they got over it. Even if they think the person who released the texts was wrong. It still had to hurt. I stammer something that might be the start of another apology, but Lee shakes his head.

"Not like that. I thought you might be overwhelmed. And Bloom said you didn't even like texts, so we figured it was a good plan, but we didn't mean to make you think we were all silently hating you."

My stomach settles a bit, even if it still seems unlikely that my friends didn't hate me for at least a second. "That's . . . Thanks. For trying, for even worrying about it at all."

Lee shrugs. "I may have miscalculated based on past trauma."

He says it casually, but it does make my heart ache over what I said. Instead of getting even more emotional, I raise an eyebrow. "Still, that's a lot of careful thought you put into the group dynamic, for a loner."

Lee smiles. "Some of us have grown over the semester."

I smile back. "Some of us are still growing."

STILL, WALKING INTO THE BAND HALL WITHOUT HAVING any sense of how much people are talking about me on Instagram feels a little like I'm walking into a dark den of snakes—a nest? Do only lions have dens? Well, a dark room full of gossiping snakes, anyway. And I have no flashlight to warn me what's ahead.

I know it's good that the account is gone. But it still sort of feels bad.

I enter the band hall. My brain is on full alert, which is why I notice the quick glances that cut away and back when I turn my head. I also see the eyes that flick to the door and then back to whatever they were doing without interest, and I think they outnumber the other kind, and I'm grateful for them.

Laylah gives me an outright smile and a wave, and I'm even more grateful for her.

Sofia doesn't look at me at all. I try to be okay with everything else that's gone so well.

Because I'm still on high alert, it doesn't escape me that

the glances and whispers totally pick up when Gilberto enters from the music closet with an armful of books. I guess by shutting down the Reflections account, he ended up the focal point of the current scandal. I should bake him some cookies or something.

I rush to release the Dragon and make it to my seat on time, sparing a second to pat its bell in apology for leaving it alone two days in a row. I take my seat next to Milo, who gives me arched eyebrows and a thumbs-up.

And then we just rehearse. More than a hundred performers, two hundred when we're joined outside by percussion and color guard, each of us with our own worries, insecurities, judgments, and feuds. We gather in our opening set, like we've done a thousand times. Ms. Schumacher nods at Gilberto, who raises his hands. We all breathe as one, play our part in the song, shape our line with careful steps to create one unified performance, something greater than the sum of its broken parts. I love finding the beat and holding it in my steps, love adjusting to my neighbor's feet and my section's curve and the whole shape of the form. It didn't happen in one flashy moment, and it crept up so slowly that I almost missed it, but I love our show.

This is even better than the solitude and achievement of the practice room. The swell of our park and play, the harmony of the Dragon with the rest of my section, washes over me. Maybe I finally found a vocation that connects me instead of isolating me. And maybe it sounds like this.

Bloom, who's been quiet all day, asks me if I have time to talk logistics after practice. He asks with his phone in his hand, eyes glued to it, voice a low mumble. I'm always around after practice anyway, and we pretty much always hang around discussing section things, so the formal invitation seems redundant if logistics was really the topic. My chest starts to feel tight.

Lee said they decided not to text me. But Bloom never answered my calls either. I wrote all those garbage things about him, and most of my "criticism" boiled down to noticing that he's kind of anxious and neurodivergent. It was horrible.

I follow him to the back hallway. There's still a lot of traffic there, so after checking over his shoulder he pulls me into a practice room instead, and now I know something weird is going down.

He's still pissed at me, and he has every right to be.

"I'm sorry," I say as soon as the door closes behind us. "I should have . . . I tried to call you . . ." No. Not excuses, not performance. I just need to tell him the truth. "I'm sorry I was so mean. So shitty. You're . . ." I struggle for the right word. "You're my co–section leader. You're my friend. I really respect and admire you, and I'm sorry I sent those messages that made it seem like I didn't. Or . . . I'm sorry that maybe at the beginning of all this, I didn't. But I do now."

Bloom blinks at me. "Okay," he says. "We can't let Sofia get away with this."

"Huh?"

"We all know it was her!" His voice bursts out higher and louder than I've maybe ever heard it. "She obviously snatched your phone when you left it out playing music—she must know your passcode, right? And then—and the jacket and the hair and all the posts about you! Ms. Schumacher and Reyes just want to say that the account's down and that's the end of it, but no! The account didn't magically access your private information—and who do they think runs the account anyway? Like, I'm sorry, but sometimes band stereotypes are true, and a secret gossip account pretty much screams flute clique, and if they need *more* proof I'm sure they could check the IP address of the updates or something, or maybe you could ask if Laylah has receipts from the flute chat, and—"

"Bloom." I hold up my hands. "Wait a second."

"And before you try that 'turn the other cheek' preaching on me, just know that my people don't really roll that way, and sometimes there needs to be some freaking justice—"

"Bloom!" I'm holding back laughter. I've never seen

him this worked up before. "What's going on? What is this? Are you— Is this you *caring* about me?"

His ears go bright red, and his hands, suspended in the middle of some dramatic gesture, drop to his sides. "It's not like . . ." he mutters. "I mean, Reyes isn't the only one who does."

This only introduces more confusion, but I find that I'm not feeling too worried about the exact meaning, because the basic idea is that Bloom isn't pissed at me, and I really, really didn't want him to be pissed at me.

"Thanks," I say. "But Gilberto Reyes did ask me if I wanted an investigation, and we both decided it was better to leave it alone. Even if . . . I don't know, I don't actually want Sofia to leave band. She's my friend."

Bloom makes an indignant strangled noise.

"Or she used to be my friend—whatever. I obviously don't want her to hack my phone or mess with my hair anymore, but I still care about her."

Bloom flips his phone in his hands without looking at it. "I mean, I *guess* . . ."

"It's fine, really." I'm laughing again, reaching out to stop his twitching hands. "Don't worry." I've said things like that a lot recently, but I haven't meant them this much in a while.

Bloom opens his mouth, then yanks his hand away without saying anything and stares at his phone.

"What?"

He shrugs. "So . . . everyone's saying . . . you and Gilberto . . ."

Wait, what? "Nooo, barking up the wrong tree on so many counts. Who's saying that? Is there a new Instagram?" My pulse spikes again.

Bloom shakes his head, hard. "No, no, no, just . . . No one's saying it really. We just all kinda thought since he made a big deal to save you . . ."

"Well, whoever thought that was wrong," I say. "I mean, I made a big deal about reporting people to save you, and I didn't like you back then." My brain must have composed that message, approved it, and sent it to my mouth for delivery, but I'm still surprised when I hear it out loud.

Bloom's quiet for a long beat. He must have heard it too. "Back then?"

Oh. Did the practice room just get smaller? Did the air just get very warm? Bloom studies the carpeted wall a few feet to the side of my head. It's nothing like the time I got an (incorrect) vibe from Gilberto, not stomach-flipping or panic-inducing. Just . . . a vibe. I could ignore it completely if I wanted to. Or . . .

"Well, does it matter?" I ask. "I seem to recall that, I don't know, the sun would never set on your indifference to that kind of thing."

"You— That's not what I said!" Bloom's phone spins

out of his fingers and clatters to the linoleum. He doesn't so much as glance toward it. "I said the stars had to align. Sometimes the stars align!"

Oh. I bite down on the half smile blooming on my lips.

Poor phrasing! No Bloom-ing on my lips! Shut up, brain!

But in spite of my brain, the vibe stays warm and light and uncrushing. I don't want to run away from it. In fact, I might want the opposite.

"Hey, so, logistics," I say loudly, watching Bloom startle and then frown at the abrupt subject change. "You wanted to talk logistics? For Homecoming, right?"

"Oh." Bloom crouches to retrieve his phone. He hides his confusion, the flash of disappointment, really well, but not well enough. "Yeah. Tomorrow's game. You didn't miss much, so I think you can just follow Lee and you'll be fine. You're a fast learner."

I recently vowed to be less mean, but here I am, teasing my co–section leader. "And Saturday?"

"Saturday?"

"Homecoming dance." I watch Bloom's frown get deeper, trying not to laugh. "Are you going?"

"I . . ." Bloom goes from brow-furrowed to wide-eyed in an instant. "Oh. I . . ." He clears his throat. "Probably it'd be good, right? Section bonding. Or, I mean, I don't know, it doesn't have to be . . ."

"Cool, so I'll see you there." I keep my smile very innocent.

"Uh . . . yeah. Definitely. I'll . . . Yeah." Bloom's eyes can't stay still, flicking to me and then to the floor and ceiling. I worry that maybe I've overdone it, put too much pressure on it, but after a second he settles on a steady smile and a tiny relieved sigh. Which makes me smile back. Which makes the practice room seem small again, but not in a claustrophobic way.

"Well, I'd better go grab the Dragon." It's time for me to use the space for its actual purpose, not teasing a star-betrayed Bloom.

"Yeah—no! Uh, yeah. But wait. First, there was something we wanted to show you." Bloom scrambles to open the practice door for me, ushering me out toward the band hall to see . . .

Sectionals? Everyone sits in a semicircle, instruments up.

"So, uh, I had been sort of playing with this arrangement just for fun, and then when everything blew up and you weren't at practice, I mentioned it and everyone agreed that we should . . . So we can play this to anyone who wants to talk bad about, you know, the section. And it's just short, because I barely know what I'm doing and we didn't have much time to learn it, and it's just a stand tune, and . . ." Bloom coughs while the rest of the boys laugh and wiggle in their chairs. "Anyway, go ahead, y'all. Uh, I mean . . ." He straightens his slouch, raises his hands, and does a quick count-off.

The boys play a slightly slow but recognizable melody that blares over at least two supporting parts. "Juice" sounds a little clunky with no higher brass, but I can't keep from beaming or from bouncing along with the beat.

"Y'all learned Lizzo for me?" I fight against my sudden tear duct activity.

"Yes, I sacrificed 'Despacito' for you," Elias says. "Please clap."

I clap obligingly while Lee points out, "You were resoundingly outvoted for 'Despacito.' And right now we're celebrating Yasmín."

"Yasmeeeen!" Neeraj calls out. I lift my chin at him, heart swelling with how much I appreciate his enthusiasm and thumping with guilt for how I mocked that. He nods back without a hint of a grudge. I don't deserve his easy warmth, but I'm glad for it.

"We all love Lizzo here," Caleb adds. "And anyway, you bought us cupcakes."

"He's trying to say he loves you too," Milo says. "And I am not at all jealous, because I am in full agreement."

"Ughhhh, y'all are too sappy," I squeal. "Somebody say something mean, quick!"

"Oh no." Jonathan shakes his head. "I've seen what

happens when someone talks bad about us, and I want no part of it."

These guys are such clowns, it's unbelievable.

THE FOOTBALL GAME ROUTINE GETS SHAKEN UP BY THE endless halftime announcements of alumni gifts and Homecoming court and whatever else the administration goes on about while we stand in place spelling KHS and playing the same D.S. al coda repetition with no coda in sight. The only entertainment we have is moving our sousaphone bells in a tiny dance along with the music, and even that gets old. Then we do an abbreviated halftime performance, slightly annoyed that we can only do a third of our show for the largest audience we'll ever have.

At least we nail it, though.

During the third quarter, while everyone scarfs the snickerdoodles Mom helped me actually bake from scratch, talk turns to tomorrow's dance, next month's UIL, and all-state band auditions.

"Do you . . . Are you going to look at the tuba étude?" Bloom asks me.

"Oh, definitely not. I'll audition on flute." I mean, obviously. I'm still objectively bad at taming the Dragon, even with our simplified parts. And I've never even touched a concert tuba, which might not be an entirely different beast but must have a learning curve.

"Sure, yeah. Well, if you haven't checked those out yet, I can send you the link . . ."

"I'm a section leader too," I remind him with a smile. "I got the same staff email reminding us to remind everyone to practice, and the link was there. But thanks."

"You won't be anymore, though, will you?" Elias asks. "Next semester you won't be flute section leader."

"Section leaders are less of a thing in concert season," Bloom says. "And Yasmín will be first chair flute."

Which is a vote of confidence, but it makes me feel weird. Will I be? Will I have to challenge Sofia to get it, or deal with her challenging me to try to take back her throne?

"So tomorrow," Elias says around a mouthful of cookie. "Homecoming part two: electric boogaloo. Are we all meeting up before? Or just at the gym?"

"It would be hard to all carpool from someone's house," Jonathan points out.

"And I want to make a grand entrance," Neeraj says. "So I can impress you all with how good I clean up."

"Literally who here do you think you're going to impress?" Jonathan shakes his head.

"I think we were going to, you know, drive together," Milo says, lacing his fingers with Caleb's.

"And I'm actually bringing someone," Lee adds. Our heads all swivel to him. "You don't know them; we met at a trans youth meetup thing, and we're probably just friends. I'm begging y'all to be cool."

"There's nothing 'just' about friends," Bloom says quietly. "Friends are the best."

"Ugh, fine, so some of y'all have significant others, and the rest of us value our platonic relationships and definitely don't feel left out at all, BUT are we just supposed to walk into the gym alone?" Elias whines. "I need a crew."

It's decided that we'll meet up in the band hall before the dance. I wave down Gilberto as we're putting up uniforms for the night and make sure we can get the doors unlocked. Turns out we are far from the first nerds to think of this.

"That's a relief," I tell him. "I was afraid I'd have to pretend to use a practice room on Saturday afternoon to convince you."

"Listen, I'm never going to argue with someone who wants to be here rather than home," Gilberto jokes with a sadly slanting smile. "But hey! Speaking of which"—he perks up—"did Ellen tell you the good news? We're both going to live at Casa for the summer, running the house and everything as full-time volunteers."

"What?" Ellen has not told me that, but to be fair I kind of monopolized our conversations this week, and then she had to close last night. "When was this decided?"

"I've known for a while," Gilberto says. "My

parents . . . Well, they approve of the Catholic part at least, and it will get me out of the house sooner. And it's good, you know? I feel like I'm actually doing something. Ellen told me yesterday. She had been half joking about it for a while, but I guess she decided for sure now that her law school apps are done."

Her law school apps? Okay, mental note to sit Ellen down soon and get some information out of her. I'm maybe trying to reform my gossip habits, but inquiring minds want to know details!

"That's so cool," I say. "What a good idea."

"Yeah, you should come work with us sometime," Gilberto says. "It's a good antidote to feeling like the church has totally forgotten that the last are supposed to be first, and that Catholicism is just, you know, the weird hang-ups about sex and the 'pro-life' but somehow anti-welfare grandstanding."

I snort. "I'm glad someone else understands my faith."

Oh. For the second time this week, my brain catches up to my mouth and realizes something very obvious.

"Hey," I say. "Do you . . . Sorry, this is weird. But, like, all my tíos and primos live in Mexico, and I've been having trouble . . . This is so weird. But would you consider sponsoring me for confirmation?"

Gilberto smiles. "Oh yeah, if you want. That would be cool. Is that next semester?"

"Yeah, and we have a couple of prep events," I say. "If you don't mind . . . It's some extra homework and a few weekends."

"I don't mind at all," Gilberto says. "That's, like, an honor. Thanks."

"I'll bring the form in next week," I say. "Have a good night."

"You too, ahijada." Gilberto winks and waves, and it gives my heart the happiest and most comfortable flutter as I turn back to my freshman boys.

Mom is thrilled that I'm going to a dance. She helps me go through practically my entire closet for options, and we both drag Ellen in to tell us everything she remembers about how formal school dances are and can I wear a nice skirt or is it, like, cocktail dresses only?

"What is Sofia wearing?" Mom asks. "Tell her to come over and get ready here so she can help us choose."

I freeze, and Ellen steps in to ask why I can't wear slacks to the dance, which predictably makes Mom defensive about the fact that I *can* if I *want* to but I'm *allowed* to wear a dress because there's nothing *wrong* with being traditional. Ellen flashes me a tight-lipped smile as she quickly backpedals, her distraction successful.

It makes me feel like a coward.

"Mom, actually, Sofia and I are . . . We're kind of in

a fight right now." I clear my throat. "Or, I don't know, we're not in a fight, but we got in a fight, and . . . I don't think she'll be coming around. I don't think we're going to be as close anymore."

"Oh no!" Mom shifts her attention from Ellen to frown at me. "But I'm sure you two will work it out soon. What if you call her now as a peace offering? Or do you want me to call Marta myself?"

"No, Mom. I don't want that. Thanks anyway."

Mom presses her lips together. She's never been great at processing things she doesn't want to hear, or surprises, or surprises she doesn't want to hear. But I don't try to find an excuse to avoid her annoyance.

"Well," she says finally, "if you don't want to now, maybe later when things cool off . . . Oh! I have some shoes that would go with this dress. Let me go look for them, and you can try them on."

I'm only a little shocked that I didn't get screamed at.

"That was good boundary-setting." Ellen nods when Mom leaves.

"Eh. I'll keep working on it," I say. "And, side note, when were you going to tell anyone about law school apps?"

Ellen jumps, then mutters, "Gilberto . . ." while I stick out my tongue. "Yeah . . . I'll have to call a family meeting next week or something. Quickly, before I start getting rejections."

"Or acceptances," I say, because Ellen would be a great lawyer, probably! All she does is read things and be mad about things and talk! "And living at the shelter, that sounds like a lot of work."

"Work, but also fun." Ellen smiles. "And not to sound ungrateful, but probably a little bit relaxing compared to living at home." She smiles, and the twist in it reminds me of Gilberto.

"It's going to be great," I say. "I'm impressed."

Ellen adjusts her topknot and smiles. "Thanks, kiddo. You know, maybe I should go talk to Dad about all of this right now . . ." She inches away from the closet in a clear ploy to escape the fashion show. I take pity on her and wave her toward the door. "Have a good dance," she says on her way out. "Tell Gilberto he's a snitch for me—and not the good kind!"

I laugh, and then I text Laylah to see what she's going to wear tonight.

WE END UP HANGING OUT IN THE BAND HALL LONGER than we meant to. First we all have to say hi, and compliment all the dress shirts and blazers, and meet Lee's date, Ash (who's so gloriously goth that they make Lee's cleaned-up grunge look positively preppy), and I have to make sure everyone appreciates my treble and bass clef earrings. Then Bloom shows up, shirtsleeves too short for his long arms and wonky tie making his collar stick up, and the boys take one look and swarm to get him straightened up. Milo and Elias each roll up a sleeve while Lee shows off his Wikipedic knowledge of different tie knots and Caleb shapes up Bloom's hair with a pocket comb and someone's abandoned bottle of water. By the time they're all finished, Bloom looks, well, still basically the same, but a lot neater. And then Neeraj finally shows up, and the greetings and meetings and outfit-showing-off start all over again, and then we finally head to the gym almost an hour after the dance has started.

We circle the dark and vaguely decorated space, finding other band kids and ignoring everyone else in big-public-school fashion. Laylah and Mia join our dance circle for a while, and Milo's clarinet friends, and some percussionists that I'm not friends with but everyone else is because I guess they're freshmen. The music is good (they play Lizzo!) and loud, and I like dancing and yelling to be heard and letting jokes fly over my head half the time. Our little band-kid circle drifts around the dance floor, dodging tech-crew circles and cheerleader circles and extremely impressive dance department circles and looser groups and flows of people who aren't totally consumed by their extracurriculars like we are. We join the trumpets, who try to start a weird dance battle, and the trombones, who start a cheese puff fight (or did Elias initiate by attacking them first?), and the color guard, who put us all to shame with their moves. And then our circle shifts, and we see the flutes in their own tiny circle, spinning and laughing and still rocking faded green hair accents.

I try to act natural and keep dancing, but nobody else does. The flutes quickly notice the mess of low brass boys standing and staring at them—not awkward at all, guys, thanks!

I'm already planning my excuse to go grab more snacks when Han steps into the circle and offers me a hand. Laylah smiles and nods at me like maybe she knows I'm afraid the invitation is a trap.

I take Han's hand. She lifts it and spins me under, to the whooping of both sections. She does a second twirl herself, and then I keep following her lead until everyone is back to dancing more or less normally.

"Sorry I called you a slacker," I whisper when we break apart.

Han smiles. "I know what I care about, and I'm not embarrassed band isn't high on the list."

"If anyone wants, I have a flask," Katrina whispers at full volume. "Just, no pictures or videos, please."

"Your hair looks so cute down!" one of the freshman flutes confides, leaning close to me and hitting me with a strong whiff of Katrina's flask. "I'm really sorry everything was such a mess at the sleepover—we were such a mess, I mean—but you pull it off so well; I want to chop mine!"

"I'm sorry too," the other freshman shouts into my other ear, "but ditto!"

Which is sweet, even if it is very loud.

But the moment isn't perfect. Because Sofia is standing at the edge of our merged circle, looking amazing in a ruffled black dress and bright red shoes, not dancing with either group and not taking the step forward that all the other flutes have taken. I catch her eye, try to beam a message telling her to just come here and give some semblance of an apology, or insult my dress in a not-actually-mean way, or something to show that we're on the track toward mending whatever's left here.

Instead, she takes a step back, removing herself more obviously from the group, removing herself from being in any sort of friendly situation with me.

And I guess I have to accept that I can't do anything about that.

So I turn my back and find Bloom hovering at my elbow, and he's leaning forward and saying something I can't hear, but I smile and half nod to show that it's fine; I'm fine; I'm sad to lose her but happy with everything I do have.

Everything is—honestly—okay.

Until a group of Model UN kids clears out and I see Andy just a few feet away and boogie-ing straight toward us, eyes and hands and lips locked with someone that I'm guessing takes AP Music Theory.

They're swaying straight toward the spot where Sofia still stands basically on her own, looking about as lost as anyone can look in their own school gym.

So of course whatever moment of clarity I just had evaporates into the inexorable need to dive across the circle to save Sofia from confronting her asshat ex alone. I end up grabbing Bloom's hand and bringing him along for the ride to form a tiny but believable dance trio, just in time for Andy to come up for air and focus his eyes on us.

"Oh," he says. "Hey, y'all. Having fun?" And then his dance partner puts her hand on his neck and they're off again. I try to glare, but I'm not sure he notices, and it doesn't really matter that much. The important thing is that I was there.

Sofia looks at Andy's retreating back, looks at me, looks at the circle of flutes and low brass, and then bolts in the direction of the bathroom.

And even though Bloom grabs my elbow, and I know exactly what he's thinking and why he's thinking it, I pull my arm away and give him a thumbs-up. I will him to trust me.

Then I follow her.

CHAPTER 19

"Can you. Please. Leave me alone?" Sofia's voice leaks out of the stall I'm standing in front of. Her red heels—visible under the foot-high gap—show that she's standing with her back against the badly fitted door.

"I can," I say. "But don't you think we should get some kind of closure?"

Her laugh is heavy. "What is this, a breakup?"

I mean, isn't it? I think about Mom's casual assumption that "you'll work it out soon." That's what's expected when two people have been so close for so long. So what else should you call it when you can't make it work anymore?

"I just want . . ." *to know what I did wrong. To know how long our fun-mean dynamic has been festering with something toxic that I didn't notice. Answers.* ". . . to talk."

"I don't really feel like I owe you an explanation," Sofia says.

"No, I guess you don't." I take a breath, trying to track the problems we've had, trying to work my way backward and find the threads I missed when I wasn't looking for them. "I wanted to say, well . . ." I want to say so many things, but I should probably start with the one I've been turning over in my brain since it happened. "Remember that night at the sleepover, with Never Have I Ever?" I think I know why I hurt Sofia that night, and I think I know what I should have said then, and I try to say it now even though it might be too late. "I wasn't judging you, or angry at you. I was angry at Andy, but I'm always angry at him, and I shouldn't have made that anger more important than your feelings. I'm sorry." That's not all, though, I know that's not all. "And I'm sorry I wasn't very good at . . . I'm sorry you couldn't talk to me about Andy stuff, this year or all summer. I'm not sure why I'm so bad at it, but I'm trying to figure it out. And of course you're allowed to be mad—"

"Shut *up*, Yasmín!" Sofia snaps, voice breaking, one heel stamping against the tile floor.

The music is muffled, and the bathroom smells exactly as slightly-worse-than-neutral as it does on a normal school day. Sofia sighs against the stall door. "What? Am I supposed to apologize now? Take credit for every mean thing someone said online about you? I just posted them; I didn't make anyone send them in!"

A tiny corner of my heart, the one that hoped that Bloom was wrong, that my instincts were wrong, drops and shatters next to Sofia's heels.

"I have to forgive you now that you kind of realized one time you were shitty? What about everything else, Yasmín? What about stalking and basing your whole life on beating me? Or kissing up to every single authority figure? You keep pretending you're perfect and your life is perfect, and they all fall for it. Am I *allowed to be mad* that you convinced everyone that you're the bigger person this time too? Because you apologized, because you're a pushover who never does anything?" Sofia chokes on her laughter. "Or do you just want me to say that I'm an evil bitch and that's why I did it?"

I didn't want any of this, no. I sort of came in here wanting to finally have a breakthrough moment. I thought maybe I even wanted to tell Sofia that I *was* too dependent on her, too jealous when she got a boyfriend, too confused about my own feelings to realize what I was doing wrong. But I don't know if that matters anymore, with how deep her hurt goes, with how my feelings have changed.

It does make me a little less heartbroken to know that Sofia is as angry and guilty and full of pain as I've been this semester. It makes me feel better that she feels bad. How's that for "being a good person"?

"I'm sorry," I say.

"No, you're not!" Sofia says, and then in a much softer voice she adds, "You shouldn't be."

"We can both be—"

"*You* didn't even do any of this on purpose, and I did. You don't get to be the one who's sorry."

"Okay . . ." I say, and a weak smile twists my lips as I read between the lines. "So you're sorry, then?"

"Shut *up*, Yasmín." But when she says it, her voice sounds so much more normal. It's a relief to hear it. I can't help it. I laugh.

Sofia stopped being my friend the moment she started harassing me on social media. I get that. But it's funny too that she's the only one who saw through me at the beginning of the year, when I was determined to deny how much I was struggling. I wish she had reacted differently. I wish she had tried to be my friend and help me through the hard time instead of wanting to show everyone else that I had it hard. None of her choices were okay. But she saw me, with all my stress and my loneliness and my ridiculous priorities. She still sees me. And I still see her.

And none of that means I need to give an entire essay of explanation, or hear one from Sofia, or keep trying to force us back to a place we've clearly outgrown. She's hurting as much as I am. We're hurting each other. I've been stubbornly trying to stay on this painful, destructive path, but maybe there's a different track, a less intense one. Maybe we can get closure.

"Look," I say. "My mom is already like, 'Do you want me to call Marta?' about this. Like it or not, they're not going to just let us disappear from each other's lives. So you don't have to be sorry, and we don't have to be . . ." *best friends*. My throat catches, so I change where my sentence was headed. "Don't have to be hanging out all the time. But I'd like to be able to interact in band, or at church, or at Costco. So . . . can we try to be on that level for a while? Not 'secret plot to humiliate me' level?"

I'm not sure Ellen would approve of my speech. I'm not sure if she would tell me to rip toxic people out of my life entirely, to not accept anyone back into my life after they tried to ruin it. But I can't be Ellen. I can only be me.

"Yes," Sofia says softly. "That wasn't— I didn't actually mean to— That's fine."

"Sure." Another tiny part of my heart breaks that she's not pushing back, not groveling to get our friendship back the way it was. But I can handle it.

"So . . . do you want to come back out and dance?" I ask. Sofia doesn't answer. I wait as long as I can, just in case her mind isn't fully made up, but then I pass the line of how long I can wait. "Okay. I'll see you at Costco or whatever."

I walk out of the bathroom, and I leave Sofia and her stubborn anger and her red shoes behind me.

Neeraj stands outside the bathroom, wringing his hands, and jumps when he sees me.

"Uh, sorry. Is she . . . ? Sorry." Neeraj looks at the ground. "We have classes together, you know? We're lab partners, and I . . ." His voice is soft. "I just want to make sure she's okay."

"It's okay," I say. "No Sofia embargos here. We're . . . basically good." Neeraj looks relieved. I wonder if he's better with a crush than he is with a euphonium, but no, I don't need to judge Sofia's potential partners. I need to find the lighter, less intense path. "I don't know if you have a shot at all, but by all means, go for it."

Neeraj smiles and shrugs. "Stranger things have happened. Remember when you showed up first day of band camp telling me you wanted to be section leader?"

"Oh wow." I'm surprised he remembers, when August feels like a crumpled granola bar shoved to the back of my mind. Some unfamiliar person tested her ambition on Neeraj that first day of band camp, and thinking about it now, I feel a little sorry for and a lot different from her. In August I didn't even think I would go to the Homecoming dance. Partly because it didn't fit on a college app, partly because the PSAT is next weekend and I could use the time to cram, but mostly because I could barely imagine it. I didn't know that by October I would want to go, that I would have people I wanted to go with. My heart was set on leading the flutes, but liking them wasn't even on my radar. In another universe, I would've eventually been the one with the password to the Reflections account.

These last three months kind of broke me. But I don't feel broken.

I let Neeraj hang back. Maybe Sofia will talk to him. Maybe she won't. Not my person anymore, so not my business.

In the gym, my friends are still dancing. They wave for me to join.

So I do.

EPILOGUE

I hold the final note as I march five, six, seven, step and CLOSE. Freeze, eyes locked on Gilberto's hands until the horns DOWN. Mark time for two and then step off toward the sideline, to the scattered applause of the other bands still waiting for their own turns in front of the judges. Posture still tense, proud, and perfect until we're off the field, out of the performance area, DONE with our UIL performance.

Mom was right about the semester ending fast. It seems like it was barely a blink between Homecoming and the Saturday morning that I sat in one of the senior English classrooms taking the PSAT, and then another blink to being here at UIL, and now we've finished our performance. Maybe time flies when you finally get a break from the constant trauma of social media targeted harassment. Or maybe I've been having fun.

"KingWOOD!" Neeraj screams in his best jock voice, and we all start to scream and jump up and down and shake out a semester's worth of nerves and a week's worth of extended rehearsals and a weekend's worth of zero sleep thanks to yesterday's late-night away game. Ms. Schumacher gives a distracted half of a speech, but we're all too excited, too anxious to get our scores back, too elated to listen.

We pack our instruments back onto the buses, hang up our jackets, and are finally set loose in our bibs and band shirts to eat or buy dinner and watch other bands and speculate about the performance. We're not going to rank in the top three of the twenty or so bands here today, or beat Cinco Ranch or anything like that, but we're hoping to match or beat our scores from two years ago. I don't know how it felt two years ago, but I think we did the best we could possibly do. I'm optimistic about our scores.

My phone buzzes. Laylah's near the front of the food truck line already—flutes are easier to pack and leave on the bus than our hulking cargo-space cases—and offering to order for me so I don't have to wait in line myself. Lifesaver.

"Should we . . . ?" Bloom asks me as we climb down

the bus steps into the parking lot. I glance around to see if our section is still mostly in one place.

"Sure. Huddle up, low brass!" I call out, then nod at Bloom once the circle is more solid.

"Yeah, great job, everyone," he says. "I, uh, overheard some of the Cinco Ranch folks talking, and they were all like, 'Oh, Kingwood didn't have a tuba section, I thought? What happened? They must have let them back in so they could compete or whatever.' So . . ."

"What voice is that?" Neeraj asks, earning an eye roll from Bloom. "Who talks like that? Do the Cinco Ranch kids talk like that?"

"The point," I say, "is that we fooled them into thinking we were a real section. So hopefully we fooled the judges as well. We should all be proud of how competent we looked."

"But our section leaders told us that competence wasn't good enough; we should shoot for excellence," Caleb calls.

"Ugh, yes, that's what I meant. Excellent."

"You don't know that until the scores come in," Lee points out cheerfully. He's gotten insufferably unbothered since he started officially dating Ash.

"We're just saying good job!" Bloom belts loudly, and then waves his hands to dismiss the huddle, giving me an exasperated look.

"I've got cookies," I call, holding up my Tupperware and then quickly passing it to Elias when everyone starts to swarm. Hopefully this makes up for keeping everyone out of the food lines for an extra few minutes.

"So what do you actually think the scores will be?" Bloom asks.

I rub my hands together, chilly now that clouds are covering the sun and I'm not insulated by stiff polyester. "I don't know. I think they'll be good."

Bloom glances at me, then back down at his phone. He unties his hoodie from around his waist and passes it to me. "Hope you're right."

I slip the hoodie on, pushing up the sleeves. "How's everyone coming along with the étude?" Since I'm auditioning for all-state as a flute and Milo as a clarinet, Bloom's been letting us skip some sectionals time to practice on our own while everyone else works on the low brass audition music.

"Uh, you know, unlikely to make it, but they're improving. Neeraj isn't even close to the strongest player anymore. Elias has that in the bag—but please don't tell Jonathan I said that, because I've been telling them it's too close to call."

"Well, not exactly. Neither of them can beat you," I say. Bloom doesn't respond, but it's true. "Maybe I should work on the étude too."

"Why?" Bloom asks, lowering his phone screen in surprise.

"I don't want to fall too behind," I say. "Chair tests for concert band are when? Last week of the semester?"

"Yeah, but . . ." Bloom stares at me until Elias comes over and tries to shove a chocolate chip cookie into his hand.

"I saved you both one," Elias says proudly. He hasn't taken the Band-Aids off his earrings yet. "These guys are animals."

Bloom ignores Elias and keeps looking at me. "Wait, aren't you . . . ?"

"I'm still going to practice my flute," I say. "I think I have a good shot to get into all-state band. And even when that's over, Ms. Schumacher is going to recommend a private teacher. But I just thought that if I have two more years of marching with the Dragon, it doesn't make sense to let my technique languish during concert season."

"You're staying?" Elias bounces between us, cookies forgotten. "You're staying in low brass?"

"Yeah," I say. "I'm staying."

"Oh shit!" Elias sprints back into the thick of the cookie frenzy. "Yasmín's staying low brass for concert season!"

"Of course she is." Lee grins. Insufferable.

"Cool," Caleb says.

"No, it isn't! Does this mean you won't let me back in after a semester with the clarinets?" Milo frets.

"Relax, Low Brassholes forever," Jonathan reassures him.

Bloom looks at me, the wind sweeping hair into his face and the sun breaking through the clouds behind him, something like stars in his eyes. "You're staying."

I smile. It's going to be a lot of work to be a full-time tuba, but I've never been against working hard. I know this will be work where I can see my progress, where I'm opening new doors instead of banging my head against old walls. And yeah, getting to stay in a section with the people I love made the decision a lot easier.

"Of course I am."

ACKNOWLEDGMENTS

This book was created during a long (and ongoing) period of isolation, but like every book, it would not exist without the hard work and support of my community. I am so grateful for all the new ways we've discovered to work, chat, and share over the past two years.

To my editor Kelsey Murphy, thank you for always being so thoughtful, curious, and kind with my stories.

To my agent Patricia Nelson, thank you for giving every new idea, plan, and contract so much attention.

To the editorial, design, marketing, and publicity teams at Penguin, thank you so much for working difficult jobs in a difficult industry that means so much to readers everywhere. Thank you especially to my cover illustrator Ali Mac, cover designer Kristin Boyle, publicist Tessa Meischeid, and all the editors and designers who have hunted down image citations, tightened and loosened lines, scoured dictionaries in English and Spanish, and generally worked incredibly hard to make these pages as polished as possible, including Krista Ahlberg,

Sola Akinlana, Monique Sterling, Abigail Powers, Kate Frentzel, and Kaitlin Severini.

Thank you to my beta readers and fellow writers. Whether you helped me with the full manuscript or a single sentence or a general concept, I could not have created this story without you. Thanks to the writing group chat, Laura Silverman, Amanda Joy, and Kika Hatzopoulou, for so many years of inspiration and motivation. Eternal heart emojis to Helena Greer, Sonora Reyes, Jonny Garza Villa, and especially to sensitivity reader A.Z. Louise, for helping shape the arcs and details of each character. Thank you to all the amazing 2022 debut authors who reminded me not to become jaded and cynical, and special thanks to Skye Quinlan for being the best ace marching band book release buddy! Thanks also to the Las Musas community and my friends from Cake Creative who continue to support me through new stages of my career.

Thank you to the teachers, librarians, booksellers, and bloggers who are tireless in getting books into the hands of readers who need them. Your adaptability and creativity in the face of this pandemic has been amazing, and I'm impressed but not at all surprised. Thanks to Mark Price and all my students for keeping me in touch with the power of reading and writing.

No one can produce without taking time for recovery, relaxation, and personal life, so thanks to my friends Claire Morice, Devon Morera, Merric Waelder, and Andrea Romero for all the Zoom and park hangouts, and for making wedding planning in a pandemic seem less impossible! Thanks to my parents and my brothers, my home base when the world gets ridiculous, and to my aunts, uncles, and cousins who have had to spend more time than I'd like at a safe distance.

Ariel, my person for so long and my husband more recently, you've been here for all of this one, avoiding the index cards all over the coffee table, delivering the late-night deadline snacks, and participating in dozens of Spanglish nuance discussions. I know you prefer quidditch, but marching band book is better because I wrote it with you.

And finally, to all the readers. I know you're tired of being resilient. I know you've been through a lot. I hope, so much, that you found hope and healing somewhere in this story. Thank you.

If you want to read Ellen's story,
pick up *This Is How We Fly*!

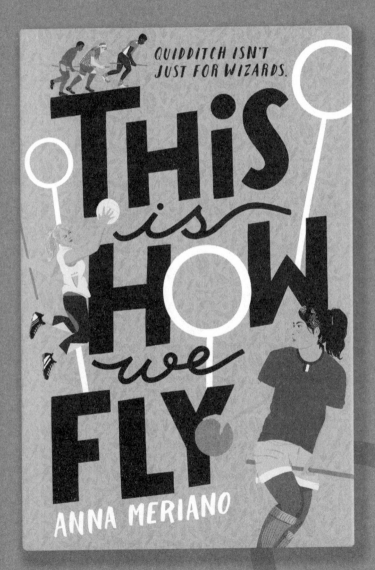

Available now!